SHADOW LINES

Sadie Gordon Richmond

All characters and events in this publication, other than those clearly in the public domain, are fictitious and any resemblance to real persons, living or dead, is purely coincidental.

Book cover design by RockingBookCovers.com

Also by this author

Front Page News
Sins of Silence
Sticks and Stones
One in a Million
I Have Never
The Ties That Bind
A Long Time Buried
Death Trap

For Mum

One

'Spiderwoman set to make a killing,' Jez read aloud over Steve's shoulder. 'When did that come out, then?'

'What?'

'Spiderwoman. I thought they were still filming.'

'It's not a review of the film. It's about Celestia Woolf.'

'Who?'

'Performance artist,' Steve replied. 'She believes she's the reincarnation of some Greek spider goddess.'

''Course she does.'

'She spins webs from things like candy floss.'

'And that's art?'

'Apparently. She's got a show coming up at the Tate Modern.'

'Unbelievable,' Jez muttered.

'Yeah, I know,' Steve agreed. 'I might've been able to get excited about it if she didn't look like a man in drag. But McRae can't get enough of her. He wants a picture collage and a half-page article, and next week I've got to interview her for a podcast.'

Jez shook his head. A moment passed before he asked, 'What would you come back as?'

'Eh?'

'If you got to be reincarnated.'

'I dunno. Someone rich and powerful, I suppose.' Steve turned in his seat. 'How about you?'

'Killer whale.'

'Why?'

'Why not?'

Priya didn't comment, wondering whether both of them didn't

deserve to come back as sewer rats. Well, maybe not both. Given that Jez wasn't a raging misogynist, she would allow him to return a little further up the animated chain of moral decline. He could be a pigeon. But a scrappy, inner-city pigeon; he was still a journalist, after all.

'How about you, Priya?' Steve asked.

Jez didn't give her a chance to reply. 'We already know what subs come back as.'

'Do we?'

'Dung beetles,' Jez went on. 'So they can continue the job of cleaning up everyone else's shit and turning it into something useful.'

Priya raised her eyes heavenwards as the two men dissolved into laughter, resisting the temptation to make the obvious point about what the remark said for the quality of their work. The subeditor, as chief editor Damon McRae never tired of telling her, is there to protect the reader from the writer. A human firewall to shield the world – or in her case, the residents of Clapham – from inarticulate writers. Until the previous year, she hadn't known it was *possible* to be a journalist if you couldn't string a sentence together. That, it turned out, was the best-kept secret of a small army of dung beetles in media outlets around the globe.

'*Et tu*, Liam?' Jez asked, looking over the top of Steve's and Priya's monitors.

'Poison arrow frog,' came the art editor's response from behind Priya's screen.

Jez didn't comment. After a moment, he leaned over Priya's desk to reach for something lying across the top of Liam's stack of filing trays. 'Is this the collage?'

'Uh-huh.'

Jez set the A3 colour printout down across the join between Priya's and Steve's desks and leaned forwards to inspect it at close range. Intrigued, Priya turned to view Liam's mock-up of the two adjoining pages, a patchwork of overlapping and cut-out photographs of Celestia Woolf. A tall, lanky woman with long, unkempt white-blonde hair, she was dressed entirely in black in almost every image – perhaps in a nod to her arachnid alter ego, or simply to provide contrast with her work. If you could call it work.

In one picture, the artist was clad in what looked like a forensic suit and laboratory safety goggles, and was flinging pink sugar syrup across a metal-framed chamber enclosed by sheets of cellophane. In another, she was weaving together long yellow strands emerging from a pasta maker. A third showed a close-up of two knitting needles, from which cascaded row upon row of intertwined headphone wires, the earpieces clustered down the sides like miniature microwave dishes on an analogue telecoms tower. The singular caption for these and the other images read *Woolf spider: Celestia will be realising her ethereal creations in the Tate Modern's Turbine Hall from 19 October.*

Priya looked up at Steve. 'Ethereal?'

'What's wrong with that?'

'Do you know what it means? Spaghetti can hardly be described as *delicate* or *other worldly*.'

'It's capellini, actually.'

'It's pasta. You'd be better off with something like eclectic.'

Steve shook his head. 'No, that doesn't work.'

Priya knew better than to ask why not, the response would more than likely be a blunt *it just doesn't.*

'Bizarre?'

'No.'

'Outlandish?'

'Maybe.'

'Gets my vote,' Jez put in. 'Seeing as we'd never get *freakish* past Damon.'

'I still don't get why we can't have ethereal,' Steve grumbled.

'People will know what we mean.'

'Because it's incorrect,' Priya persisted.

'It's hardly on a par with the Telegraph's Large Hardon Collider.'

Priya didn't reply, reaching for a red pen and ruling a line through the word *ethereal* and replacing it with *outlandish* before turning back to her work. He always used the same example, doubtless because he enjoyed having an excuse to say *hard on* to her. If he spent more time checking his facts and less repeating jokes that a more litigious woman might have used to pursue a harassment suit, he'd know The New York Times had published that particularly unfortunate typo two years ahead of the The Daily Telegraph. And he'd also know that Arachne – the spider of Greek mythology – hadn't been a goddess but a mere mortal who had gone up against one of the deities of the age. Priya could only hope he was better informed about the artist reimagining the legend for the twenty-first century.

Two

The photographer who had covered Saturday's gala dinner had already uploaded her photographs to Dropbox by the time Jez logged in on Monday morning, giving him a relatively mindless task with which to start the week. He felt grateful for the excuse to look busy, because there was no chance of his being able to focus on anything more challenging until he'd contained the potential fallout from Friday night. Assuming he was able to do as much. If he couldn't convince his friend the situation was a simple case of mistaken identity, he would need to decide on another way to handle it, and none of the options he'd come up with over the course of the weekend appealed.

He glanced up only briefly as Steve entered the office, and greeted him with a rather indifferent, 'Morning.'

'Morning sweetie!' Steve returned, with faux over-enthusiasm, dropping into the chair at the next desk. 'Didn't have much to say about your big night out, did you?'

Jez turned and gave his colleague what he hoped was a convincing perplexed look. 'What you on about?'

'Like you don't know,' Steve replied, pulling out his phone and scrolling for a moment before presenting Jez with a photograph. Jez pretended to take it in before looking back up at Steve.

'I don't get it.'

'You're telling me that isn't you?'

Jez uttered an expression of disbelief. 'What the fuck?' He responded. 'Are you on glue?'

Steve didn't reply, he simply held Jez's gaze, eyebrows raised. Jez stared back at him. At length, he shook his head slightly,

was replete with phrases like *down-to-earth* and *low-maintenance*. Tim begged to differ. Even on the occasions she opted for an uber-casual, thrown-together-in-five-minutes look, Natalie's routine took at least ten times that. Far from foregoing her protracted beauty regime, she simply opted for an alternative selection of make-up and styled her hair with a different set of tools. In the early days of their relationship, Tim had repeatedly assured her the process was wholly unnecessary for a woman who looked breathtaking without so much as a stroke of mascara. Three years on, he struggled to find anything about her attractive.

What had really interested him that day wasn't the profile of his wife – or rather, of her fictitious public persona – it was the topic covered by the preceding article. At the time, he had dismissed the idea almost as he considered it, but in the following weeks it had increasingly returned to mind. The terms of his and Natalie's prenuptial agreement stated that, should they divorce, their assets would be split fifty-fifty unless a third party was involved. Were one of them to commit adultery, the distribution would be very different. But, as far as the law was concerned, infidelity could be akin to the infallible conjecture of whether a tree falling in a deserted forest makes a sound: if nobody bore witness to it, it was impossible to build a case. And with that in mind, Tim turned off the high street and into Todd's Beanery for his first meeting of the day.

The business of making and serving various beverages, both hot and cold, along with a selection of pastries and sandwiches, occupied around half of the coffee shop's ground floor. It was just gone eight, and the area adjacent to the counter was busy with people placing and waiting for takeaway orders. Only two of the handful of tables at the front of the café were in use, although Tim guessed the others would soon fill up as the hour approached half-past.

His mouth dry, he put in his order before climbing the stairs to the first floor, where a small indoor seating area overlooked a roof terrace through floor-to-ceiling glass doors. Rather unusually, the walls were clad with six-inch-wide pinewood planks that had seemingly not been varnished or stained, lending the room the appearance of a giant packing crate. Tables and chairs of a much darker wood stood in two neat rows in front of the doors, beyond which a scattering of aluminium furniture lounged on the deserted terrace. The room itself was empty but for a slender blonde at the table farthest from the stairs. Dressed in a smart grey shift dress and matching jacket, Armani sunglasses and black patent high heels, she sat with one leg crossed over the other, scrolling through messages on a sleek black smartphone.

'Miss Allen?'

She looked around and reached to remove the sunglasses as she rose to her feet.

'Tim Bateman.' He held out a hand.

She shook it firmly. 'Nice to meet you,' she said, with a smile, before reclaiming her seat and inviting him to take the other chair at the table with a small gesture.

'My wife must never know about this,' Tim blurted, feeling uncharacteristically nervous, as he joined her.

'Of course not. Discretion is central to what I do, it's why I don't use email. I also don't send text messages or leave voicemails, and my calls will always come up as a private number.'

'Great.'

'Obviously my discretion relies on prompt payment. In cash.'

'That won't be a problem.'

Hearing a sound behind him, Tim glanced around warily to see a barista approaching with a tray. The man set a cappuccino and an Americano down on the table before asking whether they required anything else. Both Tim and his companion demurred, and the barista turned back in the direction of the stairs. No more was said until he had disappeared from view.

'So what happens now?' Tim asked, apprehensively.

'That's really up to you,' came the temperate reply. 'Why don't we start with exactly what it is you want?' She uncrossed and re-crossed her legs. 'Then I can give you some idea of what I might be able to deliver.'

Ramona silently counted each ring as she waited for an answer to her call, idly wondering why she had taken to counting from one to ten in Russian. The numbers were among the few words she could recall from a crash course she'd enrolled on a couple of years earlier, ahead of a visit to Kiev, en route to the Chernobyl exclusion zone. The purpose of the trip had been to report on a tour of the eerie ghost town of Pripyat, but her day in the derelict city had wound up inspiring another article that had drawn far more attention.

The sight of people taking gratuitous selfies in front of the skeletal remains of Pripyat's Palace of Culture had left Ramona feeling acutely uncomfortable: their behaviour seemed painfully inappropriate. Tourists causing offence by snapping selfies at Auschwitz had already made headlines, and Ramona was intrigued that anyone – save perhaps a sociopath – could visit such poignant sites and not feel the sobering weight of their atmosphere. That people had even been known to take selfies at funerals suggested the disconnect couldn't be explained simply as a result of time or distance. Perhaps, she had concluded, the all-encompassing nature of many people's smartphone use had diminished their awareness of the world beyond their screens and, with it, their capacity for empathy. It was a dismal realisation.

She replaced the receiver immediately on hearing the building's front door open. Moments later, when Steve strode into the office, she wished she had instead placed another, less private call, giving her an excuse to ignore him.

'What are you looking so guilty about?' He asked, tossing his wallet and phone onto his desk. 'Been making dirty calls to hot-muffs-are-us, I suppose?'

Had they not been alone, Ramona would have shot back a barbed remark about that being a fantasy of his, not hers. But with nobody else around, she felt too vulnerable to retaliate, and opted to say nothing. Steve's response to her silence was to lean to look at her computer monitor, the movement bringing him into uncomfortably close proximity. She instinctively recoiled.

'How safety gear designed for men puts women at risk,' he read, aloud, resting a hand on the armrest of her chair so that his arm brushed against hers. 'Don't you ever get tired of banging the same drum?'

'Having a female focus doesn't trump every other detail,' Ramona responded, turning her chair towards him to dislodge his hand and put some distance between them. 'You wouldn't lump health and safety, salary disparities and sexual harassment together if you were reporting on them from a binary perspective, would you?'

'Spare me the binary-nonbinary-pansexual crap,' Steve came back, turning around and leaning against her desk. 'The human race hasn't diversified overnight. People just like to tell themselves they're misunderstood, because it makes them feel special.'

'Yes, of course, it's that simple.'

'You're normally the one banging on about gender roles being foisted on us by societal expectations, and being nothing to do with nature,' he returned. 'But animals don't seem to have much difficulty with binary living. So by extension, all the additional categories floating around must be human constructs, too.'

Ramona struggled to come up with a response. She might not agree with him, but that didn't mean his point wasn't worthy of discussion – she just didn't want to discuss it with *him*.

'And it doesn't end there,' he went on. 'You lot yelling *me too* conveniently ignore the fact the mating game *relies* on males pursuing females.'

'Are you seriously suggesting men have been evolutionarily hardwired to harass women?' Ramona exclaimed, as, to her relief, she heard footsteps traipsing down the stairs.

Steve sighed theatrically. 'You've completely missed the point, as per usual,' he responded, as Jez wandered into the room, eyes glued to his mobile phone. 'Males coming onto females is the natural order of things, always has been. And apparently that's ok with you so long as you fancy them, but if you don't, wham! The exact same behaviour is suddenly harassment!' He pushed off from her desk and turned towards his own before adding, 'Well, not *you*, obviously. Other women.' He dropped into his chair. 'The ones who aren't the latest incarnation of Valerie Solanas.'

Three

'You keep frowning like that and I'll have to order in some Botox.'

Detective Sergeant Rebecca Palmer looked up from her desk to see Leighton Campbell leaning on the end of one of the filing cabinets that ran down one side of the open-plan office, vaguely demarcating a corridor. An easygoing young man in his mid-thirties who could politely be described as chubby, he was casually dressed in a navy polo shirt and jeans, his long dark hair untidily fastened in a low pony tail. As a Home Office pathologist, he wasn't based at Scotland Yard, yet somehow managed to spend a considerable amount of time in the building – in part, Rebecca suspected, because he was more interested in getting to the bottom of the circumstances surrounding his more challenging assignments than in ticking boxes for cut-and-dried cases, but also because he was a terrible procrastinator.

In the two years Leighton had been at the pathology unit, his boss, Professor William Maxwell – Max to his friends – seemed to have made little effort to moderate his chaotic time management, and Rebecca guessed her friend got away with it on account of being both eminently likeable and exceedingly good at his job. Presumably he did get everything done eventually – much of it, no doubt, in his own time – but his lack of focus on anything non-urgent was a frequent source of frustration for Rebecca's disciplined and conscientious superior officer, Detective Chief Inspector Lawrence Forrester.

'Whatcha up to?' Leighton asked, wandering into the office and leaning against the unoccupied desk to her left.

'Drawing up a shortlist of prospective flatmates to interview.'

'Fun. Want me to come over and protect you from axe murderers when you have them round?'

'You're the third person today who's offered their services. Perhaps I should be advertising a dating agency as well as a room?'

'Perish the thought. I'm much more interested in asking disturbing and highly inappropriate questions à la *Shallow Grave*.'

Rebecca smiled. 'And what would your first question be?'

Leighton raised his eyes heavenwards as he presumably considered his answer. 'Would you prefer cremation, burial or dissolution in acid?'

'Well, what can I say, you get the job.'

'You know it makes sense,' Leighton quipped with a grin, leaning forwards to peer through the glass door of the office adjacent to Rebecca's desk. 'Is Forrester not about? Max said he'd be expecting me.'

'I think he'll be back in a minute. He's got Jimmy with him today, so he's taken him on a tour of the building.'

'Bringing back child labour, that's what I like to hear. Or is it take your kid to work day again already?'

'I don't know, he muttered something about school holidays and a mix-up over arrangements.'

'Ah. Didn't listen to the wife, you mean.'

'Probably,' Rebecca said, thinking back to her own childhood holidays and visits to her grandparents in North Norfolk. Neither she nor her twin sister, Angela, had taken to water sports, and instead they had spent much of their time playing badminton in the garden and climbing the gnarled pine trees that clung to tracts of the coast. Then, when they grew a bit older, to complaining about how little there was to do in the area, flicking through teen magazines and chatting up boys at the local campsite. Happy memories that now made her feel quite the opposite emotion. Angela had been her best friend throughout childhood and adolescence, but more recently Rebecca had been lucky if they could manage a civil conversation.

The difficulties had begun with Elliot, Rebecca's now ex-fiancé, to whom Angela had taken a more or less instant dislike. Rebecca suspected that Angela – who since their early twenties had grown increasingly competitive – hadn't disliked Elliot as much as how happy Rebecca had clearly been with him. By the time the relationship began to disintegrate, she had been past trusting Angela with her feelings. When things finally fell apart, she had hoped relations with Angela might improve, but although her sister had been happy enough to say *I told you so*, there had been no olive branch, and at their last meeting, on their father's birthday, things had been as strained as ever. She sighed.

Leighton's eyebrows rose. 'What?'

'Ghosts of school holidays past. Where did you spend yours?'

'The beer garden,' Leighton replied, seemingly seriously, before smiling to dilute the impact of the remark. 'Cleethorpes, mostly. Granddad liked taking me and Tom on the light railway.'

Rebecca instinctively returned the smile. Given that Leighton's father was a life-long alcoholic, she suspected there was a fair amount of truth to his initial admission, and wondered, not for the first time, what it had been like growing up in the shadow of that kind of habit. During her final year with Elliot, which had been marred by his withdrawal into severe depression, he had relied increasingly on alcohol to dull his feelings. Twelve months of that had been about as much as Rebecca could take, and in the end she had called time on the relationship. Painful as that had been, as an adult she had at least had the luxury of being able to make the choice.

When Lawrence returned at five to twelve, he was alone, and Rebecca guessed that, anticipating Leighton's visit, he had left Jimmy with a colleague.

'Morning,' he greeted Leighton as he passed Rebecca's desk, glancing at his watch. 'Just about, anyway.' He continued on into his office, slipping his navy suit jacket off and hanging it up as Rebecca and Leighton followed him into the room. Sitting at his desk and turning his chair and hazel eyes simultaneously towards Leighton, he regarded him expectantly. 'So. Max left me a message earlier, something about a suspicious suicide?'

'Yep,' Leighton tossed a cardboard folder onto Lawrence's desk and dropped into a nearby chair. 'Steve Golding, age twenty-eight. Found hanged from the shower rail in his flat with his necktie. No note, no history of mental illness, nothing seemingly amiss in his life – mother wasn't satisfied with the original finding of suicide and requested a second PM.'

'A hunch that apparently wasn't unfounded,' Lawrence replied, opening the folder and leafing through the enclosed reports and photographs. 'What did you find?'

'Nothing conclusive, but I think it's worth a closer look.'

Lawrence nodded, spreading the crime scene photographs across the clear expanse of his desk.

'Unusual means of homicide,' Rebecca observed, moving around Lawrence's desk to view the file. 'Any idea how it was achieved without leaving any obvious signs of a struggle?'

'Not really, but I suspect he was strangled prior to being strung up,' Leighton returned. 'He'd clearly been hanging for some time before the body was found, so there's a lot of tissue damage consistent with that, but there's more evidence of bruising below it than I might have expected. There are also a couple of marks at the base of the skull,' he leaned over the desk and indicated two faint lines on the skin in one of the pictures. 'I think asphyxiation was achieved by looping the tie around something and pulling him back against it. But given that hypostasis wasn't inconsistent with the position he was found in, the body must have been moved fairly quickly after death.'

'Indicating a degree of premeditation,' Lawrence concluded. 'Any idea where he was moved from?'

''Fraid not,' Leighton replied, his tone apologetic. 'I might have had more idea if I'd had a chance to view the scene, but it was a rented flat and everything's already been boxed up and cleared out.'

'So what makes you so sure the body was moved?'

'I went over his socks with sticky tape. I got significantly more dust and particulate matter from the outer side of the left foot and the inner side of the right one than from anywhere else, which suggests that his feet were dragged across the floor.'

'But he was found with his shoes on,' Lawrence indicated one of the photographs.

Leighton shrugged. 'Perhaps that's why nobody thought to check his socks before.'

'Curious.'

'Someone may have been trying to avoid leaving scuff marks on the floor,' Rebecca suggested.

Lawrence nodded. 'Was he drugged?'

'No. Some alcohol in his system, but not enough to render him incapable.'

'So why didn't he struggle?'

'Good question. And one I can't answer.'

There was a moment's silence before Lawrence sat back in his chair. 'Was there anything else?'

'Possibly. Among the foreign DNA profiles I recovered was one from the genital area that tested positive for salivary amylase, so at a guess he was intimate with someone in the hours before his death. Although whether that person was with him when he died is anybody's guess.'

'Girlfriend?'

'Unlikely. According to the original police report there is a girlfriend, because she found the body, but I very much doubt it was her DNA.' Leighton paused. 'Unless she's trans, that is. The DNA I found was male.'

Lawrence and Rebecca's first stop after a quick sandwich lunch was a smart red-brick Edwardian mansion block moments from Marylebone High Street that was home to Steve's mother, Alyson Parker. From its location and what Lawrence glimpsed of the high-spec kitchen and substantial dining room on the short walk from the front door to the main reception room, he guessed the fourth-floor apartment would fetch several million on the open market.

The high-ceilinged living room was simply decorated in neutral shades, and plenty big enough to accommodate the two cream three-seater sofas that faced one another across a soft moss-green carpet, their seats littered with cushions in the same hue. Two matching armchairs stood, side by side, at angles to the sofas, looking out across the thick velvet pile and a long, glass-topped coffee table towards a substantial fireplace. The alcoves either side of the chimney breast hosted underemployed made-to-measure shelves, and the fireplace itself apparently wasn't much used, either, occupied as it was by an impressive flower arrangement.

Although tired, Alyson looked younger than Lawrence had expected, and he wondered whether she had been a teenage mother or whether her youthful appearance was a result of clean living, good skincare or perhaps even cosmetic work. She appeared quite composed, her apprehension betrayed only by the protective position in which she held her arms, gripping the sides of her knee-length belted cardigan as if it needed to be held in place manually. She offered refreshments as Lawrence and Rebecca sat down, and when Lawrence politely declined, perched on the opposite sofa, saying, 'Will's been quite non-committal. Do you think it was murder?'

A moment passed before Lawrence managed to place the alias, having never heard Max referred to by any derivative of his Christian name. Use of the familiar abbreviation of his surname apparently wasn't universal.

'At this stage we can't be sure of anything,' he said. 'Perhaps you might start by telling us why you were so convinced it was something more sinister?'

'It just didn't make any sense,' Alyson replied, hollowly. 'He was full of plans for the future – he'd just had a mortgage application approved by the bank and an offer accepted on a lovely flat in Putney, he'd booked a holiday in the Caribbean for next spring, he was applying for new jobs –' her voice wavering, she trailed off. After a brief pause, she added, 'He had all this energy and drive, and I don't see how he could have faked that.'

'We don't always know our children as well as we might like to think.'

'No, I know, but I can't believe he wouldn't have left some kind of explanation. That there was no note – nothing on Instagram or Twitter – no emails to anyone –' she shook her head slightly. 'That just seems so unlike him.'

Lawrence nodded. 'Could you give us some idea of who Steve was? His work, interests, friends – that kind of thing.'

'Yes, of course,' Alyson forced a small, artificial smile. 'He was a journalist. He was looking to get a job on one of the nationals. He'd been at a local paper, the Clapham Chronicle, for a couple of years. I think he found a lot of the subject matter rather dull, but you can't expect to start at the top, can you?'

'How about his colleagues, did he talk much about them?'

'Not really. He made the odd complaint about editorial changes he didn't agree with, but that was about it.'

'And what did he do with his free time?'

'A lot of socialising, from what I could gather. He seemed to be out every other night – dinners, drinks, galleries – occasionally the theatre, but that wasn't really his thing. He had a loose interest in rugby, but I was never sure how much that was about the game and how much it was just an opportunity to take advantage of corporate hospitality.'

'Was that opportunity available through his work?'

'No, one of his pals – a chap called Fraser. It was a perk of his job.'

'How about Steve's father?'

'He's in New York, has been for most of Steve's life. They never saw a lot of each other – Duncan's always been inclined to put work before anything else. Steve visited him a few times, and I think they kept in touch via email and Skype, but they didn't have a close relationship.'

'And when did you last hear from Steve?'

'I last saw him the weekend before he died. He came over for Sunday lunch. Then on the Monday he emailed me to say the offer had been accepted on the flat. I replied to congratulate him.'

'Do you know anything about the property, or have the name of the estate agent involved?'

'Yes, Steve emailed the spec through after his first viewing. Would you like to see it?'

Lawrence confirmed that he would, placing a copy of his card on the coffee table to provide her with an email address to forward it to before continuing.

'How did Steve seem when you saw him that Sunday?'

'He was in good spirits. Rupert – my husband – remarked that he practically skipped through the front door.'

'What was their relationship like?'

'It wasn't disastrous, but it could have been a lot better,' Alyson replied, regretfully.

'Did they fall out over anything recently?'

'Not as far as I'm aware. Since Steve left home they've generally been civil to one another, but I'd be lying if I said they got along.'

'How old was Steve when you remarried?'

'Fourteen.'

'Was there anything in particular that he and your husband argued about?'

Alyson shook her head. 'To begin with it was just about everything. Steve didn't like having another adult to answer to, which was understandable, but knowing that didn't make the situation any easier. Rupert and I had to pick our battles, and over time things did settle down.'

Lawrence nodded. 'Would you mind telling me what Rupert was doing the night Steve died?' He asked, more to gauge Alyson's reaction than to ascertain the man's whereabouts. She didn't appear unsettled by the question, and Lawrence wondered whether she had expected it.

'He was at a meeting in Birmingham on the Wednesday evening. He runs a company that develops technologies for sustainable living.'

'And you?'

'I left work about seven. I had a friend over for dinner, she left shortly before eleven, I tidied up the kitchen and went to bed.'

'What time did your husband get home?'

'You'd have to ask him. He sleeps in the spare room on the nights he's back late, because I have to be up at six.'

'So you didn't see him at all that night.'

'No.'

'Does he have any children?'

'A daughter. Jasmine.'

'And how does she fit into the picture?'

'She was at university by the time Rupert and I moved in together, so she's never lived with us. She and Steve didn't hit it off because of his attitude towards her father – she lost her mother quite young, and the two of them are very close. I shouldn't think she had any contact with Steve outside of family gatherings.'

Lawrence wondered whether an examination of Steve's email and social-media accounts would bear this out. On occasion, such applications proved very useful, but more often than not they simply served to further complicate police work, with people's contact lists frequently including friends of friends, distant relatives and at least a smattering of individuals they'd never even met. Faced with a vast, overlapping network of connections it was nigh on impossible to establish whether all of the points on the grid were genuine. Online, as Lawrence frequently reminded both his children, anonymity was a double-edged sword: one could purport to be just about anybody.

Sitting across from Steve's pretty twenty-five-year-old girlfriend, Rebecca found herself wondering what she might have to forgo to make the time to look as perfectly turned out as Mia on a daily basis. The gentle curl of her thick blonde hair might, Rebecca conceded, be a natural blessing; if not, a blow-dry would be first on the list. Given enough practice, the flawless two-tone eye make-up would presumably be relatively quick to achieve, as would the neatly plucked eyebrows. The impeccable French manicure, on the other hand, would require at least weekly trips to the salon; the subtly toned calves and upper arms, even more frequent sessions of cardio and weight training.

Rebecca's approach to exercise vacillated between determination to keep fit – usually by means of an activity such as running or swimming that didn't tie her to gym membership or a class schedule – and total inaction. Sustaining any real motivation was hard going given that she found physical activity a chore: there was no sport she felt any real passion for, and she had never experienced the addictive endorphin rush others raved about. As a result, she relied largely on dietary sacrifice to maintain her size-ten figure, and was conscious that this approach didn't represent a viable long-term strategy.

Her job demanded a relatively smart dress code, and she did go to the trouble of applying a quick coat of mascara and eye shadow most mornings; however, in her own time she rarely bothered with make-up, and her limited selection of dresses and high heels largely saw the light of day only between the opening and closing of the wardrobe doors. In an ideal world, she would have loved to look as beautifully put-together as Mia on more than the odd night out or special occasion, but, in reality, life was just too short.

Contrary to either the information originally provided to Leighton or his recollection of it – Rebecca suspected the former – Mia hadn't been the one to discover Steve's body, she had simply alerted his landlord that something might be amiss after repeated attempts to contact him had failed to raise a response. She had been present at the scene, however, and one of the officers in attendance had taken a brief statement, but Lawrence generally preferred to get a comprehensive picture of any situation in person, and Rebecca wasn't surprised when he took Mia through the basics again. With the details of the initial who, what and where clarified, he asked what she remembered of her first reaction to the news of Steve's death.

'I didn't believe it,' she replied, rather dully.

'That he was dead, or that it was of his own doing?'

'Either. I mean, I thought there was no way he'd have done that, so it couldn't be him. Not that it would've made sense for it to have been anyone else, either, but –' she trailed off with a weak shrug.

'How long had you been together?'

'Nearly a year.'

'And when did you see him last?'

seem to be able to just say what they think and move on. It seems so straightforward.' She twisted the ring on her middle finger around and around, fragments of marcasite catching the light as she did so. 'I wish girls could do that. Our friendships seem so much more complicated. If I tried to tell it like it is, I'm pretty sure I'd be labelled a bitch.'

Having gathered from Alyson Parker that Fraser Boardman was a solicitor specialising in commercial litigation, Lawrence hadn't expected to find him at his home in the leafy Richmond suburb of Barnes on a Tuesday afternoon. As Fraser showed Lawrence and Rebecca into a bright, minimalist living area overlooking a tiny courtyard garden, he explained that he was working remotely after an out-of-town meeting that morning. Inviting them to sit, he reached to close the laptop lying on the coffee table and sat in an expansive armchair, remarking, 'I'm glad someone's finally taking this seriously,' as Lawrence made himself comfortable on the sofa.

'I'm not aware of anyone taking Steve's death anything but seriously,' Lawrence returned, coolly.

'You know what I mean. Steve wasn't some pathetic loser who couldn't cope with life. There's no way he'd have done something so bloody selfish.'

'Did he ever do or say anything to give you that impression?'

'He had a few choice things to say when he was late for a mate's wedding after the Victoria Line was suspended because some waste of space jumped in front of a train, yeah.'

Lawrence nodded, but before he had a chance to continue, Fraser added, 'Nobody who knew Steve would say any different. I can't believe it's taken this long to get someone to look into it.'

Whether or not Steve's friends and family all shared Fraser's belief that Steve hadn't died by his own hand, Lawrence suspected most of them would *say* as much very differently. Alyson Parker had been unusually composed for a woman who had recently lost her son, regardless of the circumstances, and her reasoning had been very much more considered than Fraser's; Mia, meanwhile, had still seemed almost shell-shocked by recent events.

'Assuming Steve didn't take his own life, can you think of anyone who might have been responsible for his death?'

Given that Fraser hadn't seemed short on opinions thus far, Lawrence had expected him to have one on this, and felt surprised when the man simply shook his head.

'He hadn't upset anyone lately?'

'I've no idea. We were mates, not bedfellows.'

'Were you ever?'

Fraser frowned. 'What?'

'Were you and Steve ever more than friends?'

'No! Jesus, what the hell kind of question is that? I have a fiancée! Steve had a girlfriend! What is *wrong* with you people?'

'There's no need to get so uptight, none of this is personal.'

'In what fucked-up world is that not a personal question?'

'What I mean,' Lawrence replied, with thinly veiled impatience, 'Is that these questions aren't tailored specifically to you. I'm not casting aspersions, I'm simply collecting information.'

Fraser looked unconvinced, but said nothing further.

'So to the best of your knowledge, Steve wasn't at odds with anyone.'

'No.'

'Did you see a lot of one another?'

'A fair amount. Most weeks six or seven of us would get together for some beers. And we always went to Cortina in January. To ski.'

'All of you?'

'Yes,' Fraser snapped. 'And our girlfriends.'

'Presumably that included Mia?'

'It would've done, she was planning on coming this year.'

'How well do you know her?'

'I've chatted to her a few times, but I wouldn't say we *know* one another,' Fraser answered, guardedly.

'Was she faithful to Steve?'

'How should I know?'

'How about Steve?' Lawrence asked. 'Did he ever play away?'

'Not if he had any sense. Nico would have knocked his block off if he'd messed Mia about.'

'Who's Nico?'

'Her brother. He's a mate. That's how Steve and Mia met.'

'Is he another member of your group?'

'Yes.'

'Do you know how he felt about Steve and Mia's relationship?'

Fraser wrinkled his nose as he apparently considered this question. 'I don't know,' he admitted, at length. 'I guess it must be a bit weird having one of your mates shagging your sister, but Steve was a decent guy and he could afford to look after her, so unless he didn't treat her right I can't see there was a lot not to like.'

'So Nico never talked to you about the relationship,' Lawrence concluded, aloud, not sure what to make of Fraser's outdated take on brotherly outlook, and wondering whether he had any siblings of his own.

'Not really.'

'That being the case, what makes you think he would have responded violently if he'd discovered Steve was being unfaithful?'

'Would you let someone get away with it if they were doing the dirty on your sister?'

Had the question been put to him in a social setting, Lawrence might have been tempted to remark that he would have considered it karma, if such a thing existed. In her years as a single woman, his sister, Carla, had cheated on a fair few of her many boyfriends, Lawrence's friends among them. A more measured response would have been that he had generally kept well out of her frenetic love life on the basis that it wasn't his place to interfere. As it was, he chose to treat the question as rhetorical, saying instead that Fraser's response hadn't answered his and asking whether Nico had ever done or said anything to suggest he would have retaliated on Mia's behalf should Steve have betrayed her.

'Not explicitly,' Fraser conceded.

'So your projection is really based on how you might react in that situation,' Lawrence observed. 'And on that note, would you mind telling us where you were the night Steve died?'

'Thoughts so far?' Lawrence asked, as he started the ignition.

'I'm a little confused,' Rebecca replied. 'I'm sure I read that Neanderthals died out thousands of years ago, yet we've just found one living in South London.'

'We ought to notify the Natural History Museum,' Lawrence joked.

'I thought evolution was supposed to improve on what went before it,' she continued. 'But in this instance, I think chimpanzees would be within their rights to view that as an insult.'

Lawrence laughed.

'I'm not kidding. If Steve was that much of a knob I wouldn't be surprised if somebody wanted him dead.'

'That thought did cross my mind,' Lawrence admitted, glancing over his shoulder before pulling out into the road.

Rebecca sighed, resting her elbow on the narrow window ledge and propping her head up with her hand. 'Do you think that's what Mia considers *telling it like it is*?'

'Well you couldn't accuse him of mincing his words.'

'No, but being a self-assured jerk isn't the same as being honest.'

'That aside, do you think men and women are different in that regard?'

There was a pause before Rebecca said, 'I think *people* are different in that regard. Some are more forthright than others, regardless of gender.' She paused again. 'Women probably pay more attention to social niceties, but then I suspect it's largely women who are offended when those niceties are violated.'

Lawrence nodded.

'I think women rely on subtle cues that men either don't pick up on or just don't care for,' Rebecca went on. 'But the fact men communicate in a more direct manner doesn't mean they do it any more honestly.'

'Katie tells me subtlety is a waste of time where I'm concerned,' Lawrence replied. 'You'd think I'd have a handle on it by now, given the amount of time I spend trying to read people in this job, but apparently not.'

'I thought she didn't want you bringing your work home?'

Lawrence smiled. 'I'll try that line next time,' he said, wryly. 'Agreeing that subtlety is a waste of time when she could just cut to the chase and tell me what she thinks apparently wasn't the right answer.'

'No, that sounds like the kind of response that would get you into trouble.'

'Got it in one,' Lawrence said, glancing at his watch. 'I can only hope Jimmy hasn't managed to do the same while we've been gone.'

'Where's Elise today? Is she not on half term, too?'

'She's visiting Katie's folks in Whitstable for a few days.'

'And Jimmy didn't fancy that?'

'That's one way of putting it,' Lawrence replied, shortly, loath to go into any further detail. In fact, until a few days earlier, fourteen-year-old Jimmy had been due to accompany his younger sister on the visit to their grandparents' seaside home. Lawrence and his wife, Katie, had been planning to take the two children to Paris for a long weekend before dropping them off in Kent on the return journey. But, on Friday evening, just as they had been packing ahead of their scheduled early-morning departure on the Eurostar, Lawrence had received a call from the local police to inform him that Jimmy had been caught travelling in a stolen car.

It wasn't the boy's first run-in with the law. Earlier in the year, Lawrence had suffered the ignominy of having to collect Jimmy from the local police station after he was caught daubing graffiti on the wall of a church. Lawrence had paid for the damage to be rectified – after which no further action had been taken – and had hoped the shock of being arrested would deter his son from committing any further crimes. The recent discovery of several broad-tipped paint markers of the type favoured by graffiti taggers in one of Jimmy's desk drawers had been cause for concern, but had done little to prepare Lawrence for the boy's latest exploit.

Jimmy had maintained all weekend that he hadn't known the vehicle was stolen, and although Lawrence didn't for one moment believe that, he did derive some comfort from the fact his son hadn't been the one in the driving seat. As a result of this – and the lack of any real evidence to contradict Jimmy's testimony – there had been little the police could do but give the boy a stern talking to and leave the matter of any further discipline to his parents. Lawrence and Katie had spent much of the long weekend going over the various options available to them, but, by the time Monday evening rolled around, they had been no closer to a decision – and were facing the additional dilemma of what to do with Jimmy during working hours for the remaining four days of half term.

Leaving him alone at home clearly wasn't an option, and, with both Lawrence and Katie due at work on Tuesday morning, the

and in the process come across a battered – and, more interestingly, locked – cash box. Thus far, she had resisted the temptation to pick the lock, but with the cleaning finally finished and the box sitting in front of her on the kitchen table, her resolve was weakening.

She might have been better able to resist had Elliot not kept so much to himself. Throughout their three years together it had been an uphill struggle to get him to talk about anything personal, particularly his past, during which he had become estranged from his family – whether of his volition or theirs, Rebecca didn't know. She had been left with a wealth of unanswered questions, and the idea that some of them might be answered by the contents of the box was compelling, not least because the odds of her being able to put him out of her mind once his belongings were out of sight were stacked against her.

When they had met, Elliot had been working long hours as a sound engineer and DJ-ing two nights a week on top of that to pay for studio time and equipment for his band, Astatine. She'd seen him through the lengthy campaign to raise money to pay for the first album, the crazy hours in the studio recording it and the early tours to promote it. And she'd watched him go from a minor underground celebrity to featuring almost weekly in the *NME*. Now, when all she wanted to do was forget about him, he finally seemed to have achieved what he'd been chasing throughout their relationship. Astatine's latest single, *Whispers in the Dust*, had been enjoying almost hourly airplay on mainstream radio and music television, and looked set to make Elliot a household name on both sides of the Atlantic. And the sad fact was that he was now too lost in misery and oblivion to enjoy – or possibly even notice – his success.

Her curiosity getting the better of her, Rebecca set about the lock with a paperclip and a small screwdriver. Leighton had previously shown her how to pick a rudimentary lock, a skill she imagined he'd picked up as a teenager from the elder brother who had spent the better part of his adult life in the custody of Her Majesty's Prison Service. That two siblings could turn out so differently was definitely ammunition for the argument of nature over nurture, Rebecca thought, although which had been at fault in Elliot's case was anybody's guess. Her hands trembling, she flicked the paperclip to one side and was rewarded with a metallic clunk. Setting the screwdriver down, she hesitated before lifting the lid. Now that she had access to the box she wasn't so sure she wanted it. She took a deep breath before gingerly flinging it open in a manner she generally reserved for any container likely to contain a spider.

Rebecca had seen the tatty photograph at the top of the pile before. The picture – of a teenage Elliot and his younger brother on a beach with a brightly coloured kite – was the only one Rebecca had seen of Elliot before his early twenties. There was no order to the box's contents, with receipts, flyers, backstage passes, postcards and the like mixed in with other paraphernalia, which ranged from guitar picks to a frayed and discoloured tangle of embroidery threads that had, before the threads wore through, been a friendship bracelet. Rebecca wondered who had given it to him.

None of the odds and ends scattered around the box was particularly noteworthy, and Rebecca turned her attention to the stack of papers. The receipts were all for major purchases, and most of the flyers bore either the names of his friends' bands or club nights, or his own DJ name – E – which had always seemed a strange choice for the rock genre, in which MDMA had never been anywhere near as popular as alcohol and cocaine. There were several other photographs, although none of Elliot, the subjects encompassing a selection of his friends and, in two cases, Rebecca herself.

Near the bottom of the pile was a thin slip of card that came as something of a surprise: a leaflet outlining the twelve steps of Alcoholics Anonymous. Given that Elliot had steadfastly refused to do anything to help himself, Rebecca guessed it had been bestowed upon him by a doctor or a friend, and turned it over in search of an answer. A moment passed before she managed to put her finger on what it was about the front of the leaflet that wasn't right, and when she did, she felt cold. Only one of the two letters staring up at her was an *A*.

Four

Lawrence purchased two coffees and a handful of pastries before heading to join Max at a table towards the rear of the coffee shop. Max was reclining in a compact armchair, his long legs loosely folded under a small round table. Besides some loss of volume and colour to his sandy hair and the addition of a few lines to his brow, he'd barely changed in the fifteen years since Lawrence had joined CID. In those days, they had worked and socialised closely, but more recently the business of running the pathology unit had left his friend with less and less time to attend crime scenes, while the pressures of family life on both sides had restricted their opportunities to connect outside the workplace.

'Sorry I couldn't do last night, I had Jim with me,' Lawrence said, as he set the tray he carried down on the table.

'Is he thinking of following in your footsteps?'

'If only,' Lawrence replied, taking the seat opposite Max. 'In the past six months he seems to have been doing his best to get on the other side of the law.'

'Perhaps he's just trying to push back against your authority.'

'I don't know. To begin with I might have been inclined to agree, but I think it's gone beyond that now.' He filled his friend in on recent events, and the potential courses of action that he and Katie had spent the past four days discussing without coming close to a conclusion. Without knowing what lay at the root of their son's behaviour, it was difficult to gauge which option, or options, offered the best chance of success.

Lawrence's father had been all for shipping Jimmy off to boarding school after his first brush with the law; he had even offered to pay the fees, apparently having guessed such recourse wouldn't otherwise be financially viable. But it seemed to Lawrence that relinquishing responsibility for the problem would send entirely the wrong message to a teenage boy who had so far refused to take responsibility for his own actions.

With this in mind, he added, 'Packing him off to boarding school seems like a cop-out. At least, at this stage. But, at the same time, I don't know whether we can afford to give it much longer before we take some sort of drastic action.'

'What's Jimmy's response to the idea of boarding?' Max asked, reaching for a croissant and tearing the pastry in two.

'We've not broached it yet. My gut reaction is that it's not the answer. I don't want him to get the impression we're giving up on him, and while it might make for a quieter life at our end – at least in the short term – I'm not convinced it would do much to improve his prospects. There's no guarantee he'd stay out of trouble at school any more than at home. And I'm more concerned with safeguarding his future than with making my life easier.'

'Do you not think you've answered your own question, then?'

'On occasion,' Lawrence agreed. 'Then I find myself coming back to the fact we probably only have so much time to turn things around. And I feel as though I should have more idea of how to handle the situation. I'm fairly certain Katie thinks as much. But, to be honest, I'm at a bit of a loss to know what to do with him.'

'So you're keeping him under surveillance.'

'Something like that,' Lawrence sighed. 'Unfortunately it doesn't represent a viable long-term strategy. We can't watch his every move forever.' He shook his head. 'And maybe that's part of the problem, maybe I've been too strict. I don't know.'

'How old's Jim now?'

'Fourteen.'

Max nodded. 'At some point we have to recognise that they bear a certain amount of responsibility for their actions, as well.'

'I know,' Lawrence replied. 'But getting him to take responsibility is proving a challenge.' He stirred the foam head of his cappuccino into the coffee. 'How are yours?'

'Fine. Sparkling, in Lily's case – she's obsessed with body glitter. That stuff gets everywhere. It's driving Marnie mad.'

'If you've not already found you're tracking iridescent stars into work it's only a matter of time,' Lawrence replied, thinking back to the height of Elise's infatuation with anything that shimmered.

'That's going to go down well with grieving relatives,' Max remarked. 'On that note, I gather you caught up with Aly yesterday. How was she?'

'Very composed, given the circumstances.'

'Sounds like Aly.'

'How do you know her?'

'We were at school together. She married one of my mates.'

'Duncan.'

'Yes.'

'I got the impression he didn't have a lot of input into Steve's upbringing.'

'Not really, no. He buggered off to New York when Steve was three or four. The marriage didn't have the most auspicious start – Aly fell pregnant at eighteen and Duncan jumped in with both feet. He spent the next few years working ten hours a day in some dead-end job and trying to play happy families in a gloomy bedsit in Elephant and Castle before deciding to jump ship.'

'Are you still in touch?'

'Not really. I see the occasional update on Linked In – I gather he's a big shot in the advertising world – but that's about it.'

'How did Alyson cope with his departure?'

'Admirably. She's not one to mope around. She put all her

energies into building a career. I suspect Steve didn't always see a lot of her, because she was juggling studying with working her way up the ladder, but I think she viewed it as a necessary evil to provide for him.'

'Did he resent that?'

'Truthfully, I don't know. But – and please don't repeat this – I think she spoiled him to compensate. I'm afraid he got rather accustomed to getting what he wanted, when he wanted.'

'Do you think he might have had trouble handling a situation where he didn't get his way?'

'I certainly wouldn't rule it out.'

Lawrence nodded. 'Given how well both his parents have done I imagine he felt under some pressure to succeed himself.'

'I suppose so. But he never seemed short of ambition, he used to talk about the prospect of reporting from war zones and disaster-stricken regions with great enthusiasm.'

'Alyson said he had his sights set on more than local news.'

'Yes. He seemed to be getting on all right. He won a prize earlier in the year for one of his articles. It's a competitive business, and you have to claw your way up. I don't think he would have had a problem with that.'

'You mean he wouldn't have had many qualms about trampling over other people to get there,' Lawrence said.

'I suspect not. Have you spoken to any of his colleagues?'

'Not yet, that's first on our list this morning.'

'What are your thoughts at this point?'

'I've yet to gather enough information to draw any conclusions.'

'Cautious as ever,' Max observed with a knowing smile. 'Ok, let me put it another way. What's your *feeling* about it?'

Lawrence smiled in return. 'My *feeling* is that although the evidence is limited I am inclined to agree with Leighton that it warrants a closer look.'

Max nodded.

Lawrence glanced at his watch. 'Do you suppose he'll be in yet?'

Max shot him a warning look. 'We've had this conversation.'

'I didn't –'

'I am not prepared to micromanage my staff,' Max asserted. 'Particularly not the ones who regularly go way beyond the call of duty. Leighton is exceptionally good at what he does, and his understanding of analytical chemistry is a huge boon when the guys at the lab are dragging their feet. He could make a hell of a lot more money elsewhere, and I'm not about to start quibbling over his punctuality or clock-watching his lunch breaks.'

'It wasn't a loaded question,' Lawrence replied. 'I just need to pick up a report we spoke about yesterday. If he's not about I'll do it later.'

'Sorry,' Max conceded, shaking his head slightly. 'I've already had words with Pete this week about my *style of management*, as he put it. He seemed to expect me to override Jon's opinion simply because he disagreed with it.'

Lawrence suspected DCI Peter Rose felt entitled to overrule most people if their opinion conflicted with his own. He hoped he had never been guilty of such glaring arrogance. Two heads – or more – were almost invariably better than one in helping to piece together the circumstances surrounding a serious crime, and he would never want people to feel they were the subjects of a dictatorship rather than members of a team. But he didn't think a good work ethic was too much to ask for. And as far as he was concerned, that included being at work from the start – and until the end – of your contracted hours.

The Clapham Chronicle's chief editor wasn't around when Rebecca and Lawrence arrived at the newspaper's dingy and

had occurred within the penal system, which perhaps had the capacity to mimic certain aspects of depressive illness in psychopaths by robbing them of stimulation and the opportunity to experience pleasure. The ensuing boredom and frustration, coupled with the impulsive nature of the personality type, might, she supposed, be sufficient to trigger an extreme response. It was certainly an interesting question.

'Was Steve good at his job?' Lawrence asked.

'That depends on your perspective.'

Lawrence's eyebrows rose. 'Well I'm asking you, so I'd like your perspective.'

'He was good at finding stories, but his rendering of them left a lot to be desired.'

'Meaning what, exactly?'

'He was a crap writer,' Priya clarified, bluntly.

Lawrence frowned. 'But he was a journalist. I would have thought being able to write was a prerequisite.'

Priya smiled. 'Yes, you would. But really you just need to be able to turn a story in on deadline. A badly written story can be fixed; no story means a hole on the page, and that's not fixable.'

'And who fixes the badly written ones? You?'

Priya nodded.

'How do the writers feel about that?'

'It varies. By and large, the worse the writer, the more precious they are about their work.'

'Was that true of Steve?'

'Yes. He was quite resistant to a lot of my changes.'

'Did you ever fall out over it?'

'*Fall out* is probably too strong. We argued a lot over alterations, but at the end of the day we're reporting local news, not brokering world peace. It's not worth losing sleep over.'

Lawrence nodded. 'What can you tell me about Steve's relationship with the other members of staff?'

'Generally I think it was ok. Ramona's clashed with him a few times because she's a staunch feminist and Steve's chauvinist remarks were anathema to her. But more often than not I got the impression she didn't think he was worth her time.'

'How about people he wrote about, did any of them take umbrage?'

'Not that I'm aware of, but complaints don't come to me.'

'Who do they go to? The editor?'

'Yes.'

'And did Steve talk much about his personal life?'

Priya shook her head. 'He talked loosely about places he'd been – he liked to name-drop trendy bars and restaurants – and he gave the impression he got a fair amount of action, but I don't know whether that was for real.'

'Action in what sense? Sexually?'

'Yes.'

'Did you think it unlikely?'

'Not necessarily. He could be very charming when it suited him. But I know guys often exaggerate about that kind of thing.'

'So you weren't aware he had a girlfriend.'

Priya made an involuntary sound somewhere between a snort and laugh. 'Seriously?'

'Yes.'

'No,' she replied, shaking her head in emphasis. 'I was not aware of that. Although I can see he may have used the word *girlfriend* rather more loosely than many of us.' She paused. 'I wouldn't mind betting she wasn't the only one.'

By the time Lawrence and Rebecca had asked all they could of Priya, the paper's chief editor, Damon McRae, was in his office. Priya showed them in to what turned out to be another cluttered, windowless room, and introduced them before closing the door on her way out. Damon, a tall, hefty man of forty-something with wispy, receding hair stood to offer a hand. His grey suit looked slightly crumpled, as if he had slept the night in it – or perhaps just not bothered to hang it up – and the top two buttons of his blue shirt were undone, a tie lying loosely coiled in the uppermost of the three filing trays on his desk. This was awash with computer printouts, many of them annotated with red pen and several stained with what looked like coffee. Three empty mugs clustered around the rear of the desktop telephone, which bore flashing LEDs presumably indicating either waiting calls or voicemail messages.

'What's this about?' Damon asked, looking perplexed, as he sat back down.

'We just have few questions about Steve Golding,' Lawrence informed him, casually, taking a seat on the opposite side of the desk.

'Why? Do you have reason to doubt it was suicide?'

'Do you?'

There was a momentary pause before Damon said, 'Well it certainly came as a huge shock to all of us.'

'So he didn't seem distracted or unhappy in the days or weeks before his death?'

'No. Everything seemed perfectly normal until –' the man trailed off with a lift of his eyebrows.

'How long Steve had been working here?'

'Just under two years. Since he passed his NCE.'

'Which is what?'

'An exam. Set by the National Council for the Training of Journalists.'

'Did he live up to your expectations?'

'Very much so. His death was a big loss to us. He understood the importance of networking – contacts are vital to what we do – and he was a natural when it came to drawing people out. He asked the right questions and he got the right answers.'

'And what are the *right* answers?' Lawrence asked, his curiosity piqued by this remark.

'The interesting ones,' Damon replied, frankly. 'In the online world, news becomes old news in minutes – people are tweeting and blogging almost the moment something happens. Reporting the facts isn't enough anymore, we need to add value – put those facts in context, provide additional information, tell people why they ought to care. And you want quotes that bring something to the story, not just state the obvious.'

'When did you last see Steve?'

'The morning of the day he died – we had a meeting early on, after that I was out for much of the day – by the time I got back Steve had already gone to record an interview with an artist we were featuring in the paper that week.'

'Who was the artist?'

'Celestia Woolf. She has an exhibition on at the Tate Modern.'

'Do you know whether Steve kept that appointment?'

'I would assume so. I didn't hear anything to the contrary from either of them.'

'I'd like her contact details, please.'

'Certainly. Although I expect you'll find her at the Tate. She's a performance artist.'

Lawrence acknowledged this detail with a nod. He had never understood the point of performance art – or, rather, never been convinced it *was* art. In some cases it could be described as performance, of sorts, but how posturing amid props intended to be shocking, prosaic or just plain weird could be described as art was beyond him. He wasn't at all sure the medium's aficionados were really convinced, either; more likely they just wanted to be seen to understand the pretentious nonsense that a handful of astute individuals were touting as culture. It seemed like money for old rope.

'Had Steve fallen out with anyone recently?'

'Not as far as I'm aware. But I don't know much about his life outside these walls.'

'I understand that any complaints about the content of the paper come to you, though.'

'Generally, yes.'

'Did anything Steve wrote give anyone cause for complaint?'

'Not about anything of note. Being a local paper we rarely get the opportunity to break a big story that people might have strong feelings about. Most of the complaints we receive relate to silly mistakes – names spelled incorrectly, mislabelled photographs, that sort of thing.'

'Was he working on anything that might have been contentious, or that someone might have wanted to keep under wraps?'

'Nothing I'm aware of, but you're welcome to have a look through his notebooks, assuming they're still here. I would have thought any information he had would be detailed in them, for legal reasons if nothing else.'

'That would be helpful, thank you.'

'I'll see whether I can find them for you,' Damon offered, moving to stand.

'One more thing before you do. What kind of salary was Steve on?'

'I couldn't tell you the exact figure without looking it up, but it would have been in the region of twenty grand. This isn't a job people go into for the money.'

Lawrence nodded, asking Damon to let him have the precise number when he had the chance and wondering how Steve had financed the lifestyle they had heard so much about in the past twenty-four hours. In light of his earlier conversation with Max, Lawrence suspected the most likely explanation was the Bank of Mum and Dad – or at least Mum. Of course, it was also possible the high life had been funded by an increasing reliance on credit, which might provide a credible motive for suicide. After all, they only had Alyson's word for it that Steve's mortgage application had been approved, and she would presumably have taken that news on trust. It wouldn't be the first time a fantasy life had fallen foul of the unavoidable constraints of reality.

Lawrence imagined Ramona regularly found herself on the receiving end of asinine comments along the lines of *you're too sexy to be a feminist.* Au naturel, it might have been *too pretty*, but she'd chosen to overshadow the porcelain skin and pale eyes of her innate English rose with a thick aubergine bob and a dash of lipstick in an almost identical shade. Combined with a monochrome-print wrap dress that showed off her cleavage and hourglass figure, and knee-high black boots, her look was more striking than pretty.

Having established that she had been a senior reporter at the Chronicle for a little over eighteen months, Lawrence asked what her relationship with Steve had been like. Her answer was unhelpfully abrupt.

'Professional.'

'Could you expand on that?'

There was a moment's silence before Ramona replied. 'My career is more important to me than scoring points, so if need be I bite my tongue and keep things civil.'

'Did you need to do that often where Steve was concerned?'

'All the time.'

'Why was that?'

Given how carefully she had phrased her previous answers, Lawrence was surprised when she responded, bluntly, 'Because he was an arrogant, sexist bigot.'

'Strong words,' he said, hoping to encourage further comment.

Ramona shrugged. 'My job is easier if people just tell it like it is. I can't imagine the same isn't true of yours. The fact I didn't like Steve doesn't mean I wished him dead.'

'Can you think of anyone who might have done?'

'No.'

'And was there anything about Steve's behaviour that struck you as out of the ordinary in the days or weeks before he died?'

'Nothing. One day he was joking with Jez and needling Priya, the next –' she held out her hands in lieu of finishing the sentence. 'When I first heard he'd died I assumed he'd been in an accident.'

'Do you remember what he said to Priya that day?'

Ramona appeared to consider the matter for a moment before shaking her head. 'No. It would have been something inappropriate under the guise of banter, but I don't recall the details.'

'Was he often inappropriate towards her?'

'Frequently.'

'Have you any idea how she felt about that?'

'Not really. On occasion she was clearly irritated, but I don't know how much it bothered her.'

'So you and she didn't discuss it.'

'I told her a few times that she shouldn't stand for it. But then she thinks I'm an ardent feminist for saying men should always treat women with respect. I don't think that's feminism, I think it's common decency.'

'Do you think his remarks were made with malicious intent?'

'Intent is only part of the problem,' Ramona countered. 'However throwaway comments are meant, they have a cumulative effect on people's attitudes. And I think it's almost more worrying if men think remarks such as *oh ignore her, she's on the rag* are ok than if they're saying it to push your buttons. I'm not petty enough to cry sexual harassment over the odd tasteless joke, but I find phrases like *which one would you do* and *she's gagging for it* unacceptable, in or outside the workplace, and when people are regularly inappropriate it does constitute harassment, whether it's intended or not.'

Lawrence nodded. He could recall several instances when he'd had to pull junior colleagues up over comments considerably less serious than those Ramona had just outlined. In most cases no harm had been meant, but of course that wasn't, as Ramona had said, the point. And the fact that one young officer had viewed the words *I bet you looked hot in uniform* as a compliment only served to exemplify her observation about prevailing attitudes.

'How did Steve get on with the other members of staff here?'

'All right. He was Damon's golden boy, and he and Jez were pretty friendly. And I think everyone gets on with Liam.'

'What about his personal life, did he talk much about that?'

'Some, but more for show than anything else, as far as I could tell. He mentioned nights out at places like the Chiltern Firehouse and Sketch, and which celebrities he'd been rubbing shoulders with, but to be honest I didn't pay much attention. It's not as if the word *celebrity* means much anymore.'

That was certainly true, and Lawrence could understand why those who had achieved acclaim by means of talent and hard graft might object to the label. Rebecca had once related Elliot's exasperated response to being described as such in the press, which had been along the lines of 'I'm a musician, not a fucking socialite'. Although these days it seemed something of a moot point, given that the media was more interested in charting his unravelling mental health than his musical accomplishments.

'Oh, and he was on about buying a flat,' Ramona remembered, aloud, returning Lawrence's thoughts to the matter at hand. 'He brought a bottle of champagne in a day or two before he died to celebrate finding a place and getting an offer accepted. He talked himself up a lot, but his excitement about that seemed authentic. You could – I don't know – *feel* it. I remember thinking afterwards that that and suicide didn't really add up.'

'So you wouldn't be surprised if there was more to it?'

'No,' Ramona replied. 'And clearly I'm not the only one.' She tipped her head to one side. 'It doesn't take a DCI to tick boxes and close a file, does it?'

Jez – full name Jerome – turned out to be the only member of the Clapham Chronicle's staff who had known that Steve had a girlfriend, or at least something approaching one. His exact words, when questioned, were, 'Yeah, he mentioned he had a woman a few times.' When Rebecca asked whether Jez knew her name, he thought for a moment before shaking his head.

'Was that because it wasn't a serious relationship, do you think, or because he just didn't talk much about his private life?'

'I dunno. I mean, it didn't stop him flirting with other girls, so I guess –' he trailed off with a shrug.

'Do you know whether he ever took things further than flirting?'

Jez shifted position uncomfortably. 'A couple of times.'

Rebecca nodded. 'Did you see much of one another socially?'

'Kind of. I mean, we went out after work a lot, but we didn't meet up much outside of that.'

'A couple of your colleagues described the two of you as friends, is that a fair assessment?'

'Yeah, we were good mates.'

'Do you think he would have confided in you if there had been something worrying him?'

'I don't know,' Jez replied, shaking his head slightly. 'Maybe if it related to work. But I don't think he worried about much, he always seemed uber-confident.'

'So as far as you're aware, there wasn't anything on his mind in the days leading up to his death.'

Jez shook his head again.

'He hadn't argued or fallen out with anyone?'

'Well – he had a row with his stepdad over the phone a day or two beforehand – but that happened a lot. He thought the guy was a twat.'

'Is that the word he used?'

The young man's cheeks coloured. 'No.'

Rebecca raised her eyebrows. 'What exactly did he say?'

There was an awkward pause before Jez answered. 'He used the C word.'

'Do you think that was indicative of the strength of his feelings, or was it a word he used often?'

'He didn't use it every five minutes, but his stepdad wasn't the only person he described that way,' Jez said, still looking embarrassed.

'Have you any idea why he felt that way about his stepfather?'

'Not really. I think to a point they just didn't like one another, but I know some of the arguments were about money. Steve used to say the guy wanted to protect his mum's assets from everyone but himself.'

'Is that what they argued about on the phone that day?'

Jez paused, lifting a hand to rub his left eyebrow and displaying grubby grey patches on a couple of his fingernails. After several seconds, he shook his head. 'I don't remember,' he admitted, rather apologetically. 'I'm not even sure whether he said.'

'When did you last see Steve?'

'The last time he was in the office. He left a couple of hours early to do an interview, so I guess about three, half-three?'

'Did you hear from him at all after that?'

Jez responded with a question of his own. 'Do you not have his mobile?'

'Do you not remember?' Rebecca countered.

There was a brief pause before he replied. 'I don't think I had any messages from him that night, but it was more than a month ago, so I'd have to check to be sure.'

'Your *good mate* was found hanged and you can't remember whether or not you heard from him in the hours before his death?' Rebecca exclaimed. 'That's pretty hard to believe.'

Jez shrugged weakly, making no effort to try to justify his response.

'Do you remember what you were doing that evening?'

'I was at home. I spent most of the night playing on my Xbox.'

'Can anybody substantiate that?'

'Microsoft, maybe?' Jez suggested. 'I was playing live.'

'Unless they offer surveillance alongside live gaming, I suspect the most they'd be able to confirm is that *someone* was playing on your machine,' Lawrence observed.

'My landlady must have come back at some point, I suppose she might be able to remember when.'

'How about Steve's flat, did you ever go around there?' Rebecca asked.

'Now and then.'

'Ever stay the night?'

'No,' Jez replied, his eyebrows drawing together suspiciously. 'Why would I? I only live a couple of miles away.'

'So you weren't anything more than friends.'

'No!' Jez exclaimed. 'What makes you –' he stopped, looking flustered. 'Neither of us was –' he trailed off again. 'We were just mates. I went round to play video games and eat pizza once in a while.'

Rebecca nodded. 'Did you ever meet any of his other friends?'

'Not really. I made small talk with one or two during a night out for Steve's birthday, but I didn't stay long because it was at a really expensive bar and I couldn't afford to be buying drinks there all night. And some of his mates were at the Great British Beer Festival in summer, but we were there with the other guys from the paper, so I was chatting to them most of the time – when I wasn't wandering about visiting different bars. Everyone always ends up scattered around at those things.'

'Was his birthday the only time he picked a venue that was out of your price range?'

Jez shrugged. 'He liked trendy places.'

'That doesn't answer my question.'

'A few times he persuaded me to go to bars that bust my budget, yeah,' Jez admitted.

'Did you resent that?'

'No. He didn't force me to go. He usually twisted my arm by saying he'd get the drinks in.'

'And did he?'

'Yes. But I always ended up feeling I ought to pay my way.'

'He can't have been earning a lot more than you, so how do you suppose he managed to afford those kinds of places?'

'I don't know, I never asked,' Jez replied. 'Maybe he had another source of income. Or maybe he couldn't really afford it either.' He shrugged again. 'Maybe I wasn't the only one sticking it on a credit card.'

'Have you been to any of these trendy bars Ramona and Jez were talking about?' Lawrence asked, as he and Rebecca turned into the side street in which he had parked that morning.

'Hardly. The rock scene is pretty much the antithesis of trendy. I'm more at home in dark, dingy bars, leather and denim than with high ceilings, coving and sharp suits.'

This came as something of a surprise to Lawrence: he had always had Rebecca's affiliation with the rock world down as little more than an extension of her previous relationship. 'I assumed that was Elliot's influence,' he admitted.

Rebecca smiled. 'Did you imagine he lured me from some

fashionable haunt into the evil clutches of hard rock?'

In all honesty, Lawrence had never given the matter of how the two had met much thought, and now they were no longer together it seemed inappropriate to ask. But abruptly changing the subject would be awkward and obvious, and he wasn't sure how to continue. Fortunately, Rebecca resolved the matter for him, adding, 'My musical tastes have always inclined that way, but before I met Elliot I suppose I was more of a rock-scene tourist than a native. The only people I used to know at gigs and clubs were the people I went to them with, now some places are full of familiar faces.'

'That must have made the past few months difficult for you.'

'Sometimes,' Rebecca acknowledged. 'But I think if you're with someone for years rather than months you're bound to end up with overlapping social spheres. And it could be worse – I've pretty much outgrown nightclubs now, and I've made several friends through work in the past couple of years. I've skipped a couple of gigs that weren't big enough for me to blend into the crowd, and there are a few pubs I generally avoid, but I'm not going to start frequenting poncey bars populated by wankers like Steve to preclude the risk of ever running into Elliot.'

'Are there no wankers on the rock scene?' Lawrence baited.

'Like you don't know the answer to that,' Rebecca replied, pointedly. 'But they're a different breed. They're not trying so hard.' She paused. 'I guess because they're not chasing exclusivity. The real adherents of the current rock scene aren't looking to get *in* on anything because they already feel like outsiders.'

'Outsiders? In what sense?'

'Heavy rock music hasn't been mainstream in a long time. And a lot of people still seem to buy into and feel threatened by misconceptions surrounding it. Not least the fallacy about Satanism. But I've always found it a pretty accepting subculture. Elliot's inner circle were less welcoming, but that was largely because of my job and the fact so many of them were taking class As.'

Lawrence had little doubt Elliot had been among them, but didn't say as much; by the time he'd realised the extent to which Elliot's lifestyle conflicted with Rebecca's career path their relationship had been all but over, so he had never felt obliged to broach the subject.

'Musical preferences aside, I've never understood why people are prepared to pay double or treble the price for a drink just because it's served in a fancy glass in a themed room with striking but uncomfortable furniture,' Rebecca continued.

'And I thought that was just me getting old.'

Rebecca shrugged. 'It seems like style over substance.'

'I get the impression that's a description that could be applied to Steve as well as his hang-outs,' Lawrence said.

'I wonder whether Mia was just an extension of that? Trophy girlfriend to keep up with Fraser and his mates?'

'Quite possibly. It certainly doesn't sound as though he was very committed to her.'

'Worth a chat with her brother, do you think?'

'Maybe,' Lawrence nodded. 'I also want to catch up with the stepfather, see what we can get out of him about his disagreements with Steve. And I'd love to know where Steve was in the hours before he died, because it clearly wasn't, as he told Mia, at work.' He depressed the circular button on his key fob to release the central-locking system of his silver Honda as they approached the vehicle. 'But first things first,' he said, as he reached to open the car door. 'Let's find out what the Tate Modern has to offer in the way of lunch.'

Priya had been rather nonplussed when Jez asked whether she'd like to go to the Italian deli three doors down from the office for a sandwich. Although they'd eaten out a few times – and been for drinks after work considerably more often – with the other members of the team, they'd never done either alone. She wondered whether, in the wake of Steve's death, he was looking for new office buddy. Fifteen minutes later, they were sitting either side of a small table wrapped in a white paper cloth, eating panini and drinking coffee.

'Do you want to stay a sub?' Jez asked.

'For now.'

'And then what?'

'I dunno,' Priya admitted. 'I don't really have a long-term plan yet.'

'You're not looking to get into writing or editing, then.'

'I don't think so. Certainly not editing, I'm more interested in the details than the angle of the big picture.'

'You're really good at it, you know,' he said, tearing the molten mozzarella oozing out of his panino – the singular, as she regularly had to remind people – from the plate.

Priya acknowledged the remark with a polite smile; she wasn't about to give him the satisfaction of returning the compliment, even if it was true. And, to be fair, it was – he might not have the experience or contacts of Ramona and Damon, but he did have a gift for writing engaging opening paragraphs and usually managed to get his facts right. He grinned and added, 'I mean, you don't mess much with my copy, so you obviously recognise works of genius.'

Priya couldn't help but smile again, genuinely this time. 'Well there's only so much crap one dung beetle can bury in a week.'

Jez looked momentarily puzzled before clearly getting the reference and wincing theatrically. 'Sorry, did that bother you? I didn't mean to –'

'Relax,' Priya interrupted. 'I can take a joke. Besides, when you think about it, it reflects on your work more than mine. There's a reason why you can buy a cat litter called Yesterday's News.'

'Can you really?'

She nodded.

'That's funny.' He took a bite of his sandwich. 'Do you have a cat?'

'Kind of. I had one growing up. She still lives with my folks.' Priya reached for her drink. 'Are you a pet person?'

'I have a tarantula. Although my landlady's threatening to evict her.'

'I can understand why. Imagine finding something that size in the bathtub first thing!'

'Yeah, it might have been a mistake to leave her skin on the kitchen windowsill when she last shed,' Jez said, with a wry smile.

'I'm surprised *you're* not facing eviction for that.'

He chuckled. 'It was worth it.'

'So will you be going to check out spiderwoman at the Tate?'

He shook his head. 'You?'

'Nah, I'm not into that pretentious bullshit. I know it's supposed to be all about the concept, but if I could easily replicate it myself I don't consider it art.'

Jez nodded. There was a pause before he said, 'I wonder whether the cops are going to talk to her.'

Priya shrugged. 'Who knows.'

'What did they ask you?'

'Probably much the same as you. Why?'

'I'm just curious. I mean, clearly they don't think it was suicide.'

'Well we were all pretty shocked when we thought it was.'

'I know,' Jez agreed. 'I just wonder what it is that's got them interested in it now. It's been almost a month. Why didn't they ask any questions when it happened?' He set his sandwich down. 'Did they give you any idea what's behind the sudden interest?'

'No. I should think they know better than to show their hand to a bunch of hacks.'

'But despite that, you and Damon were clearly close enough to keep in touch over the years since.'

She shrugged. 'It was mutually beneficial. Artists need publicity, and journalists need stories.'

'Given your history, were you surprised Damon didn't opt to do the interview himself?'

'Not particularly. Damon has a lot of friends in a lot of places, I don't imagine he has the time to cover everything that crosses his path. Besides, he was planning on coming to the opening night here, so I suppose he thought he'd see me then.'

'You speak as though he didn't actually make it in the end.'

'No, he didn't.'

'Why not?'

'You'd have to ask him.'

'Did he not give you a reason?'

'He said something had come up. I didn't cross-examine him. A lot of people are on the list for that kind of thing, and you don't expect all of them to actually turn up.' She paused before adding, with a smile, 'And if it's a smaller event, you're quite glad when some of them don't. Otherwise there's a real risk you'll run out of wine.'

Five

EverGreener, Rupert Parker's eco-technology company, was based in a long, low building at an industrial unit on the outskirts of the Hertfordshire market town of Hitchin. The partition walls of the small open-plan office were hung with framed posters advertising the company's products, services and environmental credentials, and towards the rear of the space glass walls had been erected to section off two meeting rooms. Rupert, a tall, broad man who would tower over his petite wife, showed Rebecca and Lawrence into the nearer of the two, offering tea and coffee before sitting in one of the comfortable modern chairs gathered around the small round table. Rebecca had already surmised from its cut and quality that his charcoal grey suit probably hadn't been bought off the peg, and as he rested his forearms on the table, linking his fingers loosely together, she noticed he wore a Patek Philippe watch.

Lawrence thanked the man for making the time to speak to them before asking Rupert how he would describe his relationship with his stepson.

'Trying,' came the frank reply. 'I did my best to keep things cordial for Aly's sake, but it's not easy when someone won't meet you half way.'

'What kinds of things did you clash over?'

'Oh, all sorts. Although I think a lot of the time he was trying to wind me up, as much as anything.'

'I understand from a couple of his friends that money featured fairly prominently in your disagreements.'

'Yes.'

Steve left home, but before that things seemed fairly amicable. Obviously that wasn't always the case, but their separation was long before my time.'

'Do you know what Duncan's thoughts were on the manner of Steve's death?'

'Much the same as Aly's and mine, that writing it off as suicide was just the easy option for the powers that be,' Rupert responded, bluntly, before apparently thinking better of being so brutally honest and adding, 'I'm sorry, that sounded horribly rude – I'm in no way lumping everyone in the system into that. Will Maxwell's a great guy, and I know he thinks very highly of you. But there are always those who incline towards the lazy solution, and Aly deserves better.'

Lawrence nodded. 'Could you run us through your movements in the twenty-four hours before Steve's death?'

'Certainly. I was here first thing on the Wednesday morning – then I drove up to Birmingham for a meeting with a couple of potential investors in the afternoon – I dined with them that evening. I left the restaurant a little after ten, and I drove back home.'

'Do you remember what time you arrived home?'

'Shortly before one. I went more or less straight to bed, because I wanted to be up in time to go to the gym before I came in here the next day.'

'Did anybody see you between your departure from the restaurant and Thursday morning?'

Several seconds passed before Rupert shook his head slightly, saying, 'I've no idea. I should think I walked past several CCTV cameras between the car and the front door, and I suppose it's possible someone else in the building saw me on my way in, but I really don't remember much about it, now. Coming in and up the stairs is so routine I generally do it on autopilot.' He paused, and another thought seemed to strike him. 'And as far as I was concerned at the time, it was just another late night.'

Tim had allowed plenty of time to travel through the rush hour from Southwark to Mayfair, and arrived at Brown's Hotel with more than a quarter of an hour to spare. Feeling even more apprehensive than he had done ahead of his first meeting with Lisa, he repeatedly considered and dismissed the idea of ordering a double scotch while he waited. He scanned his most recent emails, then set his mobile down on the table beside him, his eyes wandering over the fireplace beyond it to the large oriental bronze vase that sat on the mantelpiece. The central motif was a resplendent bird, its substantial wings unfurled and its head held high, that he took to be a phoenix. The creature's elongated tail feathers rose up behind it, extending above head height, while the body of the vase around it bore abstract bronze curls that might have been clouds but were probably, he concluded, stylised trees. Tim wondered whether it was an antique or a reproduction, and, if the former, how much it might be worth.

Lisa arrived on the dot of six, impeccably dressed in a salmon pink top, black skirt suit and patent high heels, with not a hair out of place. Greeting Tim warmly, she slipped into the chair next to his, sliding a hand beneath the button that secured her jacket and releasing it in one fluid motion. As she dropped her eyes to her walnut-coloured Mulberry handbag – the tiny tree was one of the few fashion logos Tim could identify – he allowed his eyes to travel over the hint of cleavage exposed by her cowl-necked top, swiftly returning them to her face as she unfastened the bag's catch and looked back up.

'Can I get you a drink?' He offered, wondering what was appropriate in this situation. 'Wine? Champagne?'

Lisa declined with a barely perceptible shake of her head. 'No, thank you. I'm not here to be wined and dined.'

'Of course, I'm sorry,' Tim nodded, wondering even as he said it why he was apologising when *he* was paying for *her* services.

'You should feel free, though,' Lisa replied, with an encouraging smile. 'I know this is new territory for you, and you'd be far from alone in finding it nerve-wracking. Many people do.'

Tim instinctively returned the smile, grateful for the reassurance. Although stylish and poised, Lisa also had something of the girl-next-door about her, and seemed much more genuine and empathetic than he had expected. He wanted to ask what, aside from the obvious financial motivation, had drawn her to her current line of work, but she had made it clear at their previous meeting that her life was off-limits as a topic of conversation. Given some of the services she offered, he could only assume she had concocted a largely – if not completely – fictitious existence to share when the occasion so demanded. He was doubtless far from the first to wish they had met in different circumstances.

Lisa took several items from her handbag and laid them on the table before setting the bag down on the floor and gracefully crossing one shapely leg over the other, looking back up to meet Tim's eyes.

'I'm ready when you are.'

'How's it going?' Rebecca greeted Leighton, bumping into him in the corridor that ran between the lifts and CID.

'Pretty good – once I've spoken to your guv'nor I'm going to knock off and head to the pub,' he grinned. 'I'd invite you along, but you look like the walking dead. Heavy night last night?'

'Long night.'

'Is that not the same?'

'I wasn't out – I just didn't sleep.'

'How come?' Leighton asked, as they turned the corner into

Lawrence's empty office.

'I was boxing up all of Elliot's stuff, and –' Rebecca hesitated. 'I found this.' She reached into her handbag for the Narcotics Anonymous leaflet and handed it to him before dropping the bag onto a chair and sitting on the adjacent one.

Leighton looked momentarily puzzled, then his expression changed, presumably as he took in the initials on the slip of paper in his hand. 'Ah. So you've been playing *what if* with yourself.'

'Wouldn't you?'

'Probably, but don't jump the gun – it's not like he doesn't have friends dancing with Mr Brownstone,' Leighton leaned against the back of a chair. 'I've probably still got some AA leaflets in my possession from my adolescent idealistic phase when I thought I could get my dad to change.'

'I might not be so worried if –' she hesitated. 'If it didn't seem completely plausible. I know he's taken other things in the past – speed, coke –'

'There's a difference between party drugs and the hard stuff.'

'I know,' Rebecca said. 'But the party ended a long time ago. At one stage I used to look at old tramps shambling around the streets with a can in their hands and think *what if he ends up like that?* But now –' she paused. 'Now that seems almost optimistic. At the rate he's going, he'll be dead in six months.'

Leighton didn't disagree, and Rebecca realised she had wanted him to. She swallowed hard.

'There's nothing you can do if people don't want help.'

'Of course not, but I need to know about this.' She indicated the card.

'Then I think you're going to have to ask him.'

Rebecca nodded.

'Do you fancy a quick one when you're done?'

'I can't. I've a couple of people coming round about the room, and if I have time I might stop at Alec's on my way home, see whether I can get some sense out of Elliot.'

'You won't be home alone when people come to view the room, will you?'

'No, Dad,' Rebecca teased. 'I'll make sure someone's around to hold my hand.'

'And as if by magic,' Lawrence remarked, as he entered the office. 'I was just about to call you.'

'Your friendly neighbourhood genie,' Leighton quipped, holding his hands out, palms face upwards. 'I can grant you three wishes. Usual rules apply, of course.'

'I suppose it's too much to hope I could wish for you to arrive on time in the mornings?'

'Yeah, sorry about that, I had some trouble with the car,' Leighton replied, sounding unusually apologetic. Looking none too impressed with the excuse, Lawrence asked what was wrong with it.

'Brakes failed on St John's Hill.'

'The brakes?' Lawrence exclaimed. 'What happened?'

'Oh it's all right, I'm well-practised at dodging traffic,' Leighton returned, casually. 'Tom took my joyriding lessons very seriously.'

Rebecca suppressed a smile. Lawrence looked less amused, and she guessed he was none too sure that Leighton was joking. She suspected the remark wasn't entirely a fabrication; whether Leighton had ever actually driven a stolen car she had no idea, but from a couple of comments he'd made in the past she got the impression he'd been in a fair few.

'Hand brake,' Leighton added, after a tense pause.

'Are you all right?'

'Yeah. Thanks. Although pretty hacked off with the guy who signed off my MOT certificate last month. Anyway, I think this is what you were after.' He handed Lawrence a cardboard folder.

'Thank you. While you're here, I was thinking it might be

worth combing through historical PM reports in case there are more suicides out there that weren't as they appeared.'

'Woah, I'm not a real genie,' Leighton objected. 'Do you have any idea how many people commit suicide in a year?'

'How many?'

'In the UK, five to six thousand, and the majority of them are men. And more than half of those take their lives by hanging or strangulation.'

Lawrence nodded. 'How about just men in the Greater London area aged between – I don't know – say twenty and forty? Over the past couple of years.'

'You're still talking about hundreds of cases a year. But I'll see what I can do.'

'Thank you.'

'If it's any consolation, we've got to read through all these,' Rebecca put in, indicating a stack of computer printouts some three inches thick.

'What are they?'

'Articles from your local rag. Starting with –' Rebecca lifted the top page and scanned the opening paragraph, 'A sit-in at a school over the decision to ban pork products from the cafeteria.'

'Oh for goodness' sake,' Lawrence muttered, irritably. 'Next thing you know we won't be allowed to send the kids to school with ham sandwiches.'

'People are entitled not to do bacon for religious reasons,' Leighton countered, seemingly seriously, prompting Rebecca and Lawrence to eye him with a combination of surprise and suspicion.

'Whaaaat?' He responded, widening his eyes. 'All the more for the rest of us. Besides, I don't do religion for bacon reasons.'

'And there was me thinking bacon *was* your religion,' Lawrence joked.

'Well I do worship it daily,' Leighton returned, with a grin, pushing off from the chair back. 'Anyway, I'll leave you to share out the bedtime reading. If you'd like some originals, I've something of an archive under my sofa. Just give me a heads up if you're coming over.' He paused in the doorway. 'Give me a chance to hide the bodies.'

Six

Rebecca had volunteered to coordinate Thursday's newspaper analysis, along with several other office-based tasks, while her superior spoke to Steve's landlord – who also happened to be his downstairs neighbour – and led door-to-door enquiries in the surrounding area. Lawrence had assigned two colleagues the job of assisting her in tackling the stack of articles published by the Clapham Chronicle under Steve's byline before setting off for Putney. They were barely half an hour into the effort when Daniel Freeman, who had long been a friend as well as a co-worker of Rebecca's, exhaled loudly in disgust and tossed the printout he had been reading into the air.

'This is certainly reminding me why I don't read my local rag,' he remarked, leaning back in his chair and stretching his arms out above his head. 'Some of this stuff is brain-numbing. Imagine having to *write* about it.' He turned his dark eyes on Rebecca. 'What's that one on?'

'The use of pizza-delivery motorbikes in pedestrian areas.'

'Scintillating.'

'Yours?'

'A fund-raiser to save some church from Japanese knotweed. Surely all they need is a gallon or two of industrial-strength weed killer?'

'This one might be more to your taste,' Rebecca suggested, passing him the topmost page from her pile of printouts. 'It's about a microbrewery.'

'What is it, a hop-ed?' Daniel joked.

Rebecca smiled as she shook her head and raised her eyes

heavenward in response to the pun.

'That reminds me. Do you have plans for next Thursday night?'

'I don't think so. Unless I'm stuck in here.'

'They've a new quiz night starting at the Jugged Hare, I thought maybe we could check it out.'

'Sounds good,' Rebecca nodded. 'We shouldn't have trouble getting a team together – I'm sure Leighton and Jon would be up for it, and we might be able to drag one or two others along with the promise of beer.'

'I suppose it's too early for one of those now,' Daniel sighed, glancing at his watch. 'I might pop to Costa, though. Would either of you like anything?'

'I would love a skinny latte,' Rebecca replied, gratefully, as Daniel stood up and checked his pocket for his wallet. 'Do you want some shrapnel?'

Daniel shook his head, turning towards the young woman at the desk opposite his own. 'Eva?'

'Uh – no. Thanks.'

'Ok. Back in five.'

'He seems nice,' Eva observed, after Daniel had departed.

Rebecca nodded, not raising her eyes from the page in front of her. DC Eva Dixon had only started work in CID the previous week, and Rebecca was keen not to be drawn into idle chat on the first occasion she'd been left in charge of the new recruit.

'And cute,' Eva added, apparently not getting the message.

'Uh-huh.'

'So how come you shot him down when he tried to ask you out?'

The directness of the question took Rebecca by surprise. 'Excuse me?' She asked, looking up.

'Well he obviously fancies you.'

'The guys in this department are off-limits,' Rebecca replied, shortly.

Eva frowned. 'How d'you mean?'

'This job isn't without risk, and it's in nobody's interest if officers are emotionally involved.'

'You sound like a staff handbook,' Eva replied. 'Life isn't that simple.'

Rebecca sighed. 'No, it isn't. And neither is my personal life. Ok?'

'Ok,' Eva echoed, sounding taken aback. There was a long pause before she spoke again. 'I'm sorry, I didn't mean to –'

'Don't worry about it,' Rebecca pre-empted, keeping her eyes on the printout that rested on her left knee and trying – and failing – to focus on what she had been doing previously. She'd been having enough trouble concentrating on the task before the interruption.

On arrival in the office that morning, she had barely had a chance to shed her coat before Daniel had asked, 'What's up with Elliot?' Had Rebecca tuned in to the radio before leaving the house, she would apparently have already gathered that he was in hospital, although the reason why remained unclear. A brief statement on the band's Facebook page explained the situation with the catch-all 'exhaustion and depression', which her colleague had rejected with 'but that's standard record company bullshit, it's bound to translate to something else'. Rebecca suspected he was right. In light of her discovery on Tuesday evening, the question on her mind was *what.*

Lawrence returned to the office late in the afternoon to find Rebecca poring over grainy copies of what looked to be bank or credit-card statements, a yellow highlighter pen in her hand. She raised her eyes from the topmost page as he approached, and he guessed from her expression that she had uncovered something of note.

'I hope you've had a more fruitful day than I,' he greeted her, coming to a stop beside her desk and resting an elbow on the divider separating her desk from Daniel's.

'No luck with door-to-door?'

He shook his head. 'Admittedly it comes as no great surprise, given we're asking people to think back a month or so. Have you managed to get to the bottom of Steve's finances?'

'Yep. He did have the funds for a deposit on the flat – courtesy of his mother – but there are also significant quarterly payments into his account that I'm still trying to trace back to source because the description on the statements is just bank reference jargon.'

'So assuming Rupert was telling the truth yesterday, Alyson gave – or loaned – money to Steve behind his back,' Lawrence said.

'It looks that way. And on a related subject, EverGreener's finances aren't exactly what you'd call rosy. I managed to get hold of the company's accounts and a lot more money is going out than coming in.' She cast her eyes over her desk before reaching for a handful of pages held together with a paperclip and indicating a heavily highlighted negative balance.

'That's a big number,' Lawrence observed. 'I'd love to know the state of their personal finances.' He looked back up. 'How about the paper, did you find anything of note in there?'

'Not the one we were looking at. But I did come across a rather intriguing rumour online, and I followed that up with the Islington Gazette. They were kind enough to provide this,' she handed him a poor-quality copy of a portion of a newspaper page dated some nineteen years earlier and headed with the words 'Artist found hanged in notorious squat'. A quick scan of the first few paragraphs was sufficient to fill Lawrence in on the relevance of the piece, the deceased had apparently been involved in a relationship with another artist: one Celestia Woolf.

'Is there any more information on this?'

'I'm still waiting to hear back about what we have on it – if anything – but subsequent coverage by the Gazette indicates that there were a lot of unanswered questions. Nobody seems to have been able to agree on whether it was suicide, homicide or some kind of sex act gone awry. The coroner recorded an open verdict.'

'Any clues to whether this is the same property Damon shared with Celestia?'

'He isn't mentioned in the press coverage, but it seems likely. By all accounts the squat was pretty populous, which was presumably one of the problems facing the original investigation. With so many people *coming and going*, as Celestia put it, narrowing down who was where when was probably quite a challenge.'

Lawrence nodded.

'And there's someone else we might want to have another chat with at the Chronicle,' Rebecca continued. 'I finally managed to track down Steve's mobile, and he sent a rather curious text message to Jez a few days before he died,' she reached for the phone lying on her desk and swiped the screen, adding, 'I took a screenshot,' and swiping again before presenting the display to Lawrence. The message had been sent on a Saturday morning and read, 'Did you have a nice night at the station sweetie? Busted!!!' Jez had seemingly made no reply.

Lawrence glanced at his watch. 'Let's get over there now, then, catch them before they head off for the day,' he said, returning the mobile. 'We'll have a chat with Alyson Parker after that.'

'Whatever you do, don't leave me unattended on that high street afterwards,' Rebecca remarked, standing and tossing the phone into her handbag. 'My credit card might never recover.'

'I'll be sure to escort you from the danger zone.'

'Great place to live, though. If I had the cash to splash, I'd move there in a heartbeat.' She sighed wistfully. 'Where would you live, if money was no object?'

'I don't know,' Lawrence admitted, considering the matter for a moment. 'Westminster, maybe? For convenience. Although if money *and* travel time weren't an object I'd prefer to get out of London altogether – head for somewhere like Beaconsfield or Winchester.'

'Presumably the ultimate decision would hinge on which had the best golf courses?'

'Given how long it's been I'm not sure I'd remember how to play,' Lawrence returned, ruefully.

'I'm sure you'd be fine, Sir. It'd be just like falling off a bike.'

Lawrence smiled, wondering whether the remark had been a Freudian slip or an intentional joke. Either way, the mangled expression quite possibly offered an apt description of what his game might look like should he have a chance to revive it. The topic of relocation, meanwhile, was more relevant than she realised, and had been much on his mind in recent days.

He and Katie had discussed the possibility of moving in the interests of giving Jimmy a fresh start. But to stand any real chance of success, they would need to put sufficient distance between their current base in Battersea and any new home to ensure that their son couldn't easily reconnect with his old crowd, which ruled out much of South London. Moving farther out wasn't a viable option, as it would mean Lawrence spending even less time at home than he did already. That left the more affordable parts of North and West London, and the next consideration: Elise. Lawrence was loath to uproot her during her final year of primary school, but, even with Katie working part-time in Battersea Park, there would be no realistic way of keeping their daughter at her current school should they move north of the river. And the last thing he wanted was for Elise to suffer on account of Jimmy's misdeeds.

Priya was leaning against the railings outside the Chronicle's offices when Rebecca and Lawrence arrived, eyes on the screen of her smartphone. Leaving her superior to go on ahead, Rebecca slowed to a stop alongside her.

'Waiting for someone?'

Priya shook her head, glancing up from her mobile. 'No. I'm having a nicotine-replacement break.'

Rebecca raised her eyebrows quizzically.

'Liam and Damon get to take five minutes every hour or so to have a fag,' Priya added. 'I don't see why I should work harder just because I don't smoke.'

Rebecca smiled, imagining how this argument might go down with her superior. One of his perennial complaints pertained to the amount of time wasted by smoking breaks. Jamie, a colleague of Rebecca's, only dared slip out for a cigarette if Lawrence was out of the office, and Leighton had once joked that he was thinking of taking up the habit just to add to the number of breaks Lawrence perceived him as taking.

'Have you been not smoking long?' Rebecca quipped, resting an elbow between two of the spikes atop the railings.

Priya returned her smile. 'About a year.'

'I've always envied the social aspect of smoking in the workplace,' Rebecca confided. 'People seem to form unlikely friendships and alliances through being united by others' disapproval and standing out on the pavement in all weathers.'

'In a lot of places I expect it's a good way to hear rumours and gossip, as well. This place isn't really big enough for there to be much of that.'

'Really?' Rebecca responded. 'I can't imagine that. I spend so much time at work I think I'd go mad if I had to keep my life to myself. Although admittedly there are some things I wouldn't share with the lads.'

'Yeah, well –' Priya looked quickly around herself to check nobody stood to overhear before she said anything further. 'I guess it might be different if Ramona wasn't so –' she hesitated, then finished, in a lower voice, 'Scary.'

'I would have thought she'd make a good ally, given the strength of her feminist leanings.'

'She's great when the guys are pushing their luck, but a lot of the time I'm afraid I'll say the wrong thing and – I dunno – let the side down, I suppose. She does make some really good points, and I agree that if people are doing the same job they deserve equal pay, but I'm not convinced things like lads' mags are exploitative. I think if a woman wants to take her clothes off in exchange for cash – cash that comes largely from the pockets of men – then good luck to her. How is it feminist for one woman to tell another she shouldn't do that?'

Rebecca nodded. A friend of hers regularly posted feminist rants and campaign links on Facebook, and on occasion Rebecca felt guilty for not feeling more strongly about some of the issues at stake. But she couldn't subscribe to the idea that the differences between men and women were merely cultural, brought about by thousands of years of behavioural conditioning. For starters, there were obvious biological differences – from the visible physical ones to the unseen but far-reaching chromosomal ones. Male and female infants developed at different rates, and men and women didn't even have the same life expectancy. Meanwhile, the idea that the number of women should match that of men across a range of fields and employment grades seemed to her like a one-way system of political correctness gone mad: nobody ever complained that there weren't enough male midwives or librarians.

'How do you get on with your other colleagues?'

'All right. Liam's sweet, but he generally keeps himself to himself. Jez is a good laugh, although the continual jokes can get a bit wearing. It's easier to have a proper conversation with him when you get him on his own.'

'Does that happen often?'

'A bit more since Steve's not been around, I suppose, but not often. Usually there are several of us in the office.'

'You don't see him outside the office, then?'

'Not really. We went for lunch on Wednesday, but I think that was just because –' she stopped, abruptly, as if she'd been on the verge of betraying a confidence.

Rebecca raised her eyebrows. 'Anything to do with our visit?'

Priya sighed and, after a moment's hesitation, nodded. 'He wondered what had made you think it wasn't suicide.'

'Did he quiz you about what we'd asked you?'

'I wouldn't say quizzed. But yeah, it came up.'

'Did you find that strange?'

'Not really. I assumed he was thinking of writing about it, which seemed in poor taste but –' she shrugged. 'I'm not sure many journalists were near the front of the queue when moral compasses were handed out.'

Damon seemed surprised to see Lawrence again so soon, but made no objection to his arrival, immediately closing his laptop and sitting back in his chair when Lawrence asked whether he might have a few minutes. Lawrence shut Damon's office door behind himself before drawing one of the other chairs in the room up to the near side of the desk.

'I'd like to talk to you about Chet Higgins,' he began as he sat down, watching Damon closely for a reaction. There was a momentary pause before his expression changed slightly,

'What about bondage? Did she ever show an interest in that?'

'Not in any serious way.'

'Were you in the house when Chet died?'

'Most of us were, it was the middle of the night.'

'Did you see him in the hours before his death?'

Damon's eyebrows contracted as he seemingly considered his answer. 'I really don't remember,' he admitted, at length. 'But I never saw him more than in passing, so I'm not sure what difference it would make if I did. And I've no idea why the coroner was so cautious, I don't remember anyone who did know him being particularly surprised by what had happened.'

'Anyone, or Celestia?'

'She wasn't his only friend in the house.'

'That's not what I asked.'

Damon sighed. 'It was twenty-odd years ago, the details are all a bit hazy. But yes, ok, she said she wasn't surprised.'

'Twenty years is a long time to maintain contact with someone you had nothing more than a casual relationship with,' Lawrence observed. 'What made you stay in touch?'

'There's more to life than sex, Chief Inspector. That wasn't the only thing we shared.'

'So you consider her to be a friend.'

'Yes.'

'Yet you didn't make it to the opening of what must be the biggest exhibition of her career. Why was that?'

'Something came up.'

'What?'

'I don't think that's any of your business.'

'I'm afraid that's not your decision to make.'

Damon maintained eye contact with Lawrence for several seconds before capitulating. 'I had a row with my wife.'

'Did the row have anything to do with your plan to attend the exhibition?'

'In part.'

'And what was that part?'

'Joanne wasn't keen on my attending.'

'Why not?'

'I don't know, why do women do all sorts of things?'

'Surely she gave you a reason?' Lawrence returned, before adding, provocatively, 'Or do you do her bidding without question?'

'No!' Damon snapped, almost instinctively, before seeming to realise he was now bound to provide further explanation. He sighed heavily. 'A few years ago, we were at an event and Celestia was being rather – suggestive, I suppose. Now my wife's convinced she's going to try to jump me at any opportunity. I keep telling her Tia was just a bit drunk and got carried away, but Jo's having none of it.'

'Well it takes two to tango. What makes her think you'd be so easily led astray?'

'Apparently my intentions are irrelevant. As far as Jo is concerned, Tia is some kind of predatory temptress.'

'Are those the words she used?'

'No, I believe she said hypnotic.' Damon paused. 'And that she wouldn't even be surprised if Tia succeeded in casting her spell on a monk.'

'You look busy, what's the occasion?'

Leighton glanced up from the file in his lap as Jon set a coffee cup and a muffin on the adjacent desk. His own desk was piled high with cardboard folders, with more stacked in boxes around his chair. He checked his watch. 'Christ, how did it become five o'clock?'

'Well,' Jon replied, dropping into his chair, 'How it works is, the Earth goes around the Sun, and as it does that it turns –' he stopped with a grin as Leighton good-humouredly gave him the finger. 'I was hoping to entice you out for a pint and a game of pool, but it looks like you're going to be a while. What are you working on?'

'Apparent suicide, question mark homicide. I'm checking through the files for any other potentially suspicious deaths.'

'Sounds like a thankless task.'

'Yep. But I've been at it for hours, so I'm due a break. When were you planning on knocking off?'

'Half five?'

'Perfecto,' Leighton nodded, returning his attention to the file and hearing the office door open for the second time in as many minutes.

'Still not committed to the clear desk policy, I see,' Roddy remarked, sarcastically, as he made for his own desk.

'Well you know what Einstein said about that,' Leighton replied, without looking up.

Someone more astute might have had the sense to leave the interaction there, but Roddy took the bait. 'Enlighten me.'

Leighton met his eyes. 'If a cluttered desk is a sign of a cluttered mind, of what is an empty desk a sign?' He said, with just enough of a smile to take the edge off the quote. Jon almost choked on his coffee.

'Smart arse,' Roddy muttered, bending to retrieve something from his drawer.

'I'm hunting for suspicious suicides. So if anything springs to mind, please let me know.'

Roddy looked up. 'Any particular means?'

'Hanging,' Leighton revealed, his mobile interrupting before the exchange could go any further. He checked the screen before answering.

'Hi Mum.'

'Hello Lee, how are you, pet?'

'Fine, thanks. You?'

'Oh yes, I'm all right, I'm just on my way out to get some sour cream, I picked up some leeks at the market, and I thought I might make that chicken crumble I did at Easter, but –'

'Mum, I'm at work, can this wait?'

'Oh, sorry, pet. Are you on call tonight?'

'No. Why don't I give you a ring around nine?'

Lorna Campbell hesitated. 'I was hoping you might be able to pop up here,' she said, as if *here* was North London rather than South Yorkshire.

'Why, what's up?' Leighton asked, as Roddy passed him a Post-it note bearing a crime reference number. He mouthed his thanks before sticking it to the side of his laptop screen.

'It's your dad's leg. I keep making him appointments with the nurse at the surgery, but he won't go, and they won't do home visits anymore. I've tried dressing it myself but it's getting worse and I don't know what more I can do.'

Leighton didn't comment on his mother's penultimate admission. It wasn't difficult to guess why home visits to his parents had been suspended: if Glenn Campbell was half as ill-tempered and abusive towards medical professionals as he was most other people, he was lucky not to have been discharged from the surgery's books altogether. Leighton knew that any effort on his part to attend to Glenn's ulcerated leg – or any other of his myriad health problems – was unlikely to win him even grudging thanks. But, of course, his father wasn't the one asking for help.

'All right,' he conceded, reluctantly, with a sigh. 'I'll be with you when I can, ok?'

'Thank you. I'm sorry, I know how busy you are, I just didn't know what else to do, and –'

'It's ok. I'll see you later.'

'Yes. Thank you, pet.'

'Ok.' Leighton hung up, looking to Jon. 'Sorry, going to have to rain check on the pool. Family fun and games. Maybe tomorrow?'

'Sure.'

Leighton returned his eyes to the report before remembering his car was still in the garage. He swore to himself. Admittedly a fast train would get him to Sheffield quicker than the M1, but relying on public transport would also force him to spend the night up there. On the bright side, if he resisted the temptation to surf the net or chat to friends online, he could at least get some of the work he'd earmarked the evening for done on the way. And if he wasn't driving, he could have a drink or two, as well.

Before Lawrence and Rebecca had even sat down with Jez, he informed them he didn't have much time as he was due to attend a community meeting about a controversial building development within the hour. Lawrence promised not to keep him long before slipping his mobile phone out of his breast pocket and displaying the screenshot Rebecca had taken earlier that afternoon.

'A few days before he died, Steve sent you this text message. Could you tell us what it relates to?'

Jez gave the screen his attention for a moment before replying, shortly, 'No.'

'No?'

He shrugged. 'I don't know what he was on about. I assumed he'd sent it to me by mistake.'

'Did you ask Steve about it when you saw him the following Monday?'

'No. To be honest, I'd forgotten all about it by then.'

'Did he not mention it either?'

Jez shook his head. Lawrence suspected he wasn't telling the truth; from the tone of Steve's message and what he had learned over the past couple of days, he sensed Steve wasn't likely to have left it at that. As if Jez had read his thoughts, he added, 'Maybe he realised he'd sent it to the wrong person.'

Lawrence guessed from Rebecca's expression that she was no more convinced by this than he was, but moved on to his next line of enquiry without comment.

'I understand you've been curious to know what we know about Steve's death. Would you mind telling us why you've been probing your colleagues for that information?'

'I'm a curious person,' Jez replied, with a shrug. 'That's journalists for you. I didn't have an agenda, I was just – asking.'

'You went to the trouble of inviting Priya to lunch purely in the hope of satisfying your curiosity?' Lawrence asked, disbelievingly.

'I asked Priya out for lunch because I fancy her,' Jez replied, bluntly. 'I didn't do it with any particular conversation in mind.'

Lawrence raised his eyebrows. 'You've worked with her for over a year, but you only took it upon yourself to ask her out the day we turned up? That seems like something of a coincidence.'

Jez looked uncomfortable, but said nothing.

'What made you ask her yesterday?'

'Given that it wasn't exactly a normal day in the office it seemed like a good opportunity to do something out of the ordinary without being too obvious.'

'Have you really had no previous opportunities?'

Jez's cheeks coloured. There was an awkward silence before he said, 'I would have asked before, but I knew Steve would take the piss.'

'So you cared what Steve thought,' Lawrence concluded.

'That's normal, isn't it? Caring what your colleagues think of you?'

'I think it depends on the colleague. He clearly didn't care much about those around him if he would have made fun of your feelings for Priya.'

‘What, have you never made fun of your mates?’

Of course he had. And, at Jez’s age, Lawrence didn’t doubt he’d made remarks that might well have influenced friends’ decisions, just as some of theirs had swayed his. These days he was well aware banter wasn’t necessarily as innocuous as it seemed, and considerably less concerned about what anybody else thought of his life choices.

‘Let me put it another way,’ he suggested. ‘Did you resent Steve’s lack of regard for your feelings?’

‘Not really.’

‘Not really,’ Lawrence echoed. ‘So there was a part of you that did.’

‘No, not exactly – it wasn’t so much that I would have minded him taking the mick if Priya and I had got together – I was more worried about what he might say if she turned me down.’

‘That doesn’t answer my question.’

‘I don’t *know*, I honestly didn’t think that deeply about it. It wasn’t as if Steve’s opinion was the only variable I had to worry about, the fact Priya and I work together was a far bigger concern.’

‘Well that clearly didn’t concern you too much yesterday.’

‘I guess I just figured life is short,’ Jez responded, holding his hands out, palms upwards, in supplication. ‘Sometimes you have to take a risk.’ He paused, then added, with a smile, ‘*Carpe diem*, and all that. Seize the day.’

Alyson had received Lawrence and Rebecca at her front door with what looked like a Campari- or Aperol-based drink in her hand, and – perhaps as a result – seemed slightly vacant. Having shown them in, she took a seat on the sofa farthest from the living room door and set her drink down on one of the leather coasters scattered across the otherwise empty coffee table before realising, aloud, ‘I’m sorry, I didn’t offer you a drink – can I get you anything?' She moved to stand.

'No, thank you,' Lawrence said, holding up a hand to stop her and perching on the opposing sofa.

'Sorry,' Alyson repeated, as she sank back down into her seat.

'We won't take up too much of your time,' Lawrence began. 'But I do have a few questions about Steve's financial affairs.'

Alyson nodded.

'According to his bank statements, in September you transferred a considerable sum of money into his account. Is that correct?'

'Yes.'

'Presumably that was to facilitate his purchase of the flat?'

'Yes.'

'That wouldn't be any of our concern, but when we spoke to your husband yesterday, he was adamant you weren't financing Steve's step onto the property ladder, which does raise questions.'

As Lawrence spoke, Alyson lifted her carefully coiffured eyebrows a little way, nodding as he finished. 'I did mention it to him,' she replied, mildly. 'But I think a lot of what I say goes in one ear and out the other.'

Lawrence felt his own eyebrows rise, quite astonished by this response. 'You *mentioned* it?' He echoed, incredulously. 'Mrs Parker, we're talking about well over half a million pounds! Did that really merit no more than a *mention*?'

'It was a loan, not a gift,' Alyson responded, unconcernedly. 'Steve was going to pay it back within two years.'

'How? He certainly wasn't earning enough to do so.'

'Duncan's parents established a trust for him shortly after he was born. He wasn't entitled to realise the assets until he turned thirty, so I agreed to lend him the funds in the meantime.'

'I see,' Lawrence paused for a moment's thought. 'I'm sorry to have to ask, but what will happen to those assets now?'

'Offhand, I don't know. I'm not a trustee. Sorting out things like that hasn't been a priority these past few weeks.'

'I understand that,' Lawrence replied. 'But I'd be grateful if you could find out and let me know as soon as possible.'

'Of course.'

'On a related note, your husband mentioned that you're a partner in his business.'

'A silent one.'

'Do you keep an eye on the accounts?'

'If you're asking whether I'm aware the company is running a deficit, then yes, I am.'

'I was actually going to ask whether you were aware of the size of the debt that's accumulated as a result.'

'I don't know the number, because I haven't asked. I've always been mindful not to be forever looking over Rupert's shoulder.'

'That seems a rather reckless attitude, given that you're presumably liable for the debt should the company go under.'

'It's not reckless at all. The bank overdraft facility isn't unlimited, and Rupert can't extend it without my signature.'

'You still run the risk of losing a considerable sum.'

'Any business venture is an educated gamble,' Alyson responded. 'I accept that. And there's more to EverGreener than making money. But I'm not sure how any of this is relevant to you.'

'It may not be, this is simply a routine line of enquiry. Money is a common motive in homicide.'

Apparently accepting this explanation, Alyson nodded.

'Whilst we're on the subject of EverGreener, do you share your husband's passion for sustainable living?'

Alyson's momentary hesitation spoke for her, and it occurred to Lawrence that he couldn't imagine her being passionate about anything. He wondered whether her strangely indifferent manner was her way of coping with Steve's death; surely she wasn't always so detached?

'I recognise the importance of environmental sustainability and I admire what Rupert is trying to do, but in all honesty it's not something I could say I feel passionately about,' she admitted.

'Steve seems to have had quite strong feelings about it. Did he discuss those with you?'

'He didn't have strong feelings about sustainability, he had strong feelings about my investing in what he saw as Rupert's pet project. I think he'd have taken more or less the same view whatever the company's purpose. Or at least, he'd have had the same concerns about any associated deficit.'

'So he was aware of the state of EverGreener's finances.'

'It's not a secret. I imagine most journalists know their way around company accounts.'

'Was he the one who brought the matter to your attention?'

'He tried, but he didn't tell me anything I didn't know.'

'So although you weren't perpetually looking over Rupert's shoulder, Steve was. That must have been difficult for your husband.'

'I don't think either of them ever found dealing with the other easy,' Alyson admitted. 'For a long time I felt responsible for the situation, and I tried very hard to make things work between the three of us. More recently, I realised it was never going to happen,' she sighed. 'When it comes down to it, some people are like oil and water, and in the end all you can do is accept there *is* nothing you can do.'

Rebecca queued up at UCLH's main information desk to ask where she would find Elliot, and was caught off guard when the woman behind the counter asked whether she was a relative. After a moment's hesitation, she shook her head.

'Then I can't give you any information, I'm afraid. It's family only.'

Rebecca frowned. 'But he doesn't –'

'If you want to see him, you'll have to talk to his brother,' the woman interrupted, firmly.

'His *brother*?' Rebecca exclaimed.

'Yes.'

Rebecca's frown deepened. She had met Elliot's brother only once – briefly – at an Astatine gig, and given the furious response his arrival had provoked, she very much doubted he was on Elliot's list of emergency contacts. She was still digesting the information when the receptionist, apparently mistaking her consternation for resistance, added, 'Young lady, we have had a steady stream of visitors claiming to know Elliot this afternoon, and he's in no state to deal with hordes of fans, so if you're not a relative, there's no access.'

Rebecca had never felt so acutely aware that Elliot was now, in many people's eyes, public property. She briefly considered forcing the matter with her warrant card, but decided against it, and turned from the front desk feeling slightly dazed. Seeing a sign to the café, she headed towards it to buy a coffee, and as she turned a corner almost collided with Alec, Elliot's closest friend. He started slightly on seeing Rebecca, then, recovering himself, demanded, 'What the fuck are you doing here?'

'How's Elliot?'

'What's it to you?'

'I still care about him, Alec.'

'No you don't! You're just here to appease your conscience!'

'Alec, please.'

Alec held her gaze for several seconds. He looked exhausted. His sepia eyes were anxious, his long mousy hair tucked, unbrushed, behind his ears, and he clearly hadn't shaved in at least forty-eight hours. 'He's stable, ok?' He said, at length. 'So you can go now.' He turned and walked towards the doors out onto the Euston Road.

'What happened?' Rebecca asked, hurrying through the doors after him.

'That's none of your business!' Alec snapped. 'You lost the right to be a party to his private life the day you finished with him!'

'Was that before or after you rewrote history and adopted a brother?' Rebecca asked, taking an educated guess at who was really controlling Elliot's visitors.

'Well it's not like he has anyone else,' Alec retorted. 'I'm not about to abandon him to the health service!' He put a hand to his pocket for his cigarettes, heading down the steps to the pavement.

Rebecca drew a deep breath, trying to keep her cool. 'I know how much he means to you, Alec, but –'

'No you don't! You don't have a fucking clue! You know fuck all about either of us!'

Rebecca hesitated momentarily. 'Is he on smack?' She asked, the question sounding much more reasonable and matter-of-fact than she had intended.

'*What?*'

She reached into her bag for the leaflet she had come across earlier in the week. 'I found this in his stuff.'

'Well maybe he was trying to straighten Matt out.'

'I'm not an idiot, Alec.'

'And Elliot is not on smack!' Alec returned, his voice tense. 'All right?'

'So what is he doing here?'

'Like I already said, it's none of your business!'

'If you won't tell me, I'll have to ask him,' Rebecca replied. 'And your access rules aren't going to stand up to a police warrant card and the revelation he's no more your brother than mine!'

Alec didn't reply, raising a cigarette to his lips and busying himself lighting it.

'*What happened?*' Rebecca pressed.

Alec dropped his gaze to the floor as he exhaled, still saying nothing.

'It's hardly as if I'm going to broadcast it!'

'Really?'

'Oh come *on.*'

There was a long pause before Alec looked around, presumably to make sure nobody else was within earshot. 'He cut his wrists,' he admitted, at length, his voice wavering slightly. 'All right? Are you happy now?'

The news didn't come as a shock, but it saddened her. Alec returned the cigarette to his lips, his hand shaking. The pain evident in his eyes was acute.

'How is he now?'

'Out of it,' Alec replied. 'They've had him sedated most of the day.'

'And how are you doing?'

'What do you care?'

'Alec.'

He shook his head, turning away. Rebecca reached to lay a hand on his arm. Alec recoiled from her touch.

'Look, I've answered your questions, could you just go now? Please?'

With a sigh, Rebecca nodded. Then, realising Alec might not have seen the gesture, said, 'Ok. Thank you for –' she stopped, unsure how to finish the sentence. 'Thank you. I'll pop back in a couple of days' time. In the meantime, if there's anything I can do, just let me know, ok?'

'What you can do is leave him alone,' Alec responded. 'Try putting his feelings ahead of yours for once. He's in a bad enough way without having you show up to remind him of everything he's lost. Just because you have a window on his life through the media doesn't mean you're still a *part* of that life.' He paused. 'You need to get used to that.'

* * * * *

'Did you have any tea, Lee?' Lorna Campbell asked, setting a mug down on the side table near where Leighton was kneeling on the carpet, carefully applying iodine paste to the venous ulcer that ran down the inside of his father's left ankle. 'There's some leftover crumble if you're hungry.'

'Like it'd hurt him to skip a few meals,' Glenn put in, before Leighton had a chance to reply.

'I'm ok, thanks, Mum,' he said, resisting the temptation to point out that he might not have been overweight had he not spent much of his adolescence on steroid tablets prescribed to try to counteract the effect that living with two parents smoking up to forty a day had on his asthma. Saying as much would score nothing but a spectacular own goal: his father was looking for a reaction and the remark would upset only his mother. He reached for a dressing pad and peeled open the sterile packaging, asking, 'Did you see your GP about your blood pressure?'

'Ain't gotten 'round to it.'

Leighton sighed. 'Dad, you need to get it under control.'

'Can you not give him something?' Lorna asked, hesitantly.

'No,' Leighton responded, shortly, lowering the pad onto the wound.

'Fat lot of use you are,' Glenn returned. 'Then again, you always were a waste of space. If you'd been a kitten I'd've drowned you at birth.'

Leighton didn't doubt it. At the age of five or six, he'd watched Glenn do just that to the four kittens their resident mouser, Molly, had produced. Leighton had cried, and Glenn had given him a slap. Molly had disappeared a few months later. Leighton had always hoped she'd found herself a better home, but he suspected her life hadn't had a happy ending. He often wondered what sort of life his own cat, Pandora, had known before she turned up, half starved, in his garden a year earlier. This evening she would be lapping up the attentions of Margaret, an elderly neighbour who was happy to enjoy all the perks of cat ownership with none of the responsibility or expense, and regularly fed Pandora and welcomed her into her home when Leighton wasn't around to do the job himself.

'What kind of doctor can't prescribe drugs?' Glenn continued, as Leighton wound a crepe bandage around his ankle to hold the pad in place.

'I can do it, Dad, but in your case it would be unethical, not to mention potentially dangerous, given that I don't have access to your medical records. And I'm not risking my licence just because you're too stubborn – or too scared – to visit your GP.'

'I'm scared of nowt!' Glenn exclaimed, kicking out with his good leg. His heel struck Leighton's shoulder, throwing him against the side table behind him, which overturned, sending the mug of tea hurtling across the floor. Lorna hurried to fetch a cloth and Leighton pushed himself up into a sitting position before getting to his feet.

'In that case, you can go and see your GP about this,' Leighton replied. 'I am done taking crap from you.' He strode from the room without giving Glenn a chance to respond, walking through the hallway and out of the front door onto the balcony that ran across the front of the council block.

Leaning his forearms on the metal railing that overlooked the street below, he cursed himself for agreeing to come that evening, for giving in to emotional blackmail, and for feeling obliged to take responsibility for his entire family. He thought back to his conversation with Rebecca the previous afternoon. He had long since come to terms with the fact that Glenn would never stop drinking, and that, despite being subject to frequent verbal and sporadic physical abuse, Lorna would never leave her husband. What Leighton didn't seem to be able to do was stop allowing their choices to influence his. Lorna relied on him because he let her, he always had. Doubtless in half an hour or so she would persuade him to come back inside, prompt Glenn to mutter a grudging apology, and Leighton would pick up where he'd left off. And afterwards, he'd berate himself for being too weak to walk away. He'd been looking out for his mother for so long that it had become second nature. Perhaps it always would be.

Seven

Max was on the phone when Lawrence reached his office on Friday morning, and, seeing him through the glass panel in the door, waved him in.

'I'd be happy to,' he said, in a tone that implied quite the opposite, as Lawrence eased the door shut behind himself. There was a brief pause before he continued. 'A week on Monday … no, I'm not kidding. This isn't a pick'n'mix I'm running here, you know.' Another pause. 'Well then I suggest you take that up with Oxford University … no, not the former poly, the university … yes. Ok, you do that.' Max rang off without saying goodbye. 'At this rate you're going to have another homicide on your hands,' he remarked, irritably, as Lawrence took a seat.

'Don't even think about it. I've enough overtime forms on my desk as it is without you creating extra work.'

This succeeded in drawing a smile from Max, and Lawrence asked what the problem was.

'Pathological intolerance,' his friend responded, cryptically.

'Are you using *pathological* in relation to a disorder, or the field?'

'Both, I think. Although I suppose the former subsumes the latter.' He sighed. 'I'm sure Pete never used to be such an arsehole. I don't remember him quibbling over my work every five minutes.'

'Personality clash?' Lawrence suggested.

'That's what I put it down to, initially, but he seems to be clashing with just about everyone. Leighton drives him to distraction because he won't drop it when Pete tries to dismiss any findings that don't fit his hypothesis. So you'd think Pete and

Roddy would be a match made in heaven, given that Roddy would just hand over the information and leave Pete to it, but he pissed Pete off because he wouldn't do something or other that wasn't *his job*. And now Pete's picking holes in everything Jon says.'

'On what grounds?'

'Blatant racism, if that last conversation was anything to go by. To put it politely, he asked whether we don't train enough medics ourselves that we need to go to Africa for them.'

Lawrence frowned. 'I thought Jon did his training here?'

'He did! As you'd expect, really, given that he was born here.' Max shook his head. 'I know Pete's always been a control freak, but these days he seems to think he can bully his way to whatever he wants. And he might get away with it in CID, but I'm not having it in my department.'

Lawrence nodded.

'Surely MacLennan isn't oblivious to his behaviour?'

'Probably not, but Pete gets results, so –' Lawrence held his hands out.

'I don't doubt it. The question, given the way he goes about it, is how often they're the right ones.'

Lawrence conceded the point with another nod.

'Anyway, presumably you didn't come down here on the off-chance I'd want someone to moan to,' Max observed. 'Steve?'

'Yes. Or rather, his family. You said on Wednesday that your primary connection was through Duncan. How well do you know Alyson and Rupert?'

'A lot better than I do Duncan, these days. Why?'

'The first time we met, I was surprised by how composed Alyson appeared to be, but when we spoke to her last night she seemed quite detached. Almost – I don't know – blank. I'm hoping you can give me some idea of what she's normally like so I stand a better chance of working out what part grief might be playing.'

'Well I certainly wouldn't describe Aly as blank,' Max replied. 'She's never been one to wear her heart on her sleeve, but she's usually pretty dynamic and engaging. Although Rupert did say she seems to have been stuck on some kind of autopilot since Steve died. He thinks she needs to know what happened before she can start processing it, which is why he came to me.'

This was news to Lawrence. 'I didn't realise he had. As I understood it, she was the one to request the second PM.'

'She was, but Rupert asked my advice before suggesting she speak to me.'

'That's interesting,' Lawrence remarked. 'Did he say anything else memorable?'

Max appeared to consider this for a moment before shaking his head. 'Not that I recall. Most of the conversation focused on his concerns about Aly.'

Lawrence nodded. 'I know her responses to some of our questions may be affected by her current mental state, but, that aside, I'm struggling with the implications of one or two things she said last night. Were you aware Steve was buying a flat?'

'Aly mentioned he'd had an offer accepted on a place.'

'Did she also tell you she was lending him the bulk of the money?'

'No, but I can't say I'm surprised. I don't think many twenty-somethings stand much chance of getting onto the property ladder in London without help nowadays. It was tough enough for our generation.'

'Quite,' Lawrence agreed. 'What concerns me is that Rupert seemed adamant she *wasn't* funding the purchase. When I questioned her about that, she dismissed it on the basis he'd just not paid attention.'

'How the other half live, eh?' Max remarked, with a blithe smile.

'I realise what counts as significant in a monetary sense is relative, but for two individuals with years of experience in the financial sector not to have engaged in more than a passing conversation about a sum of over half a million pounds strikes me as extremely unlikely.'

'Agreed,' Max said. 'But not everybody integrates their finances when they get married. Marnie and I have a joint account for groceries, the kids, holidays and so forth, but we have our own accounts, as well. I've no idea how much is in hers. Or what she does with it.'

'And how do you think you'd feel if Marnie had a small fortune squirreled away and you learned she'd made a decision about what to do with it without discussing it with you?'

'Honestly, I don't know,' Max admitted, after a moment's silence. 'I'm not good with hypothetical questions that are so far removed from my reality. At a guess, I imagine it would depend to a large extent on our circumstances. And what she did with it. If we had a big mortgage and were struggling to give the girls what they needed, and she splashed out on something frivolous, I should think I'd take a much dimmer view of it than if we were comfortably covering all our expenses.'

'You see, I think I'd be at least as concerned by Katie making a unilateral decision behind my back as by the financial ins and outs.'

'*Behind your back* assumes intent to deceive.'

'I'm not convinced there wasn't intent in this instance. Even if it was only deception by omission.'

'I don't know,' Max replied, after another pause. 'I do take your point, but Aly had to manage by herself for a very long time, and having been left in the lurch by her first husband when she was barely twenty-one I can see why she might have felt the need to maintain her financial independence.' He paused, then, clearly anticipating a dissenting view from Lawrence, said, 'I'm not saying it's right, just that it's not incomprehensible. But I think the real question is whether Rupert would understand. And for an answer to that, I'm afraid you'd have to ask him.'

Rebecca was staring rather blankly at the noticeboard outside the pathology unit's main laboratory when a voice filtered through her thoughts. She turned to see Leighton heading down the corridor towards her, eyebrows raised expectantly.

'Sorry, what?'

'Ah, silly joke, doesn't matter,' Leighton replied, waving a hand dismissively and coming to a halt as he drew level with her. 'You all right?'

Rebecca shrugged.

'I can offer you my last Rolo, if it would help?' He offered, pulling an unopened tube from the pocket of his leather jacket. 'Although obviously you'd have to give me a few minutes to eat the rest of them first.'

Rebecca managed a smile. 'Thanks, but there's no need to put yourself out, I think the first one would do.'

Leighton handed her the chocolates before continuing on his way in the direction of the office. Rebecca followed.

'I'll give you a few minutes in case you want to talk about it,' he said, opening the office door and holding it for her. 'And then I'll get onto the pathetic effort the Owls put in against Ipswich on Tuesday.'

'What makes football fans so loyal?' Rebecca mused, as Leighton made for his desk. 'Relatively few people stay loyal to bands, or writers, or – whatever – through the years, the masses tend to jump capriciously from one to another as the style changes or the next big thing comes along. Yet with football people keep on rooting for their team year after year after year, whether it's successful or not.'

'Well I suppose that's partly because you can't support more than one team at once,' Leighton responded, dropping into his chair. 'There's no limit to the number of songs you can get into. And sport doesn't really change over time. The teams and players might get better or worse, but they're all still playing the same game. Music and literature do change – at least, the decent stuff does.'

Rebecca nodded, holding the remainder of the Rolos out for Leighton to take. He declined with a shake of his head. 'I'm guessing you might need one or two more later.'

'Thanks.' She sat in the unoccupied chair at Jon's desk.

'You look about as tired as I feel. What's up? Elliot?'

'Uh-huh,' she confirmed, with a sigh. 'I just feel – I don't know – responsible.'

'Was it self-inflicted?'

She nodded.

'You can't blame yourself, Becks. It's not your fault he's depressed, and it's quite possible he'd have done exactly the same thing if you'd still been together.'

Rebecca didn't reply.

'Have you seen him?'

'No. Alec won't let me anywhere near him. And I know he has a point, I should be thinking about what's best for Elliot, not what I want.'

'And what do you want?'

She shook her head slightly. 'I don't know. I guess to hear him say what you did. That it's not my fault. That he doesn't blame me.'

'Maybe it's nobody's fault. He's ill. It is what it is.'

Rebecca didn't immediately respond, and was just about to do so when the office door opened again, and Lawrence strode in.

'Morning,' he greeted Leighton, cheerfully.

'There's no need to remind me,' Leighton joked, with affected weariness.

'Late night, was it?'

'In a word.'

'Well we won't keep you long. How are you getting on with the archive search?'

'I'm not convinced it's not a waste of time,' Leighton admitted, sliding down in his chair and lifting his feet to rest them on the edge of the waste-paper bin beside his desk. 'I'll devote some more time to it today, but there's a limit to how many hours I can justify spending on a hunch.'

'Fair enough,' Lawrence nodded. 'Keep me posted. In the meantime, I wanted to talk to you about erotic asphyxiation.'

Leighton raised an eyebrow. 'To be honest it's not really my bag, but if you have a word with the guys over in vice, I'm sure they'll be able to point you in the direction of someone who can show you the ropes.' He grinned. 'No pun intended.'

'Thanks for the tip,' Lawrence responded, drily, as Rebecca pursed her lips to stifle a smile.

'What is it you want to know?'

'Becky dug up something on a case that might be connected to this one – a man who was found hanged in a squat some years ago. The circumstances surrounding the death weren't clear, and one suggestion was that a sex act of some sort had gone wrong.'

'Are you asking whether the same might be true of Steve's death?'

'Is that possible?'

'It's possible, but I don't think accidental death fits the bill. Nothing about the presentation of the body or the scene smacks of panic.'

'That aside, how likely is it as a cause of death?'

'I've no idea,' Leighton admitted. 'It's not exactly the kind of thing people talk about at parties.' He smiled cheekily. 'At least, not the parties I go to.'

'I was hoping for an answer from a professional rather than a social perspective,' Lawrence replied, impatiently.

'I'm not sure I can give you one. People are much more likely to end up in the hands of a pathologist if they're engaging in autoerotic asphyxiation. The risk of death is much smaller when you've two people involved. Even with the former it's difficult to make any real estimate of numbers, because some people would rather have a family member's death recorded as suicide than the result of what they see as deviant sexual behaviour.'

'You mean relatives may tamper with the scene.'

Leighton nodded. 'Yep. There was a report on this not so long ago,' he took his feet off the bin and stood up, heading for the veritable library of journals and books lining the back wall of the office. Crouching down, he ran a finger along a row of journal spines on the bottom shelf before stopping and pulling an issue out. He flicked through it, then straightened up and turned back towards his desk, holding the journal out for Lawrence to take.

'Bloody hell, if I didn't know you better I'd say you needed to get out more,' Lawrence observed, after a moment, handing the journal on to Rebecca. It was dated nearly four years previously.

'Ah, but I do, you guys work me way too hard.'

Lawrence smiled. 'Well at the risk of overloading you further, do you think you might have time to look into this at some stage today?'

'I'll do my best to squeeze it in.'

'Are we all right to hang onto this in the meantime?' Lawrence indicated the journal in Rebecca's hands.

'Providing you bring it back,' Leighton replied, reaching for his chair. 'Roddy'll go ape if he finds anything missing from the library.' He sat back down. 'So if anyone asks, I didn't give it you.' He lifted his eyebrows conspiratorially. 'Ok?'

'That didn't take long,' Daniel remarked, as Lawrence approached his desk en route back through CID.

'Eva left me a message about Steve's notebooks,' Lawrence replied, glancing at the empty desk opposite Daniel's. 'Do you know where she is?'

'No. She was here a minute ago.'

Lawrence nodded. 'Has Jim been all right for you?'

'Like a church mouse,' Daniel answered, casting an uneasy glance in the direction of Lawrence's open office door. 'I told him if he didn't behave, I'd lock him in the cells. I think he might have thought I was serious.' He affected an exaggerated wince. 'Sorry.'

'I doubt you've done any lasting damage,' Lawrence responded, unconcernedly. 'Have you had any luck establishing where Steve got to between leaving Deptford and arriving home on the night he died?'

Daniel shook his head. 'What CCTV I've been able to get hold of has been toss all use because it was raining half the night, so the only notable detail I've gathered so far is how many umbrellas are plastered with corporate logos. And obviously nobody working in the local pubs can remember one day from another a month on. But I'm still waiting on a couple of calls, so there's an outside chance I might hear something useful.'

'Ok, keep me posted.'

'Sure thing.'

Lawrence continued on his way into his office, where Jimmy was sitting at the desk, working on an item of holiday homework. The boy raised his eyes warily as Lawrence entered the room, his expression turning to one of relief when he saw who it was. Lawrence guessed Daniel had been right about Jimmy taking his joke to heart, and felt a sense of relief himself. His son might not have much respect for *his* authority, but apparently did still have some for other exponents of the law. Then again, the broad-shouldered, six-foot-four officer probably seemed intimidating to most fourteen-year-olds, whether or not they had any idea of his occupation. Either way, Lawrence concluded, the experience probably hadn't done his cause any harm.

'Don't let me interrupt,' he said, as he reached for his laptop. Jimmy obediently returned his eyes to the textbook in front of him, and Lawrence pulled a chair up to the rear of the desk, cleared a space for the laptop and logged into the system. He had scarcely registered the presence of five unread emails when a tentative knock came at the open office door, and he glanced around to see Eva hovering uncertainly in the doorway, a thick envelope file in her hands.

'Come on in,' he encouraged, with a perfunctory smile. 'Grab a seat.'

'Thanks.' She perched on a nearby chair. 'Sorry it's taken so long. I thought it would just be a matter of finding someone fluent in Teeline, but it turns out translating it isn't as easy as you'd think.'

'Oh?'

'Aside from the challenge of making sense of someone else's handwriting, a lot of Teeline's symbols can represent several different words, so you're reliant to some extent on context and memory to make sense of things – and that's not much help if you didn't write the notes yourself. The only clues we really had were the names of people and places, which were generally spelled out in Roman text, at least initially.'

'For accuracy, I suppose,' Lawrence guessed.

'So you'd think, but I spotted several mistakes. We managed to translate a lot of the notes retrospectively by cross-referencing names with articles on the Chronicle's website, and Tara – one of the press secretaries – did what she could with the rest. It's all typed up in here,' she opened the flap of the folder to display a sheath of papers. 'I've flagged a few things of interest, but most notable are a few lines about Rupert Parker suggesting he was involved in a type of stock fraud called pump and dump.'

'What does that involve?'

'Apparently you start with a low-value stock, use positive spin to push up the price, then sell your holding before the price can drop back down. And on the face of it, that's not dissimilar to what happened at EverGreener last spring,' she pulled the topmost sheet of paper from the folder and presented Lawrence with a line graph that rose steadily before falling in a series of abrupt bursts. Near the high point of the trajectory was an arrow, which Eva indicated, saying, 'That's when Parker sold almost half his stock.'

'Interesting.'

'And he wasn't the only one. Someone else who off-loaded a large holding at around the same time is a stockbroker called Eugene King, who Parker meets on a regular basis for lunch. King's currently under investigation in relation to allegations of misconduct, including deliberately mis-selling stocks,' Eva proffered a printout of a news article on the case, with several lunch dates and venues written neatly in green biro on an attached Post-it note. The names of the restaurants were immediately recognizable – they probably all featured in lists of London's best eateries – and a quick scan of the article's opening paragraph was sufficient for Lawrence to recall something of it from coverage when the story had broken over the summer.

'Great, thank you.'

'Steve also had a notebook that seems to be devoted to stories that might have had an audience beyond Clapham, and he had quite a lot of notes on Tim Bateman.'

'And he is?'

'Computer geek turned billionaire. Known largely for his marriage to the former model Natalie Keyes – she's currently trying to reinvent herself as some kind of fashion patron. Bateman runs a company called Sandbox Systems that last year secured a lucrative four-year contract to develop software for the MOD.

Sandbox wasn't the expected recipient of the contract and there were whispers about bribery. I'm not sure whether that's what this relates to, or whether this is something else,' she passed Lawrence a photocopied page headed with Tim's name and followed by a series of incomprehensible squiggles.

His eye was drawn immediately down the page to a simple flow diagram liberally highlighted in fluorescent yellow. Tim's initials formed the starting point, led on to a circled pound sign and then, by way of three divergent arrows, to two other names and a question mark. Lawrence recognised the first of the names as that of a government minister even before he'd absorbed Eva's accompanying note on the woman's job description, and wasn't surprised when the man named immediately below also turned out to be a politician. Beneath the sketch, another name – this time unfamiliar and unannotated – appeared in square brackets, along with a mobile number.

'Do we know who this is?' Lawrence asked.

'No. Do you want me to find out?'

'Please. I imagine it's the source of at least some of the other information. And is there any translation on this?' He indicated the shorthand further up the page.

'Most of what Tara could make sense of was just basic background information,' Eva replied, apologetically, handing over another page from the folder.

Lawrence nodded, casting his eyes over it quickly. 'Ok, can you leave this with me?'

'Sure,' Eva closed the folder and placed it on Lawrence's desk, getting to her feet and asking, hesitantly, 'Is there anything else?'

'Not right now, thanks.'

'Ok,' she nodded, making for the doorway and almost colliding with Rebecca as she came in the opposite direction, a cardboard tray of drinks in her hand.

'Sorry,' Rebecca apologised, turning sideways to allow Eva to pass before taking the final few steps into the room. 'Nobody warned me we were expecting the Monsoon today,' she complained as she set the tray down, her hair dripping onto her sky blue blouse and rendering the fabric over her shoulders translucent. Tossing her handbag onto a chair, she tipped her head back and used her fingers to roughly comb her dark hair into a petite ponytail. As she twisted and squeezed, rivulets of rainwater ran down her hands and wrists, and she released her grip on her hair, shaking what she could of the water from her forearms. 'And yes,' she continued, as she took a cardboard cup from the tray and set it down beside Lawrence's laptop, 'I know the word Monsoon actually relates to the prevailing wind, not the rain, but you get my drift.'

Lawrence hadn't given the matter much thought, even less been intending to correct her, but nodded obligingly as he thanked her for the coffee.

'And as we've got a visitor I thought we should have some snacks,' she added, with a smile, setting an individually wrapped chocolate brownie beside the coffee with one hand as she placed a small bottle of orange juice and another brownie in front of Jimmy. He looked up, his face brightening, and it occurred to Lawrence that in withholding the reason for his son's presence in the office he had perhaps given his colleagues the erroneous impression that the boy was unfairly paying the price of having two working parents. It would, he realised, have been pertinent to convey at least that the arrangement was intended to be one of punishment as much as convenience. Moreover, he ought to have concerned himself a little less with his own reputation and considered the message concealing the truth from his co-workers might send to his son. He was hardly leading by example.

On Rebecca and Lawrence's second visit to EverGreener, Rupert

Parker was demonstrably less welcoming than he had been previously, but voiced no objection when Lawrence asked if he could spare a few minutes and showed them into the same glass-walled meeting room they had occupied during Wednesday's visit. Taking a seat without offering refreshments this time, Rupert sat back, crossing his legs and regarding Lawrence expectantly.

'We spoke before about Steve's plans to purchase a flat, and you –'

'Aly filled me in,' Rupert interrupted. 'So I'm aware she was lending him the money. But please tell me you didn't come all the way out here just to ask about that?'

'I didn't come to ask you that at all. For one thing, I'm more interested in knowing how you feel about having been left in the dark about the loan.'

'That's rather an emotive way of phrasing it,' Rupert replied. 'I don't think it was ever Aly's intention that I be *left in the dark*.'

Lawrence wasn't convinced Rupert believed that any more than he did, but nevertheless reworded his question. 'Very well, how do you feel about the fact your wife didn't think the topic worthy of more than a passing mention?'

Rupert avoided answering directly, saying, 'You speak as if she needed my permission, Inspector. As I said the other day, I don't tell Aly what to do with her money.'

'But it's not just her money, is it?' Lawrence responded, ignoring the fact the man had – he suspected intentionally – downgraded his job title. 'You're married.'

'Legally speaking, you're correct, but that's not how we operate,' Rupert returned, sitting forwards in his chair. 'Look, I might not agree with Aly's decision, but given the circumstances I'm a lot more concerned about the fact she's lost her son than the fate of a few hundred grand! She was never good at saying no to Steve, and if that had been a deal-breaker for me we'd have divorced a long time ago! Money is not the be-all and end-all!'

you've had a chance to calm down. In the meantime, if your assistant could spare five minutes, I'd like a quick word. Then we'll be on our way.'

Tim had spent time he could ill afford with Natalie and her architect on Friday morning, and the arrival of unscheduled visitors minutes before he was due to leave the office for another meeting couldn't have been less welcome. He'd repeated *no appointment, no access* to Caroline so many times that he didn't even give her time to explain to whom she would be delivering the news, slamming the telephone receiver down, turning his chair and bending to rummage in his briefcase. Moments later, a tentative knock at the office door heralded his secretary's second attempt to waylay him.

'Caroline, what did I say?' Tim demanded, without looking around, as he heard the door open.

'Yes, I know, Mr Bateman, but –'

'Yes *but*?' Tim echoed, turning his head in exasperation; if there was one expression he detested, it was *yes but*, and Caroline knew it. 'If the but isn't world war three, I'm not interested!'

'It's the police,' Caroline replied, quickly.

'The police?' Tim exclaimed, straightening up almost reflexively. 'What do they want?'

'They didn't say,' Caroline replied, hesitantly. Tim guessed she hadn't asked.

'Fine, ok, show them in,' Tim nodded, abandoning the search of his briefcase and moving to straighten his tie.

Never mind policemen getting younger, he mused moments later, policewomen appeared to be getting prettier. The petite detective sergeant – he didn't pay attention to her name –wouldn't have looked out of place in one of Natalie's catalogues. Assuming she undid her shirt by a button or two and lost the sensible court shoes, that was. Her powder blue eyes met with his as she sat down and, although she didn't smile, he could imagine dimples puckering her cheeks when she did.

'How can I help?' Tim asked, looking from her to her superior officer. He was older, probably not far off Tim's forty-six years, with an enviably athletic build that exhibited no sign of middle-aged spread. Presumably not the type to head for the gym only to use the hot tub and sauna, as Tim almost invariably did.

'We've a few questions about Steve Golding,' the DCI began as his partner drew out a notebook.

Tim frowned. 'Who?'

The man repeated the name, adding, 'Journalist. Clapham Chronicle.'

Tim shook his head slightly. 'I'm afraid I've no idea who he is.'

'Was,' came the clipped reply. 'We're investigating his death.'

'Well I'm sorry to hear that, but I'm still none the wiser.'

'Conversely, he seems to have amassed a considerable amount of information about you.'

'As can anyone with access to Google.'

'Oh we realise that, but Wikipedia doesn't seem to cover your dealings with Geraint Pritchard and Miriam Morgan-Jones.'

'Neither does my memory, I'm afraid,' Tim replied, levelly. 'Look, I wish I could help, but I've never heard of the bloke and I'm very busy so –'

He was cut off by an authoritative, 'We'll try not to keep you too much longer,' and felt a muscle near his left eye twitch as he swallowed an indignant retort; he wasn't accustomed to someone else having the upper hand.

'Perhaps this might aid your memory,' the DCI added, slipping a photograph out of his jacket pocket and leaning forwards to push it into the centre of Tim's desk. Tim made a pretense of studying it before shaking his head and sliding it back the other way.

Eight

Priya stole a glance at Ramona as she replaced the receiver of her desktop telephone, looking pale and shaken. The hushed exchange had been largely inaudible, but what Priya had overheard had sounded like a mixture of denials and apologies.

'Are you all right?' She asked, hesitantly, after a moment.

Ramona nodded, looking anything but.

'Male?'

'What?'

'I meant was it a man who upset you.'

'Oh. Right. Yes.' Ramona tried to smile, her eyes filling with tears instead. Priya had no idea how to respond. She wasn't at all sure Ramona would appreciate a friendly hug. In the end, she pulled a packet of tissues from her desk drawer and held it out.

'Thanks,' Ramona took the packet, busying herself unsticking the tab that sealed it and taking a tissue. She dried her eyes carefully from below – presumably to avoid smudging her dark eyeliner – and returned the rest of the tissues to Priya.

'Is there anything I can do?' Priya offered, tentatively.

Ramona shook her head. 'No. Thank you.'

'Ok.' Priya gave her colleague a small smile before returning her eyes to her screen, thinking perhaps Ramona would prefer to be left to gather herself together in peace. She had almost re-submerged herself in her work when Ramona spoke again. Her words caused Priya's heart to skip a beat.

'Am I really too scary to talk to?'

Priya swallowed hard, forcing herself to take her eyes off the screen to meet Ramona's. Her throat felt tight. 'I'm sorry – I didn't mean –'

'I'd like to know.'

Put on the spot, Priya's mind went blank. She swallowed again. 'I just –' she broke off, unsure of what she had been going to say. 'I worry about saying the wrong thing sometimes. That's all. I don't want you to think badly of me because I don't always see feminist issues the same way you do.'

Ramona regarded her in silence for some moments, her pale eyes still wet. Priya wondered what she was thinking, feeling increasingly uncomfortable under the other woman's gaze.

'Do you think the way Steve used to behave was ok?' Ramona asked, at length.

'Not always. But I think it bothered you more than me,' Priya replied, before adding, quickly, 'I'm not saying you're oversensitive. Just that we're different.'

Ramona nodded. 'You found him irritating rather than intimidating.'

Priya frowned. 'Intimidating?' She echoed, not sure what to make of the remark. At times Steve's jokes and innuendo had made her cringe, but she couldn't remember him doing anything that might have been classed as intimidating, in either a physical or a sexual sense. Perhaps *oversensitive* wasn't the wrong adjective for Ramona after all, despite the fact she came across as something approaching the polar opposite. She was the kind of woman Priya's father would have described as ballsy. Priya herself preferred feisty. But in reality, it seemed Ramona was neither.

'I know some of his jokes were embarrassing, but I don't remember him saying anything particularly threatening,' Priya admitted.

'Tasteless jokes I can handle,' Ramona replied, dully, raising a hand to rub the back of her neck, ducking her head and lowering her eyes as she did so. 'I don't think they're clever or acceptable, but they're not worth losing sleep over.' She paused. 'What I found intimidating wasn't the silly stuff that people pretended to laugh about. It was the way he was when we were alone.'

A police warrant card apparently allowed the holder to jump the long entry queue to the Palace of Westminster but not the airport-style security search, and Rebecca wondered whether government employees had to endure the same inconvenience every time they entered the building. Having been relieved of the pretty glass nail file she'd only recently procured at Greenwich Market, as well as a miniature spray can of deodorant, she was issued with a visitor's pass, complete with an unflattering black-and-white photograph, and her handbag returned to her.

She set about affixing the clip of the pass to the waistband of her navy pencil skirt as Lawrence stepped through the body scanner behind her, thinking irritably that the sharp H pencil still in her possession would probably make for a better weapon than the confiscated nail file. It was a complaint she had heard more than once from Leighton, who could list at least a dozen potentially lethal everyday items that rarely, if ever, raised security eyebrows. She had once asked which among them he considered the most dangerous. Well aware that Rebecca's birthday fell on St Andrew's Day, his straight-faced reply had been 'an angry Sagittarian'.

'Sergeant Palmer?'

Rebecca raised her head to meet the russet brown eyes of a pretty twenty-something woman with barely controlled dark corkscrew curls and eyebrows that peaked quirkily towards the middle where the hairs grew against one another. Gina Wallace, Rebecca guessed, correctly – the third individual named in Steve's notes on Tim Bateman, and Geraint Pritchard's parliamentary researcher. With the introductions completed, Gina led them down several rather grand corridors before showing them into a large, unoccupied office whose décor could have been cut and pasted from the House of Commons Chamber itself. The wood panels were the same golden brown of those Rebecca had seen countless times on television and computer screens, the predominant colour in the rich wallpaper the verdant green of the benches, and the carpet, desks and chairs largely coordinated to one or other hue. Perhaps every room in the Commons was decorated along the same lines, she mused. It was the sort of thing Lawrence was almost certain to know, and she made a mental note to ask him later.

Gina gathered three chairs together on one side of the room and invited her visitors to sit. As Rebecca did so, she pulled out her notebook and the H pencil that had been the subject of her cogitations minutes earlier. Lawrence promptly held out a hand for both items, wordlessly communicating in a moment's eye contact that he intended her to ask the questions.

'We're hoping you might be able to help us fill in a few gaps in our investigation,' Rebecca began, slipping a photograph of Steve out from between the pages of the notebook before passing the latter to her superior. 'Do you recognise the man in this picture?'

Gina only had to glance at it before she nodded, saying, 'Yes. Steve.' And, after a momentary pause, 'Has something happened to him?'

'I'm afraid he was found dead a few weeks ago.'

The shock that flooded Gina's face was tinged with another emotion, and, when she asked the obvious question, Rebecca sensed an undercurrent of relief. Gina had slept with Steve, she immediately realised, and finally had an answer to the question of why he'd never called that didn't reflect on her.

Dispensing with the girl's query by way of the half-lie that they weren't certain what had happened yet, Rebecca returned to her own line of enquiry.

'Had you known Steve long?'

Neither Lawrence nor Rebecca looked to be around when Leighton dropped into CID shortly after five, but Lawrence's office wasn't deserted. Sitting in his chair, elbow on the desk and head propped up with his hand, was a dark-haired boy in his early teens. He looked bored, and was doodling on the cover of an exercise book.

'Hello,' Leighton greeted.

The boy glanced up. 'Hi.'

'Jimmy?' He guessed.

'Yeah.'

'I'm Leighton.'

Jimmy nodded disinterestedly.

'You waiting for your dad?'

He nodded again.

'Well I guess that makes two of us,' Leighton responded, concluding that if Lawrence had left his son unattended he probably hadn't gone far. He sat in a chair near the desk, setting his rucksack down on the adjacent chair and unzipping the front pocket. Pulling out a paper bag, he tipped it in Jimmy's direction. 'Cookie?'

This drew more enthusiasm, and Jimmy managed a smile as he reached to take one. 'Thanks.'

Leighton helped himself to the cookies before setting the bag down.

'Are you a policeman too?'

'No. I don't think they'd have me.'

'What do you do?'

'I'm a pathologist.'

'Do you have to cut up dead bodies, like on TV?'

'I do.'

'Isn't that kind of gross?'

'It can be.'

Jimmy didn't reply.

'How about you? What do you want to do?'

'Football.'

Leighton smiled. 'Yeah, me too, really. Who do you support?'

'West Ham.'

'Good choice.'

'What about you?'

'Sheffield Wednesday.'

'Is that where you come from?'

'Yep.'

Jimmy nodded.

'So are you on half term?'

'Uh-huh.'

'Not much of a way to be spending it. What'd you do wrong?'

There was a brief pause. 'Stole a car.'

'Christ. I was joking.'

Jimmy cast his eyes down.

'What did you steal?'

He shrugged.

'So it wasn't your idea, then.'

The boy frowned. 'How'd you figure that?'

'If you're going to steal a car you need to know which ones you can start easily and don't have a steering lock. And they're not as easy to come by as they were when I was your age.'

Jimmy eyed him suspiciously. 'You've never stolen a car.'

'No,' Leighton replied. 'I stole a lot more than one.'

'How many?'

'I genuinely don't know,' he admitted. 'Which means I owe an awful lot of people an apology.'

'Did you ever get caught?'

'No.' Leighton slid down in his chair. 'Although my brother did.'

'Did he get in a lot of trouble?'

'He got two years.'

There was a brief pause before she said, rather awkwardly, 'I'm sorry if I dropped you in it yesterday. With the police, I mean.'

'Why, what did you say?'

'Just that you'd asked what they'd asked me. I honestly didn't mean for it to come up, we were just chatting – well, I *thought* we were just chatting – and somehow we got onto the fact you and I had been for lunch on Wednesday, and –' she trailed off with a shrug.

'Ah, ambush by conversation,' Jez replied, knowingly. 'Clever coppers.'

'Sorry,' Priya repeated.

'Oh, don't worry about it.'

Feeling embarrassed, Priya needlessly stirred her drink with its straw, watching the ice cubes go round and round.

'I wasn't after some kind of scoop, though,' Jez added. 'I'm not that mercenary. I just want to know what happened.'

She nodded.

'Sometimes I think I'm the only person in the office who misses him.'

Priya wasn't sure how to respond, because she suspected that, on a personal level, he was right. She didn't doubt Damon was missing Steve from a professional standpoint; given the paper's limited budget for freelance reporting, he had been the one required to pick up the lion's share of the additional workload over the past month. Priya's job, by contrast, had been made easier by the change in personnel; Steve's articles had involved not only the most subediting, but also the most quibbling over minutiae of style and syntax that the other reporters largely accepted without question.

Seemingly realising the difficult position the remark had put her in, Jez added, 'I know he didn't exactly go out of his way to endear himself to you and Ramona, though.'

'I was never sure how much he was just trying to wind her up,'

Priya admitted. Although after Ramona's disclosure earlier in the day, she suspected Steve's intentions had been more malicious than that. Priya had never been aware of any real variation in his behavior, regardless of whether or not anyone else had been around. Perhaps the fact she'd never reacted particularly strongly to any of his remarks had worked in her favour.

'I often used to hope he was,' Jez replied.

'Really?' Priya felt surprised. 'Did it bother you?'

'Some of what he came out with, yeah. I mean, I don't think humour or satire should be ruled with the iron rod of the PC brigade, but there's a big difference between dancing on the line and leaping over it.'

'And between stating an opinion and hurling insults.'

'Yeah, I think the comparison to Valerie Solanas was the real low point.'

Priya frowned. 'Who?'

'That crazy lesbian feminist who shot Andy Warhol,' Jez replied. 'Were you not in the office when he said that?'

'I don't think so.'

'Oh, you missed a fun few minutes,' he lifted his eyebrows. 'In the same way watching the original *Halloween* movie is fun, that is. I thought she was going to explode. If looks could kill, he'd have been –' he stopped short. 'Sorry, I didn't mean –' he shook his head. 'You know what I mean. Anyway, I spent the rest of the day waiting for him to get his arse kicked by Damon, but I guess Ramona never mentioned it, because it didn't happen.'

'Did you tell the police?'

Jez looked surprised by the question. 'No. I didn't really think about it. Besides, she might be a lesbian, but she's not crazy.'

'She's not a lesbian. Not that it matters. And you hardly have to be crazy to kill someone.'

'No, but it helps,' he quipped. 'And I think there's at least an element of crazy in an elaborate sham suicide, don't you? That's about as far removed from heat-of-the-moment impulse as you can get.'

Priya didn't reply, returning her eyes to her glass. She wanted to observe that it was the job of the police to decide what did or didn't matter, but felt loath to press the point. She didn't imagine Jez wanted to rat on a colleague any more than she had – before unintentionally doing just that – and she certainly didn't like the idea of Ramona hearing she had proposed he do so. She wondered whether anyone else had been privy to the incident and, if so, whether they had brought it up. Although unless the police had interviewed the myriad freelance journalists, production staff and photographers who breezed in and out of the office from time to time, the only other person who might have had the opportunity to spill the beans was Liam. And she very much doubted he would have said a word.

Nine

'What's the prize?' Leighton asked from Lawrence's office doorway, interrupting his second read-through of a long and tedious group email from the chief superintendent. Given that Rebecca wasn't yet in, he automatically referred to his watch. It was just gone eight-thirty.

'For what, granting my wish about turning up on time?'

'Is this what on time looks like?' Leighton joked as he stepped into the office, making a show of looking around himself in awe. Although cheerful, he looked shattered, and promptly explained both this and his early arrival with the words, 'I was on call last night, so as far as I'm concerned it's still yesterday. But I do have a potential new victim for you.'

'I'm all ears.'

Leighton set a page from the classified section of the Clapham Chronicle down on Lawrence's desk. The paper was yellowing it was dated almost a year previously – and dappled with water marks, which Leighton explained with the words, 'Sorry it's rather a mess, it's been under the cat's water fountain.'

'When did you get a cat?'

'Oh – a while ago. She adopted me last year.'

'I didn't realise they'd opened a rehoming centre for medics,' Lawrence remarked. 'Did the Royal Pathological Society rescue you from an abusive home?'

'Something like that,' Leighton replied, rather dismissively, looking back to the sheet of newspaper on the desk. 'But anyway, this is what I wanted to show you.' He pointed to a small orange box two-thirds of the way down the right-hand side of the page.

and scientific terminology, and explaining how his thought processes had taken him from A to B, but when he had to write it down it seemed his hand couldn't keep pace with his mind, and much of the detail fell by the wayside. As a result, Lawrence usually found himself trying to follow a train of thought that read like a game of mental ping pong. Thus far, he had resisted asking Leighton to record his cogitations more coherently, largely because he suspected that in so doing he would be forced to admit that the younger man's mind was more agile than his own. And much as it might well be true, it wasn't something he felt inclined to acknowledge out loud.

A search of the system for the subject of Leighton's notes, one Ricardo D'Ambrosio, pulled up more than just the limited police report on his suicide. Some eight months before his death in January, Ricardo had apparently been arrested and charged after an accusation of rape was levelled against him. But since the woman responsible for the allegation had taken several weeks to make her complaint, the Criminal Prosecution Service had subsequently dropped the charges, citing a lack of evidence. Lawrence printed out both reports and added them to those on his desk before turning to Leighton's notes and wondering, not for the first time, why the pathologist always printed everything in small caps. He supposed it did at least make for a welcome contradiction to the far from unfounded jokes about the illegible nature of medics' handwriting.

An electronic squeak from his mobile phone drew his attention to the message briefly visible on the locked screen, which he half expected to be from his father, despite the man's poor proficiency with text messaging. Their lack of concordance over whether boarding school represented the best option for Jimmy had culminated in a heated telephone conversation on Friday evening. His father was always quick to offer unsolicited advice, but reluctant to accept defeat if that advice wasn't followed, and his erroneous conviction that Lawrence's opposition to the idea was borne principally of concern over the financial ramifications undoubtedly wasn't helping matters. The words *it's not your decision* had apparently made little impact, as he had already sent two emails on the subject that morning, and Lawrence's patience was wearing thin.

It came as a relief to find that the name on his mobile screen belonged to someone else, despite the fact that if Rebecca was texting him at ten to nine it was almost certainly to communicate a problem of some sort. He reached for the device to read on and have that supposition confirmed; having been forced to stop to adjudicate a road-rage dispute between a cyclist and a van driver, Rebecca was still in Highgate. He sighed, guessing she was unlikely to reach the office much inside the next hour, and turned to the copy of the postmortem report Leighton had left for him to read. That was one job he stood a good chance of accomplishing in the meantime.

Lawrence's first thought on seeing Leighton's name on his mobile phone screen shortly after midday was to wonder whether the call had been placed accidentally. He had assumed that after departing the office earlier in the day, Leighton's next stop had been home and bed. But he apparently hadn't made it that far, and was calling to ask if Lawrence was free to attend a potential crime scene in Kensal Rise.

Emerging from the lift on the fifth floor of a modern apartment block some forty minutes later, Lawrence and Rebecca found Leighton sitting on the stairs that led up to the sixth floor, clad in a paper bodysuit and holding a cardboard coffee cup in his right hand, his face pallid and eyes faintly bloodshot. Lawrence guessed the fact it was still *yesterday*, as Leighton had put it that morning, was starting to catch up with him.

'You look as if you've just been exhumed and slightly warmed,' he remarked, facetiously.

'I've barely been to bed in about three days, I think I might actually have started to decompose,' Leighton replied, wearily, rubbing his eyes with the fingers and thumb of his free hand. 'I'll have to watch they don't put the wrong man in the bag.'

Lawrence smiled. 'Who's your competition?'

'Name's Patrick Copeland. That's about as much as I know at this stage, I'm afraid.'

'Any idea who called it in?'

'Cleaner. The local plod were taking a statement when I arrived, but I'm not sure how much sense they got out of her, given the state she was in. I'm not sure how much joy you're going to get from them, either – the SIO looked none too thrilled when I said I was calling you.' Leighton rubbed his eyes again.

'Thanks for the warning.'

'And on that note, if SOCO are done in the bedroom I might go and take a nap,' he took hold of the handrail to his left and hauled himself to his feet.

'Are you going to be able to do the postmortem?'

'Today, you mean,' Leighton said. 'I'll speak to my dealer, see if I can get some speed.' He pushed open the door that led out of the lobby before asking, with a wan smile, 'D'you suppose I can expense it?'

'There are times when I'm not entirely sure he's joking,' Lawrence admitted, unfolding and shaking out a bodysuit in preparation for entering the flat.

'That's probably his intention,' Rebecca replied, as she stepped into the oversized legs of a similar garment and negotiated their passage up towards her waist, wishing she'd not chosen to wear a skirt that morning.

'I used to think the references to a delinquent past were just for effect, but I'm not convinced they are. Do you think he and his brother really did go joyriding?'

Caught between not wanting to lie and the feeling it wasn't her truth to tell, Rebecca responded with a question of her own. 'What makes you ask?'

Lawrence zipped up his bodysuit. 'Just something Jimmy said.'

'I'm sure Leighton wouldn't treat the subject lightly with an impressionable teenager.'

'I wasn't suggesting he would.' Lawrence shook his head. 'Never mind. We should take a look inside and then start working our way round the neighbours.' He headed for the door Leighton had used moments earlier. Rebecca followed him through the doorway and down a short corridor towards an open front door, which led onto a sleek open-plan living space with a polished wooden floor and expansive windows overlooking West London.

'Well, I can see why someone thought this was suspicious,' Lawrence remarked, indicating an open bottle of Dom Perignon standing on the kitchen counter to their right. 'I don't see many people cracking open a hundred-quid bottle of champagne if they're about to kill themselves.'

'Some people will drink whatever is *there*,' Rebecca pointed out, thinking back a few months. Shortly after she had broken off her relationship with Elliot, he had taken an overdose, washed down with a bottle of Jack Daniels. Having come to the end of the bottle still conscious, he had made a cocktail from the contents of the hotel minibar. She didn't suppose he would have cared whether he was downing Thunderbird or Taittinger, providing it led to oblivion.

'Any sign of a struggle?' Lawrence asked a nearby scenes of crime officer who was dusting a glass-topped coffee table for fingerprints.

'Toss all sign of anything,' came the curt reply. 'Far as I can

been primed she might well not have noticed.

'Everything's on the left.'

'Indeed,' Leighton replied. 'And lefties tend to thread their belts in the opposite direction from the majority of the population.'

'But you can't be sure *he* did,' Lawrence said.

'Ninety-nine per cent. New belts are usually straight, but once you start wearing them, they bow slightly. The direction they bend depends on how you wear them, and both of those hanging up in the wardrobe have consistently been worn the wrong way up.'

'You win,' Lawrence conceded, good-naturedly. 'Bravo.'

Leighton bowed with a theatrical flourish.

'If someone came to be dressing him, presumably there's a good chance sex was involved?' Rebecca observed.

'Quite possibly,' Leighton agreed. 'But that's a question I can't yet answer. All I can tell you at this stage is that I don't think the guy took his own life.' He bent down to reach for an evidence bag containing a garish strip of lime green and lilac fabric, and held it up. 'And that he had shockingly bad taste in ties.'

Rachel struggled to contain her excitement as she passed through the double doors into the Queens Arms; she'd been trying not to grin like a loony for the duration of the ten-minute walk from home and her cheek muscles were twitching in protest. She always looked forward to spending time alone with Jodie, but never more so than today. Spotting her friend at the bar, she waved and began threading her way through clusters of lunchtime drinkers, her elation dissipating as she neared.

Jodie apparently didn't share her enthusiasm for the rendezvous; she hadn't applied any make-up, and in the absence of foundation the only colour in her face was the mauve in the shadows beneath her eyes. Her blonde hair needed washing, and she was wearing the baggy jeans and faded jumper she usually reserved strictly for knocking around the house.

'Hey Jodes,' Rachel greeted, leaning in for a hug and trying not to feel disappointed that her friend hadn't even tried to make an effort for their afternoon out. 'You look rough, are you all right?'

'Yes,' Jodie nodded, with a small half-smile. 'Busy week. You know.'

'Yeah, been there,' Rachel replied, in what she hoped was a sympathetic tone, still feeling rather hurt. 'Have you ordered yet?'

Jodie shook her head.

'First round's on me, then. How's about we start with some fizz?' She held up her left hand, trying not to grin too widely.

Jodie stared at the ring rather dumbly for a moment before managing a rather hollow, 'Congratulations.'

'There's no need to look so happy for me,' Rachel responded, sarcastically, her excitement evaporating.

'I'm sorry – I didn't –' Jodie faltered, swallowing hard. 'I just wasn't expecting it. I am happy for you. Really.' She managed a smile, although it didn't look genuine. 'And I love the ring, it's really pretty.'

'It's an antique,' Rachel revealed, unable to stop her smile from returning as she admired the ring for what was probably the hundredth time that day. The oval-cut pink sapphire was flanked on either side by a pair of small platinum leaves set with tiny diamonds; Josh had said he knew it was perfect for her the moment he saw it, and he had been right.

'It's lovely, Rach. Congrats.' Jodie gave her another hug. Rachel returned the embrace, catching the eye of one of the bar staff as she released her friend and ordering a bottle of house champagne before perching on the bar stool next to that which Jodie was occupying.

'So, when did this happen?' Jodie asked.

'Yesterday. We had dinner at the Oxo Tower – it's not warm

enough to eat on the terrace at this time of year, but we sat in one of the windows and the view was incredible. I was dying to tell you last night, but I really wanted to do it in person. And I know we already talked about it a million times, but you will be my bridesmaid, won't you?'

Jodie nodded, blinking hard. ''Course,' she agreed, squeakily. 'Just promise me I won't have to wear pink.'

Rachel giggled. 'That's what Josh said.' She reached into her handbag for her purse as the bartender eased the cork out of the champagne bottle. 'I was thinking of picking a colour that works with pink – purple, or maybe blue – something the guys can wear as a tie, or a waistcoat, and that you can have as a dress – and then the flowers and accessories can be a mix of that and pink. You can help me work out the perfect colour scheme.' She handed over three twenty-pound notes as the bartender placed an ice bucket containing the bottle on the bar, thanking him and giving him a winning smile as he set two glasses down in front of her.

'Oh, and we're going to buy a flat,' Rachel continued, pulling a copy of the local paper from her bag. 'We've not seen any yet, but we've been looking online this morning, and there are a couple that look really nice.' She flicked through to the back half of the paper and opened it at a full-page advert for a local estate agent called Weber and Wilson. Beneath the smiling faces of three purported *agents* – probably, in reality, models who'd never even set foot in Kilburn – were six panels depicting different properties, and Rachel pointed to the lower right one, for a purpose-built two-bedroom flat on the edge of St John's Wood. 'What do you think?'

Jodie stared at the paper, her already pale face turning white.

'What's up?' Rachel asked in surprise. 'You look like you've seen a ghost.'

Her friend shook her head, pursing her lips.

Rachel frowned, Jodie's expression starting to worry her.

'Jodes, what is it?'

Jodie raised a hand to cover her face, bowing her head as she began to cry. Rachel slipped an arm around her shoulders. 'Hey, sweetie, what is it?' She asked, wondering whether she should have gathered something was wrong before now, and whether she'd subconsciously dismissed the possibility because she had been so caught up in her own news. Admittedly Jodie had seemed out of sorts the last couple of times they'd been out, but she'd explained that away on one occasion with reference to a bad day at work, and on another as PMT. And it had been some weeks since they had seen one another one-on-one, which Rachel knew was largely her fault; Josh was inclined to monopolise her free time and she rarely put up much resistance. 'I'm sorry, I didn't mean to make today all about me,' she said. 'It's just – you're my best friend, and I couldn't wait to tell you. I'm sorry.'

Jodie shook her head again. 'No,' she wept. '*I'm* sorry. I'm sorry I'm spoiling it for you!'

'You don't have to be sorry,' Rachel gave her friend's shoulder a comforting squeeze. 'What is it, Jodes? Please tell me.'

'I can't.' Jodie whispered.

'Yes you can.'

'I *can't*.'

Aware that they were, by now, the subject of sideways glances from more than one direction, Rachel guessed she probably wouldn't feel comfortable opening up in the current company, either. With this in mind, she made a unilateral decision.

'Come on, let's head back to my flat. Josh is at the football all afternoon, so we'll have the place to ourselves. We'll have some drinks and I'll make cheese toasties, and you can tell me what's going on.'

'But – you –' Jodie faltered, her tear-filled eyes flickering over the bottle of champagne and two glasses sitting on the bar in front of them.

'Oh, don't worry about it,' Rachel reassured her, gesturing dismissively at the bottle. 'It's only fizzy wine. You're a whole lot more important.' She slid down off the bar stool. 'Besides, Josh reckons most people can't tell champagne apart from Blue Nun that's been through a Soda Stream.' She smiled. 'And he's probably right.'

Waiting in the autumnal evening gloom outside a house he and Rebecca had tried with no luck earlier in the day, Lawrence glanced at his watch. It was coming up to five, and much of the afternoon had been wasted knocking on doors only to have people shrug or shake their heads in response to the bulk of his questions. Admittedly it wasn't unusual to come away from door-to-door enquiries empty handed, but that didn't make it any less frustrating. The illumination of the glass panel above the door was a prelude to it opening – although only by a couple of inches – and a face that was little more than a dark shape thanks to the light behind it appeared just above the chain.

'Yes?' Asked a woman's voice.

Lawrence displayed his warrant card and introduced himself, whereupon the door closed again before being opened properly.

'Sorry about that,' a stout forty-something woman with choppy layers cut into her red hair apologised, resting a hand on the door frame. 'What is it?'

'Could we take your name please?'

'Oh. Ok. Mikayla Kirkwood.'

'We're investigating an incident that occurred last night at a building down the road, and –'

'I wasn't here last night,' Mikayla interrupted. 'I was at my boyfriend's place in Kingston. I've only been back an hour or so.'

'Were you here at all yesterday?'

'Until about six.'

'Did you see anyone or anything that struck you as unusual?'

The woman appeared to think this over for a moment before shaking her head. Stopping suddenly with a frown, she opened her mouth as if to speak, then shook her head again.

'You don't look very sure about that.'

'It wasn't yesterday,' she shrugged.

'What wasn't yesterday?'

'Just something that seemed a bit odd. My study overlooks the street, so I often find myself watching people coming and going while I'm working.'

'And what was it that seemed odd?'

'I saw a woman – at least, I think it was a woman – getting out of a car in one of those Muslim veils.'

'A burka?'

'Yes, one of them. But I didn't think strict Muslims allowed women to drive. And she got out of the driver's seat.'

'I'm not sure that really applies these days,' Lawrence observed, thinking that the law ought to address the safety of allowing people to drive in a garment that so restricted the wearer's vision.

'I don't know. But I saw her again the next day. Or I think I did. It looked like the same car. That time, I saw her on her way back to the car, and she sat in it for ages before driving away.'

'Did you happen to get a look at the registration number?'

Mikayla shook her head. 'No. I don't even know that it was visible from where I was.'

'What can you tell us about the vehicle?'

'It was black. And small. The kind of size that can have two or four doors. Although I'm not sure which it was.'

Lawrence resisted his natural inclination to sigh: the description fitted multiple popular models of car and, with black one of the most common colours on the road, identifying the vehicle in question was unlikely to be an easy task. The only realistic means of doing so would be via CCTV and, with this in mind, he asked whether Mikayla remembered which days of the week or times of day she'd seen the woman.

Several seconds passed before Mikayla said, uneasily, 'I honestly couldn't say – it certainly wasn't yesterday – I think probably two days out of Monday to Wednesday. It was really just one of those fleeting thoughts one has. You know.'

'And do you have any idea about the time on either day? Even whether it was morning or afternoon?'

This at least prompted a definitive reply. 'Afternoon. On the first day I was eating my lunch. I usually eat at around one.'

'Any idea of her direction of travel?'

There was a pause before Mikayla pointed westwards.

'So she was driving towards Chamberlayne Road?' Lawrence concluded.

'Oh – no – that's where she went after she got out of the car. The car was going that way,' Mikayla pointed in the opposite direction.

Lawrence nodded, wondering how often the police gathered misinformation simply because members of the public answered a question subtly different from that actually posed.

'Anything else you can tell us about the woman or her car?'

'I don't think so. Sorry.'

'No, you've been very helpful, thank you. If you do think of anything else – however insignificant it might seem – please do let us know.' Lawrence handed her his card.

'Sure.'

'Thank you for your time.'

Covering the two paces between the front door and the pavement – Lawrence wasn't sure such a short distance was sufficient to be called a *path* – he felt his mobile vibrate and retrieved it from his pocket to see Leighton's name on the screen. Calculating as he accepted the call that his colleague was unlikely to have already finished the postmortem, he wondered what Leighton might have discovered that would warrant an immediate update.

'I wasn't expecting to hear from you yet,' he admitted, on accepting the call.

'Yeah, unfortunately you're not likely to be hearing from me for quite some time,' came the apologetic reply. 'We've been turfed out the building by a bunch of coppers and it doesn't sound as if we've much chance of getting back in before morning.'

'Why not?'

'I'm not sure, something about a risk of explosion. My money's on an unexploded V1.'

'Surely there are alternative facilities you can use?'

'There would be, but the body is already inside the mortuary, and I'm behind a cordon outside. I have tried to persuade them to let me in for long enough to –'

'No, no, I'm not expecting you to put yourself or anyone else at risk. Frustrating as it is, we'll just have to wait. Are you heading home?'

'Not yet, I'm going to grab a coffee and hang around for a bit longer, make sure my car really is going to be held hostage. I'll let you know if anything changes.'

'Assuming it doesn't, is there any chance of your coming in tomorrow? I'm sorry, I know it's Sunday, but –'

'No problem.'

'Thank you.'

'Ok, catch you later.'

Lawrence bade him goodbye, hanging up and giving Rebecca a brief summary of the situation. She nodded, raising her eyebrows expressively, but making no reply.

'What?'

'Nothing.'

'That sounds a lot like the kind of nothing that means

something.'

Rebecca looked uncomfortable. 'It's just –' she hesitated. 'Sometimes I think we lose track of how many favours Leighton does for us. When he rocks up a bit late, or takes an extended break, or whatever.'

'You mean sometimes *I* lose track,' Lawrence replied, guessing she had used *we* to be diplomatic.

Rebecca shrugged noncommittally.

'Point taken.'

They walked in silence for several seconds before it occurred to him to ask, 'Do you think I lose track of how many hours you put in?'

'Not at all,' Rebecca replied, smiling as she added, 'You're the one who signs off all my overtime.'

Lawrence returned the smile, but, not for the first time in recent days, found himself questioning whether his feedback to those around him – both at work and at home – was disproportionately negative. Perhaps he was inclined to focus too much on finding fault and laying down the law. His own father had taken a predominantly authoritarian approach to parenthood, and at Jimmy's age Lawrence would never have dared cross him over anything more serious than reading after lights out or fibbing about having completed his homework. And he would have been too afraid of the farther-reaching consequences to have even considered breaking the law, although in all honesty he didn't recall ever having any desire to do so.

When it came to his own children, he had never wanted to rule by fear, but he had tried to be firm and consistent about discipline and boundaries. In his presence, those still seemed to be relatively effective – Jimmy was quick to talk back, but rarely stepped too far out of line. Unfortunately, once he was out of sight, any limits were liable to go straight out the window. And much as Lawrence agreed with Max about the need for Jimmy to take responsibility for his actions, he couldn't help feeling that, one way or another, a large part of that responsibility must be his.

Imogen had put off going home for as long as possible, and drew a deep breath as she slid her key into the lock and opened the front door. She had known Lisa was angry from the icy glare she had shot Imogen over Aidan's shoulder as the two passed in the corridor outside Imogen's bedroom that morning. Shortly thereafter, the strength of that emotion had been underlined by the slam of the front door. Imogen had spent the rest of the day telling herself she shouldn't feel so guilty for doing a friend a favour and mentally rehearsing what she might say to Lisa on arrival home.

Admittedly she had agreed that she would have no male guests stay overnight – along with the myriad other conditions Lisa had stipulated – on signing her name to the lease, motivated largely by the low rent and the fact she was running out of time to find a room. Some of Lisa's demands had seemed rather eccentric, but, having lived with a couple of less than desirable housemates in the past herself, Imogen could understand her caution. And, given that Lisa hadn't seemed overly concerned when she breached a couple of the other conditions, Imogen had begun to relax and regard them more as guidelines than hard-and-fast rules. It seemed she might have underestimated the strength of the faith represented by the small pendant that hung around Lisa's neck.

Her flatmate was lying in wait on the sofa immediately opposite the stairs that led into the flat, and Imogen wondered for how long she had been sitting there.

'What did we agree about overnight visitors?' Lisa demanded, the moment Imogen reached the top step.

'I know, but –'

'What did we agree?'

'I think you know what,' Lawrence responded, trying to keep his tone relatively reasonable. 'If you're going to play at being some kind of teenage Banksy, I'd appreciate it if you'd apply a similar degree of imagination and effort, rather than defacing the walls with mindless scribble. I think you can do a lot better than this.'

Jimmy was clearly thrown by this response, having no doubt been anticipating an entirely different one. 'Yeah?' He retorted, sarcastically, recovering himself after a brief pause. 'With what? You gonna buy me some paints?'

'If you'll use them properly.'

Another pause followed. 'What if you don't like it?'

'Providing it's not rude or offensive I'm sure we'll get over it.'

Jimmy regarded him suspiciously for a couple of seconds before asking, 'What's the catch?'

'There isn't one,' Lawrence replied, shortly, turning and heading back down the stairs before his son could draw him into an argument, already wondering whether he had done the right thing. Jimmy was clearly looking for a reaction, and perhaps giving him one he didn't expect might also generate an unexpected response. With luck, providing him with a project into the bargain would serve as a distraction from whatever – or whoever – had been responsible for his more extreme acts of rebellion. When it came down to it, Lawrence concluded, it might be worth taking a leaf out of Alyson Parker's book and picking his battles: a wall few people outside the immediate family ever saw probably wasn't worth fighting for. And given that stern words, punishments and even arrests had failed to make a difference to Jimmy's behaviour, it didn't seem there was much to lose from trying an alternative tack.

'This is so not how I envisaged spending Saturday night,' Daniel grumbled, reaching for another handful of crisps without taking his eyes off the grainy image on the screen in front of him. Playing at 150 per cent of real time, the unwitting cast of the black-and-white CCTV footage moved with the accelerated speed of actors in a silent early-twentieth-century film. He had volunteered to assist Rebecca in trawling through the footage – sourced from thirteen cameras sited within a half-mile radius of Patrick Copeland's flat – largely because it would afford him an evening alone with her, and had hoped that after a couple of hours he could persuade her to take a break and go for a drink. Rebecca, however, was set on completing the task, and even a couple of jokes that she was in danger of becoming as straight-laced as Lawrence hadn't succeeded in denting her focus. It was now gone nine o'clock, and Daniel suspected that unless the CCTV threw up something relevant soon they wouldn't be doing anything else that night but heading home – in different directions – to bed.

'No?' Rebecca replied, from the next desk, her eyes similarly fixed on a monochrome movie. 'Did you think the bar staff at The Feathers could be prevailed upon to play these tapes on their wide-screen telly while we drank Jägerbombs and picked out a soundtrack from the jukebox?'

'No, but that's actually not a bad idea. What would be your first track?'

There was a pause before Rebecca asked, 'Does it need to be something you'd be likely to find on a pub jukebox?'

'Yes,' Daniel decided. 'If only so you can't pick songs by obscure rock bands nobody else has heard of.'

'You big wuss,' Rebecca returned, jovially. 'Ok, given that I'm outside Kensal Rise station, I think I'm going to ignore the fact the song's not about transport and start with *Nightrain*. You?'

'*Every Breath You Take*.'

'Please tell me you didn't pick that because it's by The Police?'

'I thought it was Sting?'

Rebecca flicked her eyes momentarily his way before raising them heavenwards and returning them to the screen, shaking her head. 'Give me strength,' she sighed.

'I remember reading somewhere that people think it's a love song and get it played at weddings, but really it's supposed to be voyeuristic,' Daniel defended his choice. 'And this task is more than a bit Big Brotherish.'

'Fair point,' Rebecca said, with a nod. 'Right. Next up for my movie is *I'm Waiting for my Man.*'

'Who's that by, then?'

'The Velvet Underground.'

'Going back a bit, aren't we?' Daniel objected. 'Could we not go –' he stopped. 'Hold on, hold on … I think this is our guy coming down the road. With a ladyfriend.' He hit pause.

Rebecca pushed off from her desk so that her chair wheeled itself in Daniel's direction. Shunting it the final couple of feet with her heels, she leaned in to get a better look at his screen, instructing, 'Ok, play.'

Daniel did as bid, and as the couple in question walked across the screen she nodded. 'Yeah, that looks like him. Play it again?'

Daniel ran the tape back thirty seconds, then restarted it. Rebecca watched intently as Patrick and his companion repeated their journey from left to right.

'Result!'

Daniel held up a hand for a high five.

'Pub?' He asked, as Rebecca's palm made contact with his.

'Let's not jump the gun,' she replied, lifting her notebook from her lap and taking a pen from Daniel's desk. 'We need to see what we can get from the other cameras first. But I think we can provisionally change that Velvet Underground track to *Femme Fatale.*'

'Teacher's pet,' Daniel teased as she noted down the time and location of the footage.

Rebecca elbowed him playfully in the ribs before starting to walk her chair back towards her own desk. 'You'll thank me for it when we don't get a bollocking in the morning.'

'I won't be here in the morning, I'm not working tomorrow,' Daniel reminded her, smugly.

'All the more reason to help me out, then,' she replied, with a mischievous grin. 'Seeing as you won't have a chance to protest if I drop you in it.'

'Sadist.'

'There's a Velvet Underground song on that theme, as well.'

'Did they write anything about beer? A nice cold one would go down a treat.'

'Well then go and get one, there's a shop just down the road.'

Daniel regarded her suspiciously, not sure whether she was serious, and after a moment, apparently sensing his gaze, she turned her head to meet his eyes.

'What?' She asked, playfully. 'We're not on duty.' She reached for her handbag and delved into it, pulled out her purse and flipped it open. Drawing a ten pound note from the back pocket, she held it out. 'My round. If they've any Kopparberg pear in the fridge, I'll have that, if not, something like Corona'll do.'

Daniel hesitated.

'*Now* who's the teacher's pet?' Rebecca smiled, clearly guessing what was on his mind. Pushing herself out of her chair, she walked the few paces to where he was sitting and tucked the note into his breast pocket. 'Like you said, it's Saturday night,' she observed, moving to reclaim her seat. 'And I won't tell if you don't.'

'Sure.'

'Eva, did you have any luck with the traffic cameras?'

'Maybe,' Eva replied, cautiously. 'Pinning down whoever your witness saw in Kilburn Lane has proved really difficult because there's no sign of anyone turning off Chamberlayne Road wearing a burka. Presumably she put that on after parking up.'

'Given the questionable safety of driving with such impaired vision, I'm relieved to hear it,' Lawrence admitted.

'But from the information we have, I think the car we're looking for belongs to a twenty-five-year-old woman named Lisa Allen,' Eva handed Lawrence what Rebecca assumed to be a copy of the relevant DVLA record.

'Any idea where her car was on Friday night?' Lawrence asked.

'No – sorry –' she trailed off, colour rising in her cheeks.

'You need to check the ANPR records.'

'ANPR,' Eva repeated, with a nod. 'Ok.'

'Automatic Number Plate Recognition,' Lawrence prompted. 'In the meantime, we'll head over to Lewisham to see if we can catch up with Lisa in person.' He reached for his car keys. 'Not least to see whether she can give us a credible explanation for what she was doing wandering around West London in a Burka.'

Lisa's Lewisham home occupied the upper floor of a small end-of-terrace house. Rather unusually, despite the presence of another flat downstairs, her apartment had sole use of the original front door, with a path leading around the side of the building presumably providing access to the lower part of the property. Behind the main door, a steep, tightly wound staircase led immediately up to the first floor, and Rebecca guessed manoeuvering any sizeable item of furniture into or out of the building would prove quite a challenge.

At the top of the stairs, she and Lawrence walked straight into what an estate agent would probably describe as an open-plan living area, given that it contained a kitchen, a sofa and a television, but was really just one room into which several functions had been crammed. It reminded Rebecca of a bedsit one of her friends had occupied a few years earlier, and she wondered what the other rooms – presumably reached through the door on the far side of the room – were like.

Lisa herself was a couple of inches taller than Rebecca's five-foot-six, and probably, Rebecca guessed, the same dress size. Her hair was styled in a short bob, with a long fringe that swept down over her right eye, her pale eyebrows indicating that she was a natural blonde. A Saint Christopher hung in the V of her cream knitted jumper, and her fingers sought it out as Lawrence introduced himself and Rebecca. Having invited them to sit down, Lisa perched on a footstool in front of the wide sash window, drawing her knees up towards her chest.

'I used to want to be a police officer,' she confessed, smoothing an invisible crease in her black trousers. Rebecca wanted to ask what had stopped her.

'We'd like to talk to you about your movements last week,' Lawrence began, instead.

Lisa frowned in consternation. 'Why, what happened last week?'

'We understand you had reason to visit Kensal Lane last Monday and Wednesday,' Lawrence continued. 'Would you mind telling us what you were doing there?'

Given the disguise reported by Mikayla Kirkwood, Rebecca had half expected Lisa to claim ignorance of the visit, and was surprised when she responded, simply, 'I was working.'

'Doing what?'

'I'm a private investigator.'

'Licensed?'

'Yes, of course, that's mandatory now.'

Lawrence nodded. 'Who do you work for?'

'I'm self-employed.'

'And what do you investigate?'

'Infidelity, as a rule.'

'And?'

Lisa looked puzzled. 'And what?'

'*As a rule* implies you cover other bases.'

'Oh. Yes. Sorry. Occasionally people ask me to try to track people down or keep an eye on employees.'

'Do you have a business card, or a website?'

'Both,' Lisa nodded, leaning to reach into the handbag that hung on the balustrade at the top of the staircase and drawing out a purse. Opening it, she pulled a pristine card from a side pocket and handed it to him. Lawrence scanned it briefly before passing it on to Rebecca. The name Calico – presumably that of the business – appeared in bold type above a quotation in italics, with a mobile phone number and web address printed in minuscule text beneath that.

'Who were you investigating in Kensal Lane?'

'A client's husband.'

'And the client's name?'

'That's confidential.'

Rebecca shot a sideways glance at her superior, wondering how he would respond to this rebuff. She suspected Lisa was sufficiently au fait with the law to know she was under no obligation to answer police questions on the subject, in which case direct pressure was unlikely to yield results.

'I do understand we're putting you in a very difficult position,' Lawrence replied. 'But it's possible you may be able to help us get to the bottom of a serious crime, so I do urge you to consider sharing at least a minimal amount of information with us.'

'I guarantee my clients confidentiality,' Lisa returned, earnestly. 'If they start having the police turn up on the doorstep, what do you suppose that's going to do for my business?'

'We will do our best to keep your name out of it.'

'That's not a risk I can afford to take. I'm sorry.'

Lawrence sat forwards, resting his forearms across his thighs. 'Miss Allen, I'm not sure you quite get the picture. If we find you've been withholding information relevant to a serious crime, there will be far-reaching consequences for you *and* your business.'

'No, I get the picture,' Lisa came back, evenly. 'And if I had information about a serious crime I wouldn't hesitate to share it. But I won't be bullied into betraying a client's trust without at least reasonable suspicion they've done something unlawful. And, right now, I don't have that.'

Apparently deciding to abandon that line of enquiry for the time being, Lawrence broached a different subject. 'Do you often wear a burka in the course of your work?'

'That depends on the job. It can be an effective means of remaining anonymous and blending into the background, but obviously it doesn't work in every setting.'

Bars and clubs for starters, Rebecca supposed – and presumably restaurants, as well. You wouldn't very well be able to eat out with the most part of your face covered.

'And can you tell us where you were between ten o'clock on Friday evening and two a.m. on Saturday?'

'Um – I was working on Friday evening – over in Balham. I don't remember what time I got home, although I know it was quite late.'

'Can you remember whereabouts in Balham you were?'

Lisa looked thoughtful. 'Yes, it was –' she frowned. 'The road had a woman's name, but I forget what it was. If I had a map I could tell you.'

'Perhaps you could look it up on Google Maps?' Lawrence replied, his tone indicating this wasn't merely a suggestion.

know, you'd have made a good goth.'

'And what makes a good goth, exactly?'

'I don't know,' Angela shrugged, after a momentary pause. 'But you look great in black. And it's not as if you've had the most conventional relationship history, is it?'

'There's a lot more to being a goth than a black wardrobe and enigmatic men,' Rebecca replied, deciding to leave the point there rather than try to explain the nuances of the alternative music spectrum to someone whose musical interests had never extended beyond what Elliot described as *pappy pop*. Taking a plump wallet of photographs from her handbag, she returned to the previous topic.

'I've a picture of me in that bridesmaid's dress in here somewhere. I don't think I took it off for about six months.'

'I remember. You insisted on wearing it on that campsite in Wales, despite the fact it rained for three days. Mum made you wear wellies underneath.'

Rebecca nodded. Somehow Angela always seemed to make her out to be the wayward younger sister: nobody would have guessed from the note of disapproval in her tone that Rebecca had been born twenty-three minutes ahead of her.

'This is one of my favourites,' Rebecca said, holding out a picture of the two of them, aged eight or nine, wearing identical fluffy violet jumpers and sitting side-by-side on the branch of a pine tree. 'I think it was Holkham Beach?'

Angela reached to take the photograph before wincing melodramatically. 'Why do parents insist on dressing twins in matching clothes?'

'As I recall, we both *saw it first*, and buying us one each was the only way Mum could keep the peace,' Rebecca reminded her.

Her sister grunted noncommittally, reaching for the next picture. 'Oh!' She exclaimed, her face brightening. 'Sammy with Nathan's snowman!'

Rebecca smiled fondly at the memory of their grandmother's gentle but greedy Border Collie devouring the snowman's carrot nose a day or two before Christmas some fifteen years earlier. Five-year-old Nathan's insistence that the root vegetable be replaced had only encouraged the animal, and before long the bag of carrots intended for Christmas dinner had been empty. Grandma had drawn the line at the idea of breaking into the parsnips, and Granddad had been tasked with finding an inedible alternative. His selection of a tapered pink candle hadn't been universally well-received.

'Not skipping school, are we?' A familiar voice interrupted Rebecca's reminiscing. She looked up to see Leighton standing at the end of the table, his long hair hanging in damp strings around his face, clearly freshly washed. He was clad in faded blue jeans and a dark grey hoodie printed with the words *Lead us not into temptation – just tell us roughly where it is*, and she guessed he had just showered after a morning in the mortuary.

'You're the one who looks as though he's not long been up,' she teased. 'Are you here for breakfast?'

'Breakfast – elevenses – lunch –' he checked his watch. 'And I s'pose it's nearly time for an afternoon snack, too.' He glanced at Angela, raising a hand in greeting. 'Hello. I'm guessing you're Angela?'

'Sorry,' Rebecca said. 'Yes. And Saffron, my niece,' she indicated, before looking to her sister. 'This is Leighton.'

Angela nodded as Saffron took the opportunity to show off her sparkly nails for a second time.

'Wow, look at those,' Leighton remarked. 'I'm very jealous, my mum won't let me wear things like that.'

'Boys can't wear glitter!' Saffron exclaimed.

'Can they not?'

She shook her head vehemently.

'That's my dreams shattered, then,' Leighton joked, with a

a private investigator?'

Turning the card back around, Leighton looked at it afresh. 'Does the company specialise in infidelity, by any chance?'

This appeared to take Lawrence by surprise, and Leighton guessed he hadn't expected the exchange to go any further. He suppressed a smile as he watched his colleague's expression change, suspecting he had embarked on a frantic mental run-through of what he knew of the three elements and their chemistry, trying to work out how Leighton had arrived at that conclusion. He waited with growing amusement for Lawrence to concede defeat and ask the inevitable question.

'How'd you guess?'

'It wasn't a chemical equation,' Leighton admitted, with a smile. 'Honey produced from the flowers of the calico bush is toxic. Two plus two equals honey trap.'

'Curious.'

Leighton glanced at the quote beneath the company name. 'The treacherous are imprisoned by their own desires,' he read, aloud. The words took him back more than twenty years.

'What's that?'

'Proverbs. Chapter eleven.'

Lawrence's eyebrows climbed. 'I thought you didn't do religion?'

'My grandmother wasn't so enlightened in the ways of bacon. But fortunately the Catholic church doesn't forbid the consumption of pork products, so I was spared a childhood of deprivation.'

'But not Bible readings.'

'Gran wasn't good at keeping track of her reading glasses,' Leighton shrugged. Or at least, that had been the pretext. Looking back, he suspected her frequent requests for him to read passages aloud had, in fact, formed a part of her effort to counteract the influence of a degenerate father and reckless elder brother. He had never had the heart to tell her that by the time he had been old enough to get up to any serious mischief he had no more believed in God than in Father Christmas or the tooth fairy, nor that foremost among the list of sins he had committed with any regularity as a teenager was lying to her about attending confession.

Her rectitude may have done little to curb his behaviour – that change had been borne largely of the sickening realisation that, had he been in the passenger seat on the night of his brother's first arrest, Tom would have faced the additional charge of causing death by dangerous driving. But without his grandmother's encouragement and her quiet confidence in him, Leighton doubted he would even have attained the requisite qualifications for medical school, much less have dared believe his application stood any chance of success. She had been his main source of stability and support throughout his formative years, and it hadn't seemed much of an imposition, in return, to respect her devotion to the faith from which she drew her strength. He only wished she could have lived long enough for him to properly repay her generosity.

'Number eleven was one of her favourites,' he continued, before his mind could gravitate further towards the memory of his grandmother's excruciating deterioration and death from bone cancer a decade earlier. 'Thirty-one verses all with the same basic message: evil begets evil. If you cut out all the repetition you could probably fit most religious texts in a match box.'

'I'll suggest it next time I speak to the Pope,' Lawrence replied, drily.

'He might need to take the matches out first.'

This drew a reluctant smile from his colleague. 'I'll bear it in mind.'

'Sorry,' Leighton shook his head, turning for the door. 'You were in the middle of something.' He returned the card to

Rebecca's desk and reached for her chair, sitting down and tipping the desk toy out into his palm. Just as he was about to begin sculpting the mass of tiny spheres into a pyramid, he spotted a flaw in the otherwise perfect cube. One of the balls was missing.

Eleven

On her return to work, Rebecca found Lawrence and Leighton adding crime scene photographs to the timeline of pictures and evidence plastered across one wall of Lawrence's office.

'Sorry, am I late?'

'Nah, I was early,' Leighton replied, leaving what he was doing and heading for one of the chairs scattered about the room. He had, she noticed, exchanged the hoodie he'd been wearing in the coffee shop for the marginally smarter option of his leather jacket. 'First time for everything and all.'

'Did you find out why you got evacuated last night?'

'Yeah, some muppet started a fire on the building site around the corner from the lab, and thanks to its proximity to a bunch of acetylene cylinders the police cleared the area.'

'Muppet?' Lawrence echoed. 'Would-be arsonist, more like. There wouldn't have been any workers on site on a Saturday evening.'

'Good point,' Leighton replied. 'You should be a detective, or something.' He grinned. 'And on that note, I guess now Becks is here we can get on to the interesting stuff.'

'By all means,' Lawrence moved to sit at his desk.

'Number one, the result on that DNA sample you queried was male. But bear in mind it may be an artefact. On the subject of Patrick, there's a small amount of bruising around his wrists, so it's likely he was restrained in some way.'

'Were there any marks on Steve's wrists?'

Leighton conveyed his uncertainty with a facial expression before saying, 'Hard to say. I didn't pick anything up on the right wrist, but his wristwatch was on quite tight, so by the time he was found there was a degree of discolouration to the left one. It's possible the watch was fastened too tight deliberately, to disguise trauma.'

'Was Patrick wearing a watch?'

'Yes, but the type of strap means it wouldn't have been easily adjustable.'

Lawrence nodded.

'Aside from that, I found several hairs down the back of Patrick's headboard. I've sent samples for DNA testing, but I'm expecting the results to show that one of them isn't human.'

'Any idea what it is?'

'Goat.'

'Goat?' Lawrence exclaimed. 'Well that's a first for me. Is there any way of knowing whether it's been transferred directly from an animal, or whether it's from a rug, or a coat or something?'

'Goat hair is often mixed in with human hair in things like hair extensions and wigs. Given that it was caught up with two other hairs that do look to be human, I'm guessing that's where it came from.'

'That is interesting,' Lawrence observed. 'What colour was the hair? Blonde?'

'Yep.'

'As per our CCTV. So perhaps, if the DNA results are right, we're looking at a man who's cross dressing – either out of preference or as a disguise.'

'Jez,' Rebecca put in. 'When I saw my niece at lunch time, she was wearing stick-on nails, and where one had come off there was this grubby sticky patch. Jez had a couple of patches like that on his nails when we first interviewed him. That might explain what Steve was alluding to in that text message.'

'Could be,' Lawrence nodded. 'It's a shame we don't know which station he was referring to, or we could check CCTV. What did the message say again?'

Rebecca reached for her phone and pulled up the screen shot. 'Did you have a nice night at the station, sweetie?'

'Who spends the night at a train station?' Leighton asked.

It was a valid point, and both Rebecca and Lawrence paused for thought.

'Well it can't be a police station, I checked and he's not in the system,' Rebecca replied.

'Could it be a venue of some sort?' Lawrence suggested.

'Maybe,' Rebecca nodded, calling up her mobile's search engine and entering a few pertinent words before concluding, moments later, 'This might be it. Central Station. It's a pub in Kings Cross that does drag shows.'

Lawrence's desktop telephone began to ring and, muttering in irritation, he reached to answer it. Rebecca looked to Leighton.

'I'm really sorry about Angela,' she said, quietly.

'Oh, don't worry about it,' he replied, appearing surprised by her concern.

'I don't know why she's such a cow.'

'It's fine, hun. If people's opinions bothered me I'd get a haircut and a new wardrobe.'

'It's not fine. It bothers *me*. I miss her. We used to be so close.'

'Have you tried telling her that?'

Rebecca nodded. 'She just brushes it off. She says it's me, but she's the one who's changed.'

'Maybe you both have.'

'She used to be on my side,' Rebecca replied, with a sigh. After a moment, she said, 'Do you miss Tom? You guys used to be close, right?'

Leighton wrinkled his nose. 'Well, we were on the same side, that's not necessarily the same thing.' He grinned and added, 'And, of course, these days he'd say I've defected.'

'Defected?' Lawrence echoed, as he replaced the telephone

receiver. 'Defected where? Not the private sector, I hope?'

'Switzerland,' Leighton replied, cryptically.

'What?' Lawrence frowned. Rebecca smiled and shook her head to indicate that it wasn't a serious conversation.

'Meanwhile, back in the UK,' she joked.

'Sorry, where were we?'

'Hair,' Rebecca reminded him. 'Jez. Cross-dressing.' She paused, another thought occurring to her. 'There's also that artist. She works with hair.'

'So she does,' Lawrence nodded.

'Which artist?' Leighton asked.

'Celestia Woolf.'

'Oh, the scarecrow woman who thinks she's a spider.'

'That's right,' Lawrence said. 'What do you know about her?'

'Only what I've read in Metro. Is Woolf her real name?'

'I've no idea. Why?'

'Female wolf spiders often eat their mates,' Leighton revealed, widening his eyes rather gleefully. 'Perhaps she's been stringing hers up for consumption later?'

'That is an alarming but not altogether unbelievable possibility,' Lawrence replied. 'Although if she is involved she presumably isn't working alone, given the DNA results.'

'I don't know,' Rebecca responded. 'She's hardly what I'd call feminine. I wouldn't be hugely surprised if she turned out to be a he. Perhaps we should find out where she was after the Tate closed on Friday night?'

Lawrence nodded. 'And see whether she'd like to donate some of her hair,' he suggested. 'Something tells me she's not going to be as keen to share as her fans.'

The peeling front door of Jez's home address was sandwiched between two shop fronts on a busy main road in Tooting, and led directly onto a dingy staircase. At the top, three doors, labelled A, B and C, huddled around a cramped first-floor landing, lit by a lone bulb that Lawrence guessed couldn't be emitting more than 60 watts. Unlocking the door to flat C, Jez continued up another flight of stairs to a marginally larger landing, where he opened a door onto an untidy bedroom. Hurriedly straightening the navy bedclothes, he held out a hand to invite Lawrence and Rebecca to sit down before perching on a battered wooden ottoman beneath the window that looked as if it was probably older than he was.

Sitting on the bed, Lawrence took in the rest of the room's contents. A wall-mounted clothes rail just beyond the foot of the bed provided hanging space for a selection of shirts, a couple of pairs of trousers and a suit jacket, and was flanked by posters for the films *Avatar* and *The Hobbit*. The floor space at the end of the bed was occupied by a series of plastic crates, stacked three deep and topped with books, a tangle of charger leads and a biscuit tin. Aside from the bed and the ottoman, the only other item of furniture in the room was a chest of drawers, which supported a large glass tank that appeared to be empty but for a few inches of soil, a hunk of tree bark and couple of small plants. Noticing Lawrence inspecting it, Jez said, 'Rosie's hiding out at the moment.'

'And what is Rosie?'

'A Chilean rose-haired tarantula.'

Rebecca, who had yet to sit down, made a rather strangled sound that Lawrence could only assume to be an exclamation of alarm, immediately retreating to the doorway and prompting an amused smile from Jez.

'It's ok, she's harmless.'

Rebecca clearly wasn't reassured, and Lawrence struggled not to laugh at her barely contained expression of horror. Looking back to Jez, he tried to focus on their reason for being there.

'Could you tell us what you did after leaving work last Friday?'

'I went to the pub.'

'Which pub?'

'The Sun, it's about five minutes walk from the office.'

'Who were you with?'

Jez's cheeks coloured slightly. 'Priya.'

'And what time were you there until?'

'Um – about nine.'

'What did you do after that?'

'I walked Priya to the station, then came home.'

'Which station?'

'Clapham Common.'

'Can anyone account for where you were after you left there?'

Jez seemed to consider this for a moment before shaking his head. 'I don't think so. My landlady's away this weekend. What happened on Friday?'

'We'll come on to that later,' Lawrence replied. 'First we'd like to talk about your predilection for cross dressing. Or, more specifically, how you reacted when you learned from his text message that Steve knew about it.'

Jez sighed, dropping his eyes to the floor. Several seconds passed before he said, 'It's not a big deal. I do stand-up comedy, and one of my routines is a drag act called Sweet Rosie.'

'If it's not a big deal, why didn't you tell us last time we asked?'

Jez shrugged.

'And you described Steve as a *good mate*, but you didn't tell him either, did you?'

'I didn't want him spreading it around the office because of the connotations.'

'So you're embarrassed by the connotations,' Lawrence concluded.

'No!' Jez objected. 'I just didn't want Priya to get the wrong idea!'

'And what would that be?'

'If you do a drag act, the assumption is that you must be gay. If Steve had told everyone, Priya would probably have assumed as much, and if I'd made a move after that she'd have thought it was to try to quash that rumour rather than because I genuinely like her.'

'Did Steve mention it to anyone?'

'I don't think so. I played dumb and gave him a hard time about being at that kind of venue in the first place – I guess I embarrassed him sufficiently for him to keep his mouth shut.'

'Would you mind telling us what your costume for Sweet Rosie comprises?'

'It'd be quicker to just show you a picture.'

'By all means, if you have one.'

Jez reached for his mobile phone, and after a few seconds of tapping and scrolling held it up to display the screen. Lawrence's first thought was to wonder how Steve had succeeded in identifying Jez from his alter ego, because he wasn't sure he would have managed to pick the photo out of a line-up even in the knowledge that Jez was among those pictured. The second thing to cross his mind was how easily Jez might be able to pass himself off as a woman if dressed accordingly. In the photograph, his make-up, stance and expression were all deliberately exaggerated, but the silver sequin sheath dress he wore skimmed his lean frame surprisingly well, and his slender calves appeared to fit quite comfortably into knee-high black stiletto boots. The look was completed by chunky diamante earings, a pink feather boa and an untidy blonde wig.

'Would you mind sending me a copy of this picture?' Lawrence asked.

'If you want,' Jez replied, sounding rather nonplussed. 'If you give me your email address I can do it now.' He fiddled with the phone for a moment before handing it to Lawrence, the cursor flickering in the 'to' field of a Gmail template. Lawrence filled it in before hitting 'send' and returning the phone to its owner.

'Do you keep your costume here?'

Jez nodded.

'Can we see the wig?'

'Sadly, no,' Jez replied, ruefully. 'I lost it the last time I had it out. I'm not sure whether I left it at the venue or dropped it on the way home, it was rather a drunken night. It's a shame, it was a nice one.'

Whether or not that were true, Lawrence guessed the wig *would* be irretrievably lost long before he could get his hands on a search warrant.

'Where did you get it?'

'A charity shop down the road. Why?'

'Never mind,' Lawrence dismissed the question. 'And just one more thing, does the name Patrick Copeland mean anything to you?'

Jez didn't appear to react to the name, looking thoughtful for a moment before shaking his head. 'Sorry, no. Should it?'

'Not necessarily.'

He looked relieved. 'I come across so many names in the course of my job that I start to lose track,' he admitted. 'Sometimes I even forget the names of people I've interviewed just a week or two earlier.' He rubbed his chin before adding, sheepishly, 'Which can be really embarrassing when they turn up at the office unannounced and know exactly who I am.'

Having timed their second visit to the Tate Modern to coincide with closing time, Lawrence and Rebecca were two of the few people not making for the exits as they walked towards Celestia Woolf's growing exhibition. The macrame web she had been weaving on Wednesday had since been attached, at varying levels, to several of the Turbine Hall's huge steel supports, so that it extended across the width of the gallery. What she had been doing since its completion wasn't clear, because as they arrived she was in the process of packing whatever it was away. Seemingly sensing their approach, she glanced up, looking considerably more tired than on their previous visit, which, combined with her all-black ensemble and total absence of make-up, conspired to give her a rather haggard appearance. She looked to be wearing exactly the same outfit as before, and Rebecca found herself wondering whether the woman's wardrobe contained any colour whatsoever.

'I suppose you're after more than a private view?' Celestia remarked, tossing several props into a large wooden trunk before giving Rebecca and Lawrence her undivided attention.

'I'm afraid so,' Rebecca replied, apologetically. 'Could you give us a brief account of where you were on Friday evening, please?'

'I was here. The gallery doesn't close until ten on Fridays and Saturdays.'

'And after ten?'

'I got a cab home and went to bed. I was due back here yesterday morning for another twelve-hour day.'

'It sounds like quite a gruelling schedule,' Rebecca replied, with as much sincerity as she could muster, given that she frequently worked at least as many hours for considerably more than two days in a row. 'Hopefully we won't need to take up too much of your time. Do you know a man named Patrick Copeland?'

Celestia drummed her fingernails on the lid of the trunk, her long, slender fingers leading Rebecca to think of Jez's unusual pet. There was something slightly spooky about them – perhaps owing to their similarity to the elongated digits of many a supernatural cartoon character – but, Rebecca conceded, nothing masculine. Shaking her head, Celestia concluded, 'Doesn't ring any bells.'

'How about Chet Higgins?'

'Chet?' She exclaimed. 'Why on earth –' she stopped herself, finishing, after a pause, 'I knew Chet, yes.'

'Am I right in thinking you and he were once involved?'

'We took a lot of ecstasy and we had a lot of sex. If that's what you call involved, then yes, I suppose we were.'

'Were you with Chet the night he died?' Rebecca asked, trying not to show any reaction to language she suspected was chosen wholly for effect.

'I wasn't with him at the time,' Celestia replied. 'But I did see him during the evening beforehand.'

'And how did he seem?'

'Horny.'

'Anything else?'

Celestia shook her head.

'He didn't seem anxious or distressed?'

'Not that I recall.'

'Did that not strike you as strange? After the event, I mean?'

'Not really. He was never very demonstrative.'

'What was your first thought when you heard about his death?'

'I didn't *hear* about it,' Celestia returned, shortly. 'I found him.'

'I'm sorry, I didn't realise,' Rebecca replied. 'That must have been very upsetting.'

Celestia shrugged affirmation.

'I'm sorry to ask you to relive it, but did you ever have reason to doubt his death was suicide?'

'No. Although your lot tried to make out it was something more.'

'Can you think of anything that might have given that impression?'

'Oh, I don't know, I guess it wouldn't do for us bohemians and misfits to be too vanilla in our fantasies, it might make us seem almost like human beings.'

Rebecca chose to ignore this emotive – and presumably deliberate – redirection. 'So as far as you can remember there wasn't anything particularly notable about the circumstances you found him in?'

'No.'

'And how about Damon, what was his reaction to Chet's death?'

'Damon?' Celestia echoed, with an inflection of seemingly genuine surprise. 'I don't recall him having much of any sort of reaction. I don't think he and Chet really knew one another.'

'But they were both involved with you.'

'Not in any serious way.'

'Just drugs and sex all round, was it?'

'No, I didn't need to be high to get off when I was with Damon,' Celestia replied, with a coy smile. 'Besides, he didn't really approve. He's quite conventional at heart.'

Rebecca noted this last comment with interest, thinking it didn't really square with Damon's contention that he had had no qualms about sharing Celestia with another man – or perhaps even other men. She nodded, saying, 'I think that's everything. Thank you for your time.'

Celestia returned the nod, turning to continue with what she'd been doing before their arrival. As she did so, Rebecca added, as if as an afterthought, 'Oh – before we go, would you mind providing a DNA sample?'

Celestia's expression as she swung back around answered the question before she did. 'I think my DNA's my own business,' she snapped, rather defensively.

'It's only to enable us to exclude you from any further enquiries. Unless you have something to hide, there's really no reason not t–'

'Don't waste your breath,' Celestia interrupted. 'I'm not about to be tricked into being catalogued forevermore on some state database.'

'That's really not how it works. We're only permitted to retain DNA samples that can be linked to a crime.'

'What you're *permitted* to do maybe, but that guarantees me nothing. The police hardly have an unblemished record where honesty and transparency are concerned!'

'Ms Woolf, under the law –'

'Under the law, I'm obliged to provide nothing unless I'm arrested,' Celestia came back, tartly. 'Do you have any grounds for that?' She didn't pause to allow Rebecca to answer, instead doing it for her. 'No. So: no arrest, no DNA. Capisce?'

Since his release from Wakefield Prison several months earlier, Tom had taken to regularly turning up at Leighton's front door unannounced – more often than not when Leighton was on call or had already made plans – and interpreted any objection to the impromptu nature of his visits as ungracious and dismissive. And much as the two of them had once been, to paraphrase Rebecca's description, *on the same side*, the same could be said of Britain and the Soviet Union for the most part of the Second World War. There was a world of difference between being allied and being close, and these days he and Tom had even less in common than they had done as teenagers. But in the wake of his visit to Sheffield earlier in the week, Leighton had been glad of the unexpected opportunity to share his frustrations with the only other person who could ever really understand the family dynamic.

Tom had come armed with beer; they subsequently moved on to the bottles in Leighton's fridge and ordered pizza. As midnight approached the scotch came out, and Leighton was on the point of asking whether his brother wanted to stay the night when Tom said, 'Can I ask a favour?'

Leighton raised an eyebrow, wondering whether this was Tom's real reason for visiting. 'You can ask.'

'Could you lend me some money?'

'Is that what all this is about?' Leighton replied, indicating the empty beer bottles and pizza boxes on the coffee table with sweep of his hand.

'You know I wouldn't ask if I didn't have to.'

'Like this is the first time I've heard that.'

'Please. I'll pay you back. I promise.'

'I'm a scientist, Tom, I don't believe in miracles.'

'Don't be like that.'

Leighton sighed. 'How much do you need?'

There was a pause before Tom said, 'Twenty grand.'

'Twenty *grand*? Jesus Christ, what do you take me for, the World Bank?'

'I know, I know, but –'

'I do not have that kind of money!'

There was another pause, and Leighton silently dared his brother to bring up the value of his car. Eventually Tom said, 'Can you borrow it?'

'No, I bloody can't! I already have a mortgage and a car loan, the bank isn't going to lend me any more!'

'Well how much do you have?'

'What am I, the family cashpoint?'

'Come on, Lee, you owe me!' Tom returned, sitting forwards in his chair. 'I took shit from Dad on your behalf for years!'

'And vice bloody versa! Who do you suppose he took it out on when you went down?'

'Well at least I didn't take you with me! I never said a word to the filth about you!'

'Oh don't make me laugh! As if they didn't already know full well what we'd been getting up to! They just never caught me! And if you'd not been so bloody stupid, they might not have caught you, either!'

'Don't you *dare* call me stupid!' Tom flared. 'Just because you've got a bunch of degrees and some fucking letters after your name you think you're so fucking superior! You're quite happy

Twelve

Considering how rarely it was necessary to visit an estate agent in the Internet age, the sleek, high-spec décor common to the sector's high street offices seemed to Rebecca an unnecessary luxury. No doubt that was where letting fees – an invention seemingly dreamed up during the decade in which she had been renting in London – had been going. Once upon a time, agents had been content to rip off only the property owners, but apparently they'd since realised they were selling themselves short and could take a cut from both sides.

The Kilburn base of Patrick's former employer, Weber and Wilson, was typical of the type: glass desks and stylish office chairs lounged on a black marble floor that gleamed under fierce spotlights while wide-screen televisions on the walls showcased available properties. Little wonder rental costs in the capital were what they were.

Patrick's colleagues had learned of his death only half an hour before Lawrence and Rebecca's arrival, and were clearly still rather shell-shocked by the news. Initial enquiries quickly established that the best place to start was likely to be with Hari, a suave young man in a slim-fitting black suit and flamboyant purple shirt who had been out with Patrick the previous Friday evening. Taking up residence on a couple of the boxy, contemporary sofas gathered just behind the Perspex-mounted displays in the front windows, they focused immediately on the details of Patrick's last ever night out, starting with where he and Hari had gone after leaving the office that day.

'The King William. It's fifty yards up the road on the other side of the street, you can see it from outside the door.'

'What kind of time was that?' Lawrence asked.

'As soon as we'd finished up here, so ten past – maybe quarter past – seven.'

'Was anyone else with you?'

'Not at that point. My girlfriend and a few of her mates joined us a bit later on.'

'When?'

Hari blew out a breath as he considered this. 'I don't know,' he answered, eventually. 'Eight, half-eight maybe?'

'Did anyone come or go from the group after that?'

'No, but we weren't all together all the time – you know how it is when you're out in a busy pub – groups get fragmented and you lose track of people. When I left, Pat was chatting up some blonde bird.'

'Can you describe her for us?'

'Blonde. Fit-looking. I didn't really look, to be honest.'

'You didn't really look?' Lawrence echoed, disbelievingly.

Hari shrugged. 'My missus is a bit sensitive about me checking out other women. Besides, the girl had her back to me – I just caught Pat's eye from across the room and indicated we were off,' he jerked a thumb over his shoulder as if in demonstration.

'Were you in a rush?'

The man sighed, casting his eyes down. 'Mel – that's my girlfriend – and I had a bit of a row,' he admitted. 'She stormed out, so I went after her.'

'What time was that?'

'Just gone ten, I think. We were home by half past, so it can't have been much after the hour.'

'Do you remember what the blonde woman was wearing?'

He paused for thought. 'There were tables and people in the way, so I only saw her from about the waist up. She had a dark top on – black, I think.'

'And how long was her hair?'

'Long. To about here,' he indicated a point several inches below his shoulders.

'You mentioned that your girlfriend brought some friends along to the pub, were any of them still there when you left?'

Hari raised his eyes ceilingwards as he apparently thought this over. 'I'm not sure,' he concluded, at length. 'I wasn't paying much attention to anyone else towards the end of our time there.'

'We'll need those individuals' names and contact details.'

'I'll have to give Mel a call, I'd only be able to give you first names.'

Lawrence nodded. 'I'd appreciate it if you could do that now.'

'I'll try,' Hari replied, awkwardly. 'I'm not sure how quickly I'll get an answer, though. She doesn't have a desk job, so I tend to have to leave messages.' He shifted position uncomfortably before adding, 'And I'm not her favourite person right now, so it might be a while before she picks them up.'

Being presented with a full-page newspaper advert for Weber and Wilson scarcely twenty minutes after leaving the estate agent's office struck Lawrence as more than a little surreal. He and Rebecca were standing in a back office at Kilburn Police Station with Sergeant Brandon Locke, who had been the first officer to arrive at Patrick's flat on Saturday morning. The advert featured photographs of three members of the estate agent's staff, including Patrick, and it was to his picture that Brandon was pointing.

'We had a young lady walk in a little while ago with this. Said she'd like to talk to someone about this man.'

'And what did she have to say?' Lawrence asked.

'Nothing, yet – we thought you'd want to ask the questions.'

Lawrence gave the other man a look that he hoped conveyed

his considerable scepticism; no doubt in reality Brandon and his colleagues didn't want to risk being landed with any more paperwork than absolutely necessary.

'In that case, I'd like to make a start straight away.'

'She says she'll only speak to a female officer,' Brandon replied, his tone a touch apologetic.

'So if I hadn't by chance had DS Palmer with me I'd have wasted a good hour of my morning,' Lawrence said, irritably. 'Do you have a video link I can observe the interview through, or am I going to be sitting here twiddling my thumbs and waiting for an undrinkable cup of coffee to go cold?'

'I'm sure I can sort something out. Why don't you take a seat, and I'll let you know when we're good to go?'

Lawrence sighed pointedly, nodding by way of agreement. Brandon turned to go, then doubled back on himself. Apparently oblivious to Lawrence's last remark, he asked, 'Can I get you anything? Tea? Coffee?'

Lawrence looked to Rebecca. 'Muddy cup of something masquerading as a caffeinated beverage, Becky?'

Rebecca shook her head, the set of her features indicating she was stifling a smile.

He returned his eyes to Brandon. 'No thank you.'

The man nodded and hurried towards the office doorway. As he disappeared from view, Lawrence drew breath to speak and Rebecca pre-empted with, 'I know what you're going to say.'

He said it anyway. 'Too bad we can't charge him with wasting police time.'

'It can't be any more of a waste of time than the visit to the estate agent. We learned precious little there we'd not already figured out from CCTV.'

'True.'

'Do you think it's a coincidence he's in an advert in the local paper? Given Ricardo had one in the Chronicle, I mean.'

'I don't know,' Lawrence replied, thinking he ought to have made the same connection. 'I don't suppose Patrick was the one who put the ad in, but it wouldn't hurt to cross-check staff lists past and present to see whether there's any overlap between the two publications. I'm sure ours isn't the only profession where you can't swing a cat without running into a familiar face.' He leaned against a filing cabinet. 'And if there isn't a direct link, perhaps there's an indirect one.'

There were two young women sitting on the padded chairs of the small meeting room, the petite blonde clutching her brunette companion's hand tightly enough to turn the latter's unpolished fingernails dark pink. The blonde didn't visibly respond to Rebecca's arrival, keeping her bloodshot eyes fixed on the coffee table, but the brunette looked around almost in curiosity, leading Rebecca to guess she was there merely to provide moral support. And, much as Rebecca understood Lawrence's frustration at being called in without any real explanation, she could also appreciate why Brandon might have suspected the woman huddled in the chair closest to the wall was likely to prove more than a minor witness.

'Hello,' Rebecca began, as she sat across the table from the women, meeting the brunette's eyes and giving her a polite smile. 'I'm Detective Sergeant Palmer. Can I take your names?'

'I'm Rachel,' the brunette offered, in return. 'Rachel Benson.'

Rebecca nodded, transferring her attention to the pinched face of the girl next to her. There was a pause before Rachel looked in the same direction, seemingly prompting her companion to speak.

'Jodie,' she revealed, in little more than a whisper.

'And your surname?'

'Yarwood.'

'I understand you wanted to talk to somebody about this man,'

Rebecca set a photograph of Patrick Copeland on the table between them.

Jodie nodded.

'Could you tell me what you wanted to talk about?'

'It was about six weeks ago,' Jodie began, her voice shaking. There was a long silence before she continued. 'I met Rachel – and some other friends – after work. At the pub. And –' she drew a long, slow breath. 'And I –' she closed her eyes, bowing her head.

'Do you remember the name of the pub?' Rebecca asked, thinking the girl might find it easier to focus on specifics.

'Yes,' Jodie nodded, looking up. 'The King William. We go every Wednesday.'

'Is that in Kilburn?' Rebecca checked, guessing it was the same pub Hari had talked about scarcely an hour earlier.

Another nod.

'What time did you meet?'

'Six-thirty? Seven?' Jodie's eyes flickered towards Rachel as if for confirmation before she shrugged weakly. 'I don't know, exactly. We just meet from work.'

'So what happened on this particular occasion?'

Slowly and falteringly, Jodie gave her account of the evening, wiping her tears away with the fingers of her right hand, still clutching Rachel's with her left. Patrick had been at the next table with some colleagues – she'd seen them in the pub before – and had struck up a conversation. The two of them just seemed to click – they had so much in common and didn't stop talking all night – Jodie had felt quite guilty about abandoning her girlfriends. At the end of the evening, Patrick had taken her number and suggested they go out for dinner at the weekend. Then he'd offered to walk her home.

They'd chatted and kissed for a while at the door, and he'd tried several times to persuade her to let him in. When Jodie persisted in saying no, he'd called her a tease and forced his way in before raping her on the floor of her bedsit, tearing her dress and squeezing her breasts so hard they were left covered in bruises. He'd called her a whore. And she'd been too scared to scream. She should have fought harder, she should have screamed. Maybe it was all her fault, maybe she –

'It wasn't your fault,' Rebecca stopped her, firmly. 'You weren't to blame for any of what happened.'

Jodie hiccupped.

'I realise how difficult this must be for you, and I'm sorry to have to ask you anything more, but what made you decide to report the assault now?'

'I saw his picture,' Jodie replied, weakly. 'In the paper. Rachel said if I didn't report it he'd – he'd do it – again.'

'Are you sure it's the same man?'

'Yes. I know he works at the estate agent. He told me.'

'Do you know where he lives?'

'No.'

Rebecca nodded. 'And have you seen him since the night he assaulted you?'

'No,' Jodie swallowed. 'I've not been out much.'

'Understandably,' Rebecca responded, gently. 'Have you talked about it with anyone? Besides Rachel, that is.'

'Lisa,' Jodie replied, rubbing her eyes. 'I didn't know what to do – I didn't think anyone would believe me – I called one of those helplines for – f –' Jodie broke off. Rebecca suspected she couldn't bring herself to use the word *rape*. 'I was too scared to do anything else. Will I have to –' she gulped. 'Do I have to – show anyone –' she shrugged, biting down on her lower lip.

'We won't need you to undergo an examination,' Rebecca replied, guessing that was what Jodie was trying to ask. Patrick was dead, there was no case to answer. Which brought her on to a new line of questioning. 'But would you mind telling me what you were doing last Friday evening?'

Jodie frowned. 'Friday? Why?'

'Please just answer the question.'

'Um – Friday – I had a meeting – in Newcastle – I didn't get back til late. I got a cab home from Kings Cross.'

'What sort of time?'

'Elevenish, I guess. The train was due in just after nine but it was delayed. What happened on Friday?'

'We're still trying to establish that. Patrick was found dead on Saturday morning,' Rebecca revealed, watching Jodie closely for her reaction.

There was a shocked silence. Jodie stared at her for a moment before starting to shake her head. She tried to speak more than once before she managed to form any identifiable words. 'You mean –' she managed, eventually, her uneven respirations audible. 'This was for *nothing*? You let me sit here – and – and – when you already *knew*?'

'What you've told me may turn out to be very important,' Rebecca replied. 'I do appreciate how hard this must have been for you, and –'

'Really?' Jodie demanded, her eyes filling up as shock gave way to emotion. 'Has it happened to you? Or is that just the line you feed to everyone?'

'I'm sorry if that sounded glib,' Rebecca replied. 'It wasn't intended that way at all. I'm under no illusion about what it must have taken for you to talk me through what happened. And I realise the news of Patrick's death has come as a shock, but it doesn't make your experience irrelevant to us.'

Jodie bowed her head, saying nothing, and drawing an unsteady breath as a tear dripped onto her jumper. Rachel slipped her arm around her friend, resting her head against Jodie's shoulder.

'I'm sorry, Jodes,' she murmured, her expression pained.

Having been the one to persuade Jodie to report the incident, Rebecca suspected Rachel now felt a wholly undeserved burden of guilt over the unexpected outcome. 'I'm sorry,' Rachel repeated, softly. 'But you're safe now. And he's never going to be able to hurt you again.'

'Becky?'

Rebecca raised her eyes from the table of the empty meeting room to see Lawrence standing in the doorway. She had been re-running the recently concluded conversation with Jodie in her head, wondering how she might have done things differently.

'You all right?'

She nodded. 'Yeah. Just feeling I could've handled that better.'

'How so?' He asked, heading for one of the unoccupied chairs and adding, perhaps in response to her look of confusion, 'The sound kept cutting out on the video feed. Although I got the gist of her account.'

'I think she felt she'd gone through telling me the story for nothing, given there's no risk of a dead man reoffending.'

Lawrence sat down, placing his mobile phone on the table. 'That's hardly your fault.'

'No, but I can't help thinking I could have broken the news differently, or made her feel less – I don't know – violated by the whole process.'

'It's never easy conducting that kind of interview. And she'll have the option of accessing victim support if she wants to, so it's not as if she's on her own with it now.'

Rebecca didn't reply, still feeling rather disconsolate.

'You don't doubt her claim is genuine, then.'

Rebecca frowned. 'Do you?'

'I'm not questioning your judgement, Becky, I'm asking for your opinion. I wasn't the one in the room with her.'

‘Sorry,’ she sighed. ‘I do believe her, yes.’

Lawrence nodded. ‘I suspect it may not be a coincidence that both Patrick and Ricardo have been accused of the same crime. Nor that, by all accounts, Steve had precious little respect for women.’

‘Do you think he might have been guilty of something similar?’

‘It’s certainly possible. And revenge is a strong motive.’

‘But they can’t all have attacked the same woman, so how are they meeting the same end? Aside from Ricardo, there’s no public record of any of them being accused of anything, so it’s not as if we’re likely to be dealing with some sort of vigilante. And Jodie’s hardly been running around telling people.’

‘She wasn’t necessarily Patrick’s first victim,’ Lawrence replied. ‘But I agree, we need to establish how a connection might have been made between victims. The Internet, maybe?’

Rebecca nodded. ‘There are forums and chat rooms out there for just about everything. Although I don’t know where we’d even start with looking for something like that.’

‘I’ve no idea either,’ Lawrence admitted. ‘I’ll see whether someone in e-crime can give us a few pointers. We also need to try to track down the woman who accused Ricardo, find out what she might be able to tell us. But while we’re up this way, I’d like to pop into the pub Patrick was at last Friday, see whether anyone working there can tell us more than Hari could.’

‘Ok.’

He held up his mobile. ‘According to the website, it’s another half hour before they open. I think the best way to fill that time is probably to go in search of a double hazelnut latte.’

Rebecca managed a smile at the mention of her favourite hot drink, appreciating her superior’s attempt to cheer her up. Lawrence returned the smile, slipping his phone into his pocket and pushing himself up out of his chair.

‘Come on, then.’

scratchings mandatory in all licensed premises.'

Lawrence smiled. 'Now there's a change to the licensing laws I'd support.'

Rebecca's eyes flickered in the direction of the door Wes had passed through moments earlier. 'Do you think there's time for me to run to the ladies while we wait?'

'Again?' Lawrence exclaimed, before he could stop himself; she'd already made use of the facilities at Kilburn Police Station that morning.

'Mouse bladder,' she shrugged, colour rising in her cheeks. 'Plus coffee.'

'Go on, then.'

'I'll be quick,' she replied, as she turned to go. 'I promise.'

As in so many pubs, the toilets were below stairs, and the air was redolent of endemic damp. Cursing the lack of hooks in toilet cubicles – at one point they'd been almost ubiquitous, now they were something of a rarity – Rebecca sat down with her handbag in her lap. Her eyes were immediately drawn to the graffiti scrawled in thick black pen at knee level and she smiled: the words 'BEWARE LIMBO DANCERS!' were accompanied by an arrow pointing to the four-inch gap at the bottom of the door. At eye level, someone had added the more cryptic declaration 'my inner child likes to play with matches', while further up a small rectangle had been penned beneath the pertinent remark 'coat hook goes here'.

The door also bore a smattering of stickers: one advertising a local drug and alcohol treatment centre, another bearing the telephone number of a helpline for rape victims, and a third warning, ungrammatically, of the dangers of using unlicensed taxis. *Illegal minicab drivers commit eleven sexual assaults a month!* the bold red and black letters screamed, tabloid-style. You didn't need to be a subeditor to spot the glaring error in the wording, which someone had corrected in a scrawl of ballpoint pen and exclamation marks on the door beside it: Eleven sexual assaults a month are commited by illegal minicab drivers. To read the original, one might almost conclude that each driver was obliged to fulfil some sort of obscene monthly quota.

Pulling her mobile from her bag, Rebecca sighed as she saw the number of messages she'd received in the previous couple of hours, guessing none of them would be the one she was waiting, not particularly optimistically, on. Over the weekend, the media had succeeded in getting hold of information about the circumstances of Elliot's hospitalisation, and thanks to a brief article in that morning's Metro it was now general knowledge among Rebecca's friends and co-workers. Several had since sent messages fishing for more information under the guise of asking whether she was all right, but there was still nothing from Alec, who hadn't been taking her calls, nor responding to text messages. If she wanted any real information about how Elliot was, it seemed she would have to force the issue.

Lawrence had been left with little choice but to write off the first of the two CCTV tapes acquired from the King William more or less immediately: thanks to a direct hit by a defecating bird on the tinted plastic dome protecting the camera lens, all that was identifiable in the recorded footage was passers' lower legs. His trawl through the second tape was no more enlightening, and with a sigh he left his desk to see how Rebecca was getting on with security footage from elsewhere. She was lying back in her chair, eyes on the screen, giggling to herself.

'You seem to be having considerably more fun than I,' he remarked. 'I'm not sure I can allow that.'

She glanced up with an impish smile. 'Jez certainly wasn't lying about seeing Priya to the tube,' she replied, turning her laptop so that Lawrence could see the images captured by one of Clapham Common station's security cameras. 'Although he did leave out a few details.'

The field of view covered a landing between two staircases, one ferrying human traffic up to and down from street level, the other – according to a sign just visible on one of the walls – funnelling customers to and from the ticket hall and trains below. Given the number of people merging abruptly into and out of view in the lower right-hand portion of the screen, Lawrence surmised that there was a second staircase to the street opposite the first. It took him several seconds to pick Jez and Priya out of the numerous monochrome figures weaving around and between one another like ants swarming in and out of a colony, and his natural reaction on doing so was to smile. Priya was leaning against the wall that faced the lower portion of the staircase, Jez directly in front of her, and the two were engaged in a passionate kiss.

'Well well,' he responded, lifting his eyebrows. 'That didn't take him long.' Then, as another thought occurred to him: 'I wonder whether he's told her about his alter ego yet?'

'That wouldn't be the Rosie I'd be concerned about if I were her,' Rebecca replied, returning the screen to its original position.

Lawrence smiled again. 'I thought you were made of sterner stuff than that.'

'Homicidal maniacs I can handle, leggy arachnids not so much.'

'You did all right interviewing Celestia yesterday.'

Rebecca sniggered. 'Perhaps I should have trapped her under a glass and threatened to put her out the window. That might have got us a DNA sample.'

'Is that how you deal with spiders at home?'

'Pretty much. Although if anyone else is around I get them to do it for me.'

'Ah, so that's why you've been looking for a flatmate.'

'Absolutely.'

'How's that going?'

'A friend of a friend moved in yesterday. Guy called Perry. Fingers crossed we don't end up killing each other.'

'Is that how it usually ends when you live with people?' Lawrence joked, before realising that against the backdrop of Elliot's drastic response to the end of their relationship it wasn't the most sensitive thing he could have said.

Fortunately Rebecca either didn't make the connection or chose to gloss over it, saying, 'Only if they steal my chocolate.'

'Death by chocoholic.'

'Something like that.'

'So what does Perry do?'

'He's a food stylist,' Rebecca revealed, raising her eyebrows pertinently, no doubt anticipating his incredulous response.

'A *what*?'

'He arranges food for photographs. For restaurants, magazines, catering companies, that kind of thing.'

'They pay people to do that?'

'Apparently so. He trained as a chef, so presumably it's not as easy as it sounds.'

'Ah, a spider-catcher who can cook,' Lawrence remarked. 'It sounds like you've hit the flatmate jackpot.'

'Yeah, that's what I was thinking until he told me some of the tricks they use to make food more photogenic,' Rebecca responded. 'I don't think he's going to be bringing anything tasty home with him. He said a lot of food isn't actually cooked properly before they photograph it, and by the time they're done it contains stuff like glue and lighter fuel.'

'Lighter fuel?' Lawrence exclaimed.

'They chuck it over anything they want to flambé, apparently.'

Rebecca pulled a face to convey her disgust. 'And to stop things like pancakes absorbing syrups and sauces, they spray them with Scotch Guard.'

'Nice.'

'Yes. Although in a way it's quite reassuring,' she observed. 'At least now I know I'm not entirely to blame for the fact my cooking never looks anything like the picture in the book.'

Jon Adeyemi regarded the pop-up message in the lower right-hand corner of the screen informing him that he had a new email from DCI Peter Rose with a sigh. The man seemed to view forensic science as an optional extra in the pursuit of justice, and repeatedly disregarded or disputed any findings that didn't align with his interpretation of events. And, much as Jon wanted to be heard, copying his boss in on all correspondence with Peter – as requested by Max after a particularly heated disagreement the previous week – seemed to Jon akin to the actions of a schoolboy telling tales.

Hearing the main door to the office open, he glanced around, feeling glad of the distraction, to find Lawrence Forrester standing behind him.

'Afternoon,' Lawrence greeted him, releasing his hold on the door and advancing into the room. 'Sorry to interrupt. Do you know where Leighton is? When I called earlier Ana said he was in, but he's not answering his mobile and I've had no response to any of my messages.'

'I'm not sure, I've not really seen him today,' Jon admitted. 'But he is about somewhere. Shall I ask him to call you?'

'If you wouldn't mind. And if you can instill some sense of urgency in him then please do.'

'There are a lot of other people chasing his time as well, you know,' Jon defended his friend.

'All I'm after is a quick phone call, it's not a lot to ask, is it?'

'I'm just saying.'

'We're all busy, Jon, but until the day comes when –' Lawrence broke off as a door the other side of the office opened and Leighton appeared, a carrier bag in one hand and a coffee in the other. 'Ah, the elusive Dr Campbell,' Lawrence continued. 'I've been trying to get hold of you for hours. Is there something wrong with your phone?'

'I've been in a meeting,' Leighton responded, shortly, setting the coffee down on his desk and tucking the bag into the footwell.

'All day?' Lawrence exclaimed.

Leighton apparently didn't feel the need to explain himself further, replying, rather curtly, 'What did you want?'

'I was hoping you might have the DNA results back for Patrick Copeland.'

'Not yet.'

'Have you chased the lab?'

'They're aware it's urgent,' Leighton returned, irritably, as he sat down. 'It may come as a surprise to you, but we're not the only ones wanting DNA results immediately if not sooner.'

'Is there anything through on that hair sample yet?'

'No.'

'And how about the body, have you checked for any delayed bruising?'

'No, I thought I'd do a half-arsed job,' Leighton snapped, with uncharacteristic sarcasm. 'I don't repeatedly question your ability to do your job, it might be nice if the same courtesy was extended in return.'

There was a tense silence, and Jon guessed Lawrence was taken aback by this response. He obviously decided not to comment, however, at length saying instead, 'Ok, well can you let me know as soon as you do hear from the lab?'

'Will do.'

'Right,' Lawrence replied, rather awkwardly, turning to go. Jon looked around in time to see him disappear through the door and, as it swung shut behind him, shifted his attention to Leighton. His friend was frowning at the screen of his mobile, scrolling down furiously with the middle finger of his right hand.

'You all right?'

Leighton sighed, tossing the phone onto his desk. 'Yeah,' he nodded, before turning his head to meet Jon's eyes. He looked tired. 'Sorry.'

'Bad day?'

'I've had better.'

'Want me to draw a face on the polystyrene box my new monitor came in so you can throw sharps at it?'

This succeeded in eliciting a smile from Leighton. 'You know full well that would contravene workplace health and safety,' he said, mimicking Roddy's West Country accent.

'That's more like it.'

'Sorry,' Leighton repeated, shaking his head slightly.

'What's up?'

'I just –' he sighed again. 'Sometimes I really do understand what makes people up and leave without a word.'

Jon raised his eyebrows. 'Well, if you decide to join the ranks of the missing, have the decency to leave your fingerprints and DNA profile on file, save the rest of us some work, eh?'

'Lazy git,' Leighton returned, amiably.

'Oh, and leave your car keys on my desk, will you? It'd be a crime if that went to waste.'

'Thanks, yeah, I'll miss you too.'

'Who is it you're looking to get away from? Forrester?'

'Nah, he's all right, really. Working with him's just a bit like being on a long car journey with a restless kid.'

'How so?'

'Are we there yet?'

Jon laughed. 'At least you're not in the car with Rose.'

'I don't think there is a driving analogy for him,' Leighton responded. 'Working with Rose is more like sharing a tent with a boa constrictor.'

'Yeah. The stuff of nightmares.'

'Painful and suffocating,' Leighton added, leaning back in his chair and rubbing his eyes with the thumb and middle finger of his left hand. 'With a good chance at least one party won't come out alive.'

The drizzle that met Rebecca at the door to the street was deceptively heavy, and after just a few steps she hesitated, debating whether to return to the office for an umbrella or cross her fingers that the rain didn't intensify in the time it took her to travel between St James's Park and Highgate stations. She had just plumped for the latter option and picked up her pace when she came face-to-face with Priya hurrying in the opposite direction. Turning around, she re-entered the building and showed the subeditor up to a small meeting room via the coffee machine. Sitting in one of the easy chairs, she gave Priya a chance to make herself comfortable before asking the reason for her unscheduled evening visit.

'It's rather tricky,' Priya admitted, uneasily. 'If I tell you something, will you have to tell other people – aside from your colleagues – what I say?'

'That rather depends on what it is,' Rebecca replied, feeling intrigued. 'But if you think we ought to know something we don't, then I think you have a duty to tell us, don't you?'

'Yes, I know, but if it turns out to be irrelevant I'm going to be putting myself in a really difficult position for nothing.'

'Well I can try to keep your name out of it,' Rebecca conceded, hoping she wasn't going to regret saying as much. 'But without knowing what it is I can't make any promises.'

Priya nodded, dropping her eyes to the floor.

'So,' Rebecca prompted, after several seconds had passed in silence. 'What is it that's on your mind?'

Priya sighed. 'Ramona and I had the office to ourselves on Friday afternoon, and Steve came up in conversation. I said I thought the sexist jokes and innuendo had bothered her more than me, and she replied that they hadn't concerned her nearly as much as the way he behaved when they were alone.'

'And how did he behave in those circumstances?'

'I'm not sure, she didn't say much more. I got the impression she'd assumed I'd had similar experiences with him, and when she realised I hadn't she clammed up. She did admit she found him intimidating, which I'd never have guessed. Although the other day Jez was telling me about something Steve had said in his presence that sounded pretty out of order, so I guess maybe he was nastier to her than I realised.'

'And what did he say?'

'Apparently Steve likened her to a radical feminist called Valerie Solanas. I don't know whether you've heard of her, she was the woman who shot Andy Warhol. I looked her up online and apparently she was a paranoid schizophrenic.'

Rebecca nodded, she recognised the name, it appeared alongside a feminist quote on the sleeve of one of the albums in Elliot's vinyl collection.

'I asked Jez whether he'd told you, and he didn't seem to think it mattered. I didn't want to go behind his back, and I don't want Ramona thinking I might believe she could actually be capable of killing someone, but it's been bothering me all weekend.'

'But clearly a part of you does believe Ramona might be capable of murder,' Rebecca observed. 'Otherwise you wouldn't be here.'

'I don't know,' Priya admitted.

'And how about Jez?'

'Oh, he just said *she's not crazy*, like it's black and white.'

'I meant do you believe he might be capable of murder?'

Priya looked taken aback. 'Wha– that's not –' she swallowed. 'Why would he? He and Steve were mates.'

'That's not what I asked.'

There was an uncomfortable silence before she conceded, 'I don't know. I don't think so, but I've read a lot of true crime, and sometimes even people's spouses don't seem to be able to believe what their partners have done, so –' she trailed off with a weak shrug.

'You were out with Jez on Friday evening,' Rebecca remarked.

'Yes,' Priya said, clearly unnerved by the comment. Apparently Jez hadn't mentioned his Sunday afternoon visit from the police.

'What time were you with him until?'

'A bit after nine. I was meeting friends in Covent Garden.'

'Did you hear anything from him later in the evening?'

'He sent me a photo of a badly worded roadworks sign he saw from the bus on his way home.'

'Do you still have the message?'

'Yes.'

'Would you mind sending it on to me?'

Priya frowned. 'Why?'

'I'm just looking to confirm what he told us.'

She nodded, but her expression remained wary.

'While we're on the subject of Jez, did he or Steve ever mention Rosie to you?'

'The spider?' Priya asked, clearly increasingly puzzled by the direction the interview was taking.

'No, not the spider,' Rebecca replied, wondering how to explain further without revealing more than necessary. 'Rosie's a comedian.'

Priya looked blank. 'I've never heard of a woman called Rosie.

Has something happened to her?'

Rebecca shook her head, dismissing the subject and turning the conversation back to the original topic of Ramona. Much as Jez's female alter ego ticked a number of the boxes on the list of what they knew of Patrick's Friday-night companion, Rebecca couldn't see how he would have been able to transform himself so completely – and travel across London – inside an hour. And while Steve could have made life uncomfortable for Jez if he'd revealed the details of his friend's stand-up routine to their colleagues, she couldn't see that being sufficient motive for murder in twenty-first century London. Bullying and harassment, on the other hand, were potentially powerful drivers.

Rebecca had still heard nothing from Alec by the time she finally left the office, and decided to stop off at UCLH on her way home in the hope he might be more forthcoming in person. Having built herself up for the encounter, she was left feeling rather deflated when the woman at the hospital information desk told her Elliot was no longer a patient. Guessing where he and Alec were likely to be, she headed up the Hampstead Road towards Camden on foot, turning into Oakley Square just fifteen minutes later.

Her first knock at Alec's basement front door went unanswered, and she continued until the door finally opened. Alec looked even more tired and dishevelled than when Rebecca had seen him last, and, on seeing her, closed his eyes momentarily in exasperation.

'He's not here,' he said, wearily, before Rebecca could launch into her prepared speech explaining that she hadn't come to see Elliot, she just wanted to know how he was.

'Is that the best you can do?'

'Come in and search the place if you want,' Alec snapped.

Rebecca felt tempted to take him up on the offer just to see his reaction.

'Well then where is he?'

Alec leaned against the door frame, saying nothing.

'According to the latest update on the band's Facebook page he's still in hospital, but he isn't, is he? I've just come from there, and they said he'd discharged himself.'

Alec folded his arms pointedly, still making no reply.

'Do you even *know* where he is?' Rebecca asked, beginning to feel concerned. 'Alec, he shouldn't be out there alone!'

'No shit,' came the irritable response. 'I seem to recall having to tell *you* that not so long ago.'

'Look, if he's gone AWOL I can help track him down, but only if you tell me what's going on!'

'If he'd gone AWOL do you seriously think I'd be wasting my time standing around talking to you?'

'So *where* is he?'

'You can't visit him.'

'That's not what I asked.'

Several seconds passed before Alec yielded. 'Private hospital. Ok?'

'Who's paying for that?'

'What's it to you?'

Rebecca sighed. 'How is he?'

'Do you really need me to answer to that?' Alec demanded. 'How the hell do you *think* he is? He's in fucking bits! He's not eating, he's not sleeping, he can barely string a bloody sentence together, and he needs to be somewhere with enough staff to keep an eye on him that he can't wander out to the nearest off licence the minute I have to go to work!'

'*What?*'

'I came home at three-thirty on Sunday morning to find him passed out on these steps in the pissing rain! And if I find out which fucking moron thought it was a good idea to sell someone wandering around barefoot in pyjamas a litre of vodka, I will fucking kill them!' There was a momentary pause before his expression changed and he added, 'In fact, if I do find out, can you charge them with anything?'

Rebecca wished she could answer differently as she admitted, 'It's unlikely.'

'And there was me thinking you might be able to make yourself useful for once.'

'I can give them a bollocking and discourage them from doing it again,' Rebecca countered, hoping the suggestion might encourage Alec to stay in touch. He responded with a noncommittal grunt, and, having succeeded in obtaining the update she'd been seeking, Rebecca decided to call it a day.

'I'll leave you in peace,' she said, turning through ninety degrees before adding, 'But please keep me in the loop about how Elliot's doing.'

Alec grunted again, this time in incredulity. 'And why would I want to do that?'

'Because if you do, I'll do as *you've* asked,' Rebecca answered, bluntly. 'And I'll leave him alone.' She raised her eyebrows pointedly. 'Ok?'

Alec held her gaze for so long that Rebecca began to feel like an unwitting contestant in a staring competition. At length, he sighed heavily, nodding in agreement.

'Ok,' he confirmed, grudgingly, before turning on his heel and closing the door abruptly behind himself. Rebecca started up the steps to the street, feeling relieved Alec hadn't put up more resistance. Admittedly only time would tell whether he would be as good as his word, but Rebecca felt optimistic. When it came down to it, Alec's concern for Elliot far outweighed the animosity he felt towards her, so if the occasional text message was all it took to keep her out of sight – and perhaps by extension out of mind – she felt fairly certain he could be relied upon to stick to his side of the bargain, type out a few words, and hit send.

Thirteen

Lawrence and Rebecca arrived at the Clapham Chronicle's offices on Tuesday morning to find Damon and Liam standing in the street outside, cigarettes grasped loosely between their fingers, the editor laughing at something the art editor was saying. Liam, who was leaning against the railings that safeguarded one of the building's lightwells, was the first to spot them, and on so doing immediately fell silent. Following the direction of his colleague's uneasy gaze, Damon turned, his expression changing as his eyes met with Lawrence's.

'Morning,' he greeted, cordially. 'I'm starting to think it might make things simpler if we just found you a desk.'

'I was hoping to speak to whoever deals with your advertising,' Lawrence replied, stopping by the railings as Rebecca headed for the door into the building.

'Oh, right,' Damon looked surprised. 'That doesn't actually happen here. Admin, accounting, advertising and HR are based down in Streatham.'

'Why's that?'

'Cheaper. It's not as if they need to be in the thick of things.'

'I see,' Lawrence nodded. 'Presumably you see the classified pages, though? Do you lay those out?' He looked to Liam, who shook his head mutely.

'We have nothing to do with any of that,' Damon answered for him. 'All we need to know is where any full- or half-page ads will go and how many pages of classifieds, legal notices and recruitment we need to factor into the issue plan. We then make sure all the rest of the pages are filled one way or another, and fire those off to the printers. They're the ones who pull everything together.'

'So who does lay out those pages? Someone in Streatham, or the printers?'

'I'm not actually sure who physically makes up the pages,' Damon admitted. 'Does it matter?'

'It might.'

'Well I can find out for you. Or I can give you the contact details for the guys down in Streatham, if you want to talk to them yourself?'

'I may need to have a chat with them, but before we get onto that, do the names Sulina Grafica or Ricardo D'Ambrosio mean anything to you?'

Damon didn't appear to react to either, but Lawrence caught a flicker of recognition in Liam's expression, which quickly turned to caught-in-the-headlights panic when Lawrence's gaze fell upon him. He began shaking his head even before he opened his mouth.

'I don't – it's just –' he stopped. 'I know the road name. That's all.'

'Which road name?' Lawrence probed.

'Sulina Road.'

'And why is that familiar?'

Liam swallowed. 'It's where I live.'

'How long have you lived there?'

'Forever,' Liam replied, snatching a quick pull on his cigarette before stammering, 'It's my parents' house.'

Lawrence nodded, wondering whether any member of the Chronicle's staff could be relied upon for an honest answer to the question of whether Liam was always so ill at ease. He had been similarly on edge when Lawrence and Rebecca had interviewed him the previous Wednesday morning, and Lawrence didn't want to waste time trying to get to the bottom of that if the explanation was something as simple as social anxiety.

Drawing a handful of folded pages from his jacket pocket, he leafed through them before presenting the young man with a photograph of Ricardo. 'Does he look familiar?'

Liam drew on his cigarette again before shrugging weakly. 'I dunno – I mean, I don't think so –' he licked his lips nervously. Lawrence didn't reply, hoping an expectant silence might prompt a more definitive evaluation. It didn't: after an awkward pause, the young man simply shook his head and repeated, 'I dunno.'

'If anything comes to mind, please do let me know,' Lawrence replied, moving to replace the picture in his pocket, then stopping as Damon held out a hand for it.

He regarded the photograph closely for several seconds before returning it to Lawrence, saying, apologetically, 'Not a face I recognize either, I'm afraid. Who is he?'

'A graphic artist called Ricardo D'Ambrosio,' Lawrence replied, before adding, in the faint hope it might take him closer to an answer, 'I'm trying to establish whether he and Steve ever had any contact, or shared any contacts.'

Damon appeared to think this over for a moment before turning to Liam. 'What was the name of that guy who kept bugging us about infographics when we were running that series on council services last year?'

Liam looked blank.

'We did a double-page spread every issue for six weeks,' Damon reminded him. 'We covered education, housing, recycling –' he counted them off on his fingers, hesitating before abandoning the list unfinished and continuing with the overarching story. 'With a half-page infographic for each one. And each week we got a letter from some bloke criticising our graphics and detailing how *he* thought we should have represented the information. He even did little colour sketches, and –'

'Oh, the pictures that always looked like they'd been drawn by someone on LSD,' Liam realised, aloud.

'Yes!' Damon exclaimed, triumphantly. 'Those. What was the guy's name?'

Liam shrugged.

'Have you still got the letters?'

He shrugged again. 'I dunno. Maybe.'

'D'you want to go and have a look?'

Liam nodded, tossing the remains of his cigarette onto the pavement and starting towards the front door of the building before doubling back, retrieving the cigarette butt and crushing it into the small metal ashtray attached to the railings to the left of the door. Lawrence wondered whether he'd previously been pulled up or fined for dropping one.

'Is he always so jumpy?' He asked, as the door closed behind Liam.

'Not always, but it doesn't take much. I think authority figures make him nervous,' Damon added his cigarette end to the box Liam had used seconds earlier. 'It took me the best part of six months to get more than two words at a time out of him.'

'What's he like with the other members of staff?'

'All right, I think. He's an obliging kid and he's quite personable one-on-one, once he gets to know you. But he's more of an observer than a participant in office life. I get the impression he struggles with being the focus of attention.'

'Has anyone ever exploited that for a cheap laugh?'

'Not that I'm aware of, but I'm probably not the best person to ask. I'm in and out quite a lot, and there's only so much I pick up on from my office, even when the door's open.'

Lawrence nodded, conscious that he certainly wouldn't be the best person to answer questions about day-to-day interactions in CID. Rebecca often commented on amusing incidents that had apparently occurred in his presence but of which he had absolutely no recollection, and from Katie's remarks – and, on occasion, complaints – it seemed he often didn't pay much attention to what was going on around him at home, either. He probably relied more than he realised on Rebecca to keep him abreast of affairs not detailed in departmental memos and emails, he reflected. She wouldn't, he suspected, ever betray colleagues over minor infractions or missteps, but he felt fairly certain he could rely on her to bring inappropriate or unfair behaviour to his attention. All the same, she couldn't be everywhere at once, and he perhaps ought to address his shortcomings in the domain before anything serious bypassed his radar. The question was where to start.

Ramona had brought a mug of coffee with her into the meeting room, and sat with both hands wrapped around it, the tips of her fingers interlinking on the far side. At the height of his drinking, Rebecca had often seen Elliot hold his morning coffee in the same fashion in an attempt to conceal the fact his hands were shaking, and she wondered whether Ramona was using the mug to steady hers.

'When we spoke last week, you implied that Steve's behaviour towards you and Priya constituted sexual harassment,' Rebecca began, crossing her legs and resting her notebook on the uppermost one. 'Is that an accurate evaluation?'

Ramona nodded.

'Did you make any effort to address that? With Damon, or with HR?'

'I was keeping a log of the more serious incidents, but I hadn't spoken to anyone about it yet.'

'Why not?'

'I wanted to have enough evidence before I said anything. The media might be quick to take a woman's side nowadays, but you need more than hearsay where workplace disciplinary procedures are concerned. There are still plenty of people who confuse having feminist views with being a man-hater, and given my reputation I didn't want to be dismissed as making mountains out of molehills.'

'So the potential repercussions made you reluctant to push the matter.'

'Yes.'

'Was it something you ever tried to discuss with Steve?'

'On occasion I let him know that a remark was out of line, but it didn't make any difference to his behaviour. If anything, it probably encouraged him.'

'Did you ever feel threatened by him?'

Ramona's hesitation spoke for her. 'On occasion,' she admitted, at length, her cheeks colouring.

'Enough to make you consider leaving?'

'Yes. But to be honest, I hoped he might do the leaving. He was pretty ambitious.'

'And you're not?'

'When I leave I want it to be for the right opportunity, not because I feel the need to escape.'

Rebecca nodded. 'Would you mind running through what you did after you left the office last Friday?'

'Friday?' Ramona frowned. 'Why?'

'Please just answer the question.'

Ramona looked put out, but complied with Rebecca's request. 'I met a woman I'd arranged to interview for a magazine article I'm writing. We met at the Sacred Café in Ganton Street at around seven and sat downstairs. At about half nine we walked up to Oxford Circus tube. I took the Bakerloo Line to Maida Vale, got in shortly after ten, microwaved some dinner, read for a while and went to bed.'

'Well, you certainly didn't need to think too hard about that,' Rebecca remarked, thinking Ramona seemed prepared for the question.

'If you'd rather get my answers piecemeal, I can make it like pulling teeth,' she returned. 'I just assumed you'd find that kind of interview as frustrating to conduct as I do.'

It wasn't an unreasonable point, but Rebecca didn't acknowledge it, instead flicking back through her notebook. Maida Vale didn't ring any bells, and she wondered whether Ramona had given them the correct details on their initial visit to the Chronicle's offices the previous week. On that occasion, Lawrence had questioned how Steve had financed an extravagant lifestyle on a journalist's salary, so she thought she would have been sufficiently surprised by Ramona reporting an address in such an affluent neighbourhood to at least recall the fact. Either way, the mile-long stretch of the A5 that bore the same name as the West London district of Maida Vale connected the Edgware Road to Kilburn High Road – putting Ramona within easy walking distance of the King William pub on Friday night.

'Last week, you told us you live in Dorking,' she said, on finding the relevant page of her notes. 'Now apparently it's Maida Vale. Could you explain that?'

'The place in Maida Vale isn't mine. It's my father's.'

'Can he confirm you were there?'

'Only insofar as I told him I was. He's in Fuerteventura with his third wife.'

'If nobody was home, why did you go round?'

'I'm there more than he is. It's not his home either, he just stays there when he's in town.'

'So why did you not provide us with that address last week?'

'You asked for my home address. That's in Dorking.'

'And what were you reading?'

It seemed to take Ramona a moment to register what Rebecca was referring to. 'What, on Friday night?' She asked. 'Silent Spring.'

'Did you leave the flat at any time that night?'

'No.'

'You didn't go to the King William pub?'

'*No*,' she stressed, her eyebrows drawing together into a frown. 'I read my book and went to bed. I didn't go anywhere, see anyone or do anything!'

She sounded unnecessarily insistent, her voice slightly strained. Feeling sceptical, Rebecca asked why she'd stayed in London on a Friday night if all she was going to do was read a book and go to bed.

'I was tired and it was convenient,' Ramona responded, sounding exasperated. 'I don't know, I really didn't think that much about it! I didn't know I was going to get the third degree. If I had, I might have chosen differently!'

Lawrence glanced up in response to an unnecessary knock on his open office door to see Leighton hovering in the doorway, his expression slightly sheepish – perhaps as a result of the tense exchange the previous afternoon, or possibly owing to the fact he was attired unusually smartly in a suit and tie. Presumably he had either just returned from giving evidence in court or was on his way to do so; given that it wasn't quite midday and that he hadn't yet shed the tie, the latter seemed more likely. Lawrence sat back in his chair, bidding his colleague a good morning.

'I've never been convinced those two words go together,' Leighton returned, with a quirky smile, as he advanced into the room. 'But on this occasion I might be willing to make an exception, seeing as I've just had some results from the lab.'

'And you have a DNA hit?'

'Two, actually, so you can be doubly sure it's right.' He smiled again, although it didn't quite seem to reach his eyes. 'A salivary sample that matches the one on Steve's genitals – although this

Fourteen

A movement at the edge of her field of vision caught Rebecca's eye and she raised her eyes from her screen to see Jamie surreptitiously trying to catch a glimpse of Lawrence's office through the open doorway. She guessed he'd just been for a cigarette and didn't want to catch up with their superior while the fact was still evident; when, moments later, he leaned against the side of her desk, the accompanying smoky haze proved her hunch correct.

'He'll be back any minute,' she warned her friend, nodding in the direction of Lawrence's empty office.

'Lunch break,' Jamie excused himself, drawing a pack of menthol gum from his pocket and taking a piece before offering it to her. 'Any news?'

'Yep. Traffic unit picked her up in Hoxton,' Rebecca updated him, declining the gum with a shake of her head. 'That's not going to fool him, you know. He's not daft.'

'Indeed he isn't,' Lawrence remarked, as he strode into view. 'But right now he's more interested in Lisa's mobile phone log than in discussing the misuse of police time. Anything so far?'

'Jodie's number, not surprisingly,' Rebecca replied. 'More interestingly, Tim Bateman's number is also in there. And whereas Jodie is named as a contact, Tim isn't – despite his number coming up under both outgoing and incoming calls several times within the past week alone. Most recently on Friday afternoon.'

'Is it saved to the phone rather than the SIM?' Jamie asked.

Rebecca shook her head.

'Ok, let's find out where he was on Friday night,' Lawrence

looked to Jamie. 'Can you take care of that?'

'Sure.'

'And if his story doesn't check out, bring him in.'

Jamie nodded, turning to go.

'Are there any pictures on there?' Lawrence asked Rebecca, indicating the disassembled mobile phone lying on her desk.

'Not of note. She had a quality digital camera with her, though, Danny's been going through the photos. Presumably she'll have more on a computer at home.'

'Ok. Once you and he are done with what we've got here, I want you to head over to Lewisham and take her place apart. In the meantime, I'll see what I can get out of her.'

'*The expectation of the wicked is retribution*,' Lawrence read aloud from his notes before fixing his eyes on Lisa. 'So it says in the same chapter of Proverbs that the quote on your business card comes from. Is that your view? Is that why you've been tracking down men you believe to be guilty of sexual assault?'

Lisa shook her head slightly, her pale eyes caught in a perplexed frown. 'What?'

Lawrence placed the photograph Rebecca had taken of the sticker on the toilet door at the King William on the table between them. 'Do you have any training that qualifies you to run this kind of service?'

'I'm not aware of any law that says it's an offence to provide empathy and support to people in distress.'

'I didn't ask about the legalities of the situation, I asked whether you have any training in victim support.'

'Not everybody needs training to be able to connect with people.'

'I'll ask one more time. Answering only yes or no, do you have any training in this area?'

'No,' Lisa admitted, coolly.

'And do you think it's appropriate to take responsibility for someone else's emotional welfare without it?'

Lisa tipped her head to one side. 'Did you have any training on how to handle others' emotions before you had children, Chief Inspector? Because that seems like a pretty big responsibility to me, but nobody ever checks whether people are capable of undertaking that one. You have to jump through more hoops to adopt a rescue pet than to have a child.'

Lisa's assumption – or perhaps even knowledge – of his personal circumstances was presumably intended to be unnerving, and Lawrence resisted the automatic urge to react, saying only, 'Yes or no?'

'Not every question can be answered as simply as that.'

'I'll take that as no comment. Let's move on to Patrick Copeland.'

'Who?'

'Patrick Copeland. The estate agent Jodie Yarwood claims raped her. You do at least know who Jodie is?'

'I know *a* Jodie.'

'Jodie Yarwood has called your mobile multiple times in the past month, and you've called her on several occasions. As a number of the calls lasted well in excess of thirty minutes, I think it's safe to conclude you've been speaking to the same Jodie we have.'

Lisa's response was a shrug so small that the movement was barely discernible.

'I also understand from Jodie that she's told you all about the night Patrick walked her home, forced his way into her flat and raped her. Did you, at any time, encourage her to go to the police about that attack?'

'It's not my place to tell people what to do.'

'Fine, if you want to play word games I can rephrase. Did you ever raise it as a possible course of action?'

'She was afraid nobody would believe her. Perhaps if society wasn't so quick to make women out to be responsible for the crimes men commit against them, more women would feel able to come forward to report sexual assaults to the police, and more of those reports would lead to convictions.'

It was an argument Lawrence had heard countless times before. Survey after survey reported that a significant minority of the population – female as well as male – believed rape victims bore at least partial responsibility for their plight on account of a whole range of variables. And although there were clearly those who took the view that by dressing immodestly or being out alone late at night women were *asking for it*, he was never sure how many respondents of polls on the matter were truly of that opinion and how many had simply failed to adequately differentiate between *blame* and *risk*.

As far as Lawrence was concerned, the blame for any crime rested firmly with the perpetrator – a pickpocket was no less guilty of theft than a bank robber simply because the item stolen had been within easy reach – but that didn't mean people bore no responsibility for their own safety. Where crimes as emotive as rape were concerned, however, it was a debate beset by grey areas, and not a subject he was inclined to discuss with anyone, least of all Lisa.

'So with society as it is, what?' He asked. 'You've been seeking to redress the balance? Doling out dues to those you believe deserve them and ensuring they'll never have the chance to reoffend?'

'I offer support to victims, that doesn't –'

'And in the process have the opportunity to collect all manner of details about their supposed attackers. But there's only so much they can tell you. Have you ever considered the implications of getting it wrong? Of targeting the wrong person? What about the potential for flaws and falsehoods in the accounts of your purported victims? You've no evidence that a voice at the other end of a phone line is genuine!'

'Why would anyone call a helpline to talk about something that *didn't* happen?'

'Offhand I can think of several reasons. Delusion? Attention? Twisted fantasy? With no relevant training, how do you even begin to tease out mentally ill from traumatised victim? There are always two sides to a story. Did you even think to *ask* Patrick for his version of events before you plotted his demise?'

'I didn't plot anything.'

'But you know who did. You did that person's research. That's what you were doing in Kensal Lane last week.'

'I was there on behalf of a client,' Lisa returned, her voice sounding strained. 'I've already told you that.'

'Which client? Jodie?'

'Jodie's not a *client*! I don't charge women like Jodie for my time!'

'So whose research were you doing?'

'We've been through all this before! I won't breach my clients' confidentiality on the basis of an unsubstantiated theory!'

'Miss Allen, I think we're a bit past that point, don't you? We have your mobile phone records, and we're perfectly capable of identifying and tracking down every single person you've been in contact with. And if you don't start to cooperate, I won't hesitate to tell each and every one of them who is responsible for my turning up on their doorstep.'

'If you want to waste police resources on a wild goose chase, go ahead.'

'You might also want to bear in mind that if there are legal ramifications as well as professional ones, your non-cooperation will do you no favours in court.'

'I'm not going to roll over just because you threaten me.'

Lawrence regarded Lisa closely for several seconds before raising his eyebrows and returning his eyes to his notes. He waited a few more moments before concluding, gravely, 'I do hope you don't come to regret that decision.'

Rebecca and Daniel arrived at Lisa's Lewisham home shortly after five to find the lights on, although they had to ring the bell twice before it drew any response. At length, the sound of a window opening served as a prelude to the appearance of a woman's head and shoulders at first-floor level, a haphazard grey towelling turban binding her hair.

'Hello?'

'Police,' Rebecca replied, displaying her warrant card. 'Could we come in, please?'

'Oh – right – ok. Hang on.' The head withdrew. Seconds later, Rebecca heard footsteps behind the door before it was opened by a petite woman not much taller than five foot, clad in a burgundy dressing gown and white fluffy slippers. Rebecca guessed from their unsullied appearance that they must be more or less brand new.

'Sorry – we get a lot of people trying to borrow money from us at the door,' the slippers' owner explained, using her forefingers to draw inverted commas in the air as she spoke the word *borrow*. 'Come in.' She turned and began making her way back up the flight of stairs immediately inside, leaving Rebecca and Daniel to follow.

At the top of the stairs they crowded into the limited available space between the kitchen units, the sofa and the stand that supported the television, and Rebecca introduced herself and Daniel before asking the woman her name.

'Imogen Telford.'

'Are you Lisa's flatmate?'

'Yes.'

'Would you mind answering a few questions for us?'

'If I can,' Imogen replied, uneasily. 'Um – do you want to sit down?' She gestured towards the sofa.

Rebecca took a seat and, as Daniel joined her, Imogen settled herself on a large floor cushion, holding on to both sides of her satin dressing gown as she did so to preserve her modesty.

'Have you lived here long?' Rebecca asked, conversationally.

'About five months.'

'Did you know Lisa before that?'

Imogen shook her head. 'I found the room through Gumtree.'

'Would you say you've become friends since then?'

Imogen's eyebrows contracted in concern. 'Is Lisa ok?'

'She's fine,' Rebecca responded. 'We just need to have a chat with her about her work. Does she talk much about it with you?'

'No. She says it's confidential.'

'But you do know what she does?'

'Yes. She's a private detective. Although that's all I know, really. She keeps her work life very much to herself.'

'How about her social life? Have you met any of her friends?'

'No,' Imogen replied, sounding a little surprised by this realisation. 'I'm sure she has some, though, she goes out often enough, and she's always chatting on the phone.'

'Does she have a boyfriend?'

'I don't think so. Although, if she did, I'm not sure she'd bring him home. I had a friend stay over last week and that didn't go down well at *all*.'

'Why not?'

'I did kind of agree not to have guys stay over when I moved in,' Imogen admitted, with a half-hearted shrug. 'But he missed his last train, so I was in a bit of a bind. It's not like we *did* anything, I didn't think it was a big deal.'

It didn't sound like a big deal to Rebecca, either. 'Did Lisa say why she didn't want you having men staying over?'

'No. I think maybe it's a religious thing. She always wears a Saint Christopher.'

'Does she go to church?'

The question appeared to take Imogen by surprise. 'I've no idea,' she admitted, after a moment. 'That sounds ridiculous, doesn't it? We do get on well, she's a nice girl, I just –' she shrugged, her eyebrows contracting into an anxious frown. 'I guess when I think about it, I don't know a whole lot about her.'

'What the hell is all this about?' Tim demanded, the moment Lawrence and Jamie joined him in the interview room.

'What do you think it's about?' Lawrence countered, pulling a chair out from the table and sitting opposite the man.

'If I had the first clue I wouldn't need to ask!'

'We'll come on to the first clue in a minute. In the meantime, perhaps you might start by telling us the nature of your relationship with Lisa Allen.'

'Lisa?' Tim exclaimed, incredulously.

'Lisa,' Lawrence echoed. 'You've made calls to and received them from her within the past week, so clearly you're acquainted.'

'Only in a professional capacity.'

'In what sense?'

'In the sense that I engaged her services.'

'Could you please expand on exactly what those were?'

'She's a private detective, what do you think they were? I paid her to investigate something for me!'

'Which was what?'

'That's none of your damn business!'

'I'm sorry about that, but I'm afraid we need you to answer the question.'

Tim crossed his arms pointedly, saying nothing.

Tim muttered something under his breath, closing his eyes momentarily. A brief silence followed before he sighed and admitted, 'I went to a strip club, ok?'

'And why did you feel it necessary to conceal that from us?'

'Why the hell do you think? My bloody wife was in the next room!'

With Natalie supposedly embroiled in an extramarital affair, this seemed something of an unnecessary concern. When Lawrence said as much, Tim replied, as if it ought to have been obvious, 'Yes, but *she* doesn't know I know that!'

Lawrence frowned. 'So let me see if I understand correctly: you paid Lisa to provide evidence of your wife's affair, which she did, but a week later you're yet to do anything with that information?'

'Not exactly. It's not as simple as that.'

'Right,' Lawrence responded, doubtfully.

'I can show you the damn pictures if you're so interested!'

'We'll come onto those later. First of all I'd like the details of where you were between nine-thirty on Friday night and two a.m. the following morning.'

'Gaslight. In Duke of York Street.'

'Were you there alone?'

'Well I *arrived* there alone, but I didn't spend much of the time I was in there unaccompanied. That's the point of those places, really, isn't it?'

'And can you name anyone who might be able to verify that for us?'

'Lainey,' Tim replied, surprisingly readily, before adding, awkwardly, 'She knows me. We've – spent time together – before.'

Lawrence nodded, wondering whether Jamie had any more idea than he did of what that might mean in context, having never visited a gentlemen's club – a misnomer if ever there was one – as a paying customer. He suspected that, even with the help of a few drinks, he would feel too self-conscious to enjoy the experience, and given Katie's overt antipathy to the industry had generally been happy to dismiss any opportunity to find out without much consideration.

He hadn't been single since the age of nineteen, and at that stage of life lads' nights out had usually comprised beers at one student bar or another followed by a couple of hours in whichever relatively generic nightclub someone had managed to gather discounted flyers for. The only further expenditure he remembered anyone contemplating had involved fast food of varying levels of unappealing en route back to halls. It hadn't taken long for him to tire of that particular routine, and he had been more than happy to exchange most such outings for evenings alone with Katie even before they graduated. Thereafter, she had proved a credible excuse to decline the bulk of undesirable invitations, and where venues such as strip clubs were concerned he didn't imagine he'd missed much as a result. Certainly nothing he'd not seen in the course of his job.

Rebecca had searched countless homes and bedrooms during her time in CID, but Lisa's was one of the most extraordinary – made more so because, although exceptionally tidy, at first glance nothing about it seemed out of the ordinary. The small double bed just in front of the window was covered with a pretty purple woollen throw, and a single matching cushion stood on one corner, leaning against the pillows. Above the headboard hung a wide canvas print depicting a spray of five magenta orchid flowers, and to the left a bedside unit held a digital clock, a tissue box and a coaster, all colour-coordinated with the bedding.

The wall opposite the window was furnished with a sizeable wardrobe and a matching shelf unit, the latter stocked in a manner not dissimilar to that in Rebecca's own bedroom. Several of the shelves bore neat rows of books – admittedly more highbrow than those in Rebecca's collection – and another a small stereo unit and a self-supporting calendar. The uppermost one was empty but for a subtly scented reed diffuser. To the left of the shelves, beside the door frame, was a compact chest of drawers scattered with the usual miscellany of the female dressing table – a hairbrush, a handful of hair clips, deodorant, moisturiser, cleanser – and, at the back, a petite, perfectly proportioned succulent in a plain white china pot was reflected in the mirror on the wall behind.

None of the belongings on view caught Rebecca's attention, which, in itself, struck her as strange. There were no knick-knacks or personal items – no soft toys, ornaments, picture frames – in fact, almost nothing that said anything about Lisa. Even the calendar was merely functional, a grid of dates on a plain background, unadorned and unmarked. And although books could be viewed as offering some insight into a person's psyche, it was impossible to know whether the selection of familiar titles on display represented Lisa's personal choice or was merely a job lot of popular classics.

A search beneath the surface revealed a little more. Lisa clearly had expensive tastes, and her impeccably ordered wardrobe was stocked almost entirely with designer names: Armani and Joseph suits; dresses by Alexander McQueen and Missoni; shoes by Christian Louboutin; and handbags from the likes of Bottega Veneta and Mulberry. Her make-up box was similarly cluttered with famous names: Dior eyeshadow, Chanel lipstick, highlighter by Saint Laurent. In the drawer alongside it were three pairs of designer sunglasses and several purses, but no jewellery; apparently the Saint Christopher around her neck was the only piece she owned. And while her possessions shed light on her shopping preferences, the drawers and cupboards mirrored the room's visible surfaces in holding no belongings particular to Lisa. Rebecca unearthed nothing that looked like a memento, no letters or cards, no address book – although that information could conceivably be stored in the woman's phone or computer – and no photograph albums. The room could almost have been part of an exceptionally detailed show home, with all the appearances but none of the personality of its lived-in counterpart.

Perhaps Lisa was just completely unsentimental. Rebecca knew not everybody shared her tendency to hoard souvenirs of their own personal history, from a childhood night light and a favourite teddy bear to the wooden tulips bought on a teenage holiday in Amsterdam and a bracelet passed down by her grandmother. When she had lived at home, her mother had despaired of dusting her cluttered shelves, and Elliot had once tentatively suggested she consider making some of her accumulated keepsakes 'redundant' in the interests of saving space – before almost immediately back-tracking for fear she might instead opt to make *him* redundant.

Perhaps Lisa had severed all links with her past, and rid herself of anything that might serve as a reminder. But hadn't Elliot done just that? And, quite aside from the fact he'd *still* kept hold of a photograph and a broken antique pocket watch, it hadn't stopped him collecting bits and pieces relating to his new life. Besides, personal possessions weren't only about memories: Elliot's everyday belongings also revealed glimpses of who he was, from the handful of heavy metal badges pinned to his leather jacket to the slogans on his t-shirts.

Even in the relatively impersonal environment of the office people's desks generally said something about them: Lawrence had a small picture frame containing school photographs of Jimmy and Elise; Daniel a Doctor Who Tardis mug; Leighton a coaster stamped with Sheffield Wednesday's owl logo. All one could really take from the sum total of belongings in Lisa's bedroom was that she had expensive tastes and probably liked purple.

'It's a pretty important thing to miss, though, isn't it? And I didn't follow up on the helpline, either. It occurred to me to take the photograph, at the very least I should have called to get more details.'

'Don't beat yourself up about it. If you'd not thought to take the picture we'd still be none the wiser.'

Rebecca dropped her eyes to the floor. 'I feel like I've let you down.'

'Things always seem obvious with the benefit of hindsight, Becky. And it wasn't your fault you ended up conducting a difficult interview alone. At most, all we've really lost is twenty-four hours. Worse things have happened.'

Rebecca didn't reply.

'Go home and get some sleep. We'll give –'

'Sir!'

Lawrence turned his head in the direction of the shout to see Jamie bounding down the corridor towards them.

'According to the security camera on Gaslight's main entrance, Bateman didn't arrive until ten to one on Saturday morning,' Jamie announced, rather breathlessly, as he drew level with them. 'So we're still three hours short.'

'Why does that not surprise me?' Lawrence responded, drily. 'Put him in an interview room and I'll be along in five minutes. We'll do one more round before we call it a night.'

Jamie nodded, turning back the way he had come.

'With a bit of luck, the temptation of getting home by bedtime will work in our favour.'

Fifteen

'Mr Bateman, I'm only going to ask where you were between ten p.m. on Friday and one a.m. on Saturday once more before I charge you with wasting police time!' Lawrence informed the man on entry to the interview room, taking a seat at the table. 'We've checked Gaslight's security tapes, and you didn't arrive there until twelve-fifty! So where did you go after you left work at nine-thirty?'

Tim muttered something under his breath.

'I'm waiting,' Lawrence pressed, when the man didn't immediately answer. 'And believe me, I am not overwhelmed with patience at this stage of the game.'

'I have a girlfriend,' Tim admitted, eventually.

'A girlfriend,' Lawrence repeated, coolly. 'So your wife isn't the only one playing away.'

'Spare me the moralising,' Tim retorted. 'My marriage is none of your business, and it isn't your job to sit in judgement! If that's what you want to do, you need to retrain as a priest!'

'A priest?' Lawrence echoed. 'Are you a Catholic, Mr Bateman?'

'What the hell does that have to do with anything?'

'I'll ask the questions. That, as we're on the subject, *is* my job.'

Tim didn't reply, and Lawrence repeated his question.

'No, I'm not.'

'Do you believe sinners get due reward?'

'Eh?' Tim frowned, clearly confused. 'What is this?'

'Let's go back to your girlfriend. You brought her up in reference to Friday night, can I take it she can vouch for where you were during the hours you've so far failed to account for?'

'Yes.'

'What's her name?'

'Ramona.'

'Her full name.'

'Ramona Weaver.'

'So you *are* familiar with the Clapham Chronicle,' Lawrence concluded. 'That's very interesting. Aside from Steve, do any of her colleagues know about your affair?'

'What do you mean, *aside* from Steve?' Tim demanded. 'Nobody knows! Or at least, until you stuck your nose in nobody knew!'

'Right,' Lawrence replied, cynically. 'Either way, presumably you were aware of his death, and our investigation, before we arrived at your office?'

'Actually I wasn't. We have better things to talk about than our work colleagues.'

Lawrence regarded the man for a few seconds, unconvinced, before deciding to come back to the subject of Steve later on.

'So where did you and Ramona meet on Friday evening?'

'Her place. Maida Vale.'

'Whereabouts in Maida Vale?'

'Elgin Avenue.'

'What time did you get there?'

'I don't know, exactly – probably a bit after ten.'

'How long were you there for?'

'I ordered a cab for half twelve.'

'And what did you and Ramona do during your time there?'

'What do you *think*?' Tim demanded, sarcastically.

'What I *think* won't be included in your statement,' Lawrence returned, irritably. 'We work on facts, not assumptions.'

Tim wet his lips before he answered. 'We had a drink and we went to bed. Ok?'

'What kind of drink?'

'Wine. White wine.'

'Can you describe Ramona's bedroom?'

'Is this really necessary?'

'Yes.'

Tim sighed. 'I don't know, the décor's never really been of much interest to me when I've been in there. It's a woman's bedroom. There's a bed, a wardrobe, a chair – a mirror on the wall –' he shrugged.

'Do you recall the colour of the bedclothes?'

'They're a light colour – green or blue, I think.'

'What kind of property is it? House? Apartment? One bed? Two?'

'It's a two-bed flat in a mansion block a couple of minutes' walk from the tube station.'

Lawrence nodded. When he didn't immediately ask anything further, Tim raised another question of his own.

'Are we done?'

'Good question. I'd like the answer to that one myself.'

'You've got what you wanted!'

'That remains to be seen.'

The man frowned. 'I've told you where I was! And given the hour, I'd like to get home to bed!'

'I'm sure you would, but we need to speak to Ramona before we release you. If you'd told us the truth earlier, we'd probably have been able to do that this evening, but *given the hour*, as you put it, we'll now have to wait for the morning.' He pushed his chair back from the table. 'So until then, you're going nowhere.'

By eight-thirty on Wednesday morning, Lawrence and Jamie were back in the interview room they'd only left just before midnight. Lawrence had barely set a bottle of water, a stack of plastic cups and a cardboard file down on the table before Lisa said, 'I want to speak to a solicitor.'

'And I've already outlined why we can't allow that at this stage,' Lawrence replied, taking a seat opposite her. 'If you had difficulty grasping that, perhaps you'd like me to have DS Lanson here photocopy the relevant section of the Code of Practice for you?'

'You can't deny me access to a solicitor!'

'No, you're right, I can't. But my boss can. And he has.' Lawrence poured a glass of water. 'If you'd like to expedite your access to legal advice, the name of your accomplice would be a good place to start.'

'I don't *have* an accomplice!' Lisa returned, sounding exasperated.

'So you were working alone?'

'That's not what I meant!'

'I'm confused. Do you have an accomplice or not?'

Lisa started to answer, then stopped herself and began again. 'I've done nothing, with *or* without assistance. And I won't be tricked into saying otherwise.'

'On the off-chance you are protecting someone else, I feel bound to point out that cooperation would work in your favour when it comes to sentencing. Particularly if you weren't the one who caused death to occur.'

There was a pause before Lisa said, 'I've always wondered whether real police officers bullshit people the way the fictional kind do on TV. Conspiracy to murder carries a maximum sentence of life imprisonment and – forgive me if I'm wrong – as we no longer have the death penalty in this country, that's the same as the maximum penalty handed out for murder.'

'I'm intrigued by the fact you had cause to look that up.'

'If reading the news counts as *looking things up*.'

'Regardless of your source, as you're apparently so well informed you're presumably also aware that the legal system doesn't work in absolutes, and that there are all manner of variables that impact on sentence duration. Hence the use of the word *maximum*. But I'm not going to be sidetracked by quibbles over technicalities. If you don't want to help yourself, that's your call.' Lawrence dropped his gaze to the folder on the table and flipped back the cover. Making a show of leafing through some papers, he said, with a momentary glance in Lisa's direction, 'Remind me what it was you were doing in Kensal Lane last week?'

Lisa sighed pointedly. 'I was there on behalf of a client.'

'Was that client Tim Bateman?'

'No.'

Lawrence replaced the papers and shut the file before giving Lisa his full attention once again. 'But Mr Bateman is a client of yours.'

'Is that a question or a statement?'

'Yes or no?'

'Yes.'

'What did he engage you to do?'

'That's confidential.'

'Of course it is,' Lawrence replied, sarcastically. 'Ok, how about you tell me what you provided to him in the way of evidence for whatever it was he asked you to investigate?'

'Reframing the question doesn't change the answer.'

'I'm not asking for the details, just the format you supplied the information in. Photographs, documents, that kind of thing.'

'How is that relevant?'

'Indulge me.'

'What, so you can use the information against my client? I don't think so.'

'Fine, have it your way. I'll serve your client with a search warrant and we'll see how he likes that.'

'I've no idea what you're expecting that to achieve, but I can't stop you wasting police time. Although I did think that was an offence in itself?'

It was hard to know whether Lisa meant the comment to be provocative or just distracting, but Lawrence didn't waste time on the matter, asking another question of his own. 'Whilst we're on the subject of your clients, I'm curious to know whether honey trapping is a service you offer as standard, or whether it's something you reserve for your victims?'

'I'm not sure where you got the idea I'd do it at all.'

'That's rather disingenuous. It's implicit in the name of your business.'

'Is it?' Lisa replied, innocently.

Lawrence regarded her in silence. Lisa simply stared back at him. He was fast coming to the conclusion she suffered from some sort of personality disorder, although his knowledge of the subject was too sketchy for him to hazard a guess at which one. Establishing the specifics would be a job for a psychiatrist – assuming Lawrence was able to build enough of a case to bring charges against Lisa in the first place. He suspected that would happen only if he could catch her out or if more evidence came to light. He was certainly under no illusion she was likely to break and confess any time soon.

'I imagine it's a very effective means of operation,' he continued, after a good ten seconds had elapsed. 'There aren't many men who wouldn't be flattered by the attentions of an attractive young woman, and I should think a good number of those would be only too happy to invite that woman back for a night cap. It happens in bars across the country every night, and I'm sure it's not difficult for a suspicious wife or girlfriend to find a private investigator prepared to entrap men using just that modus operandi.' He rested his forearms along the edge of the table, linking his fingers together. 'But the provision of honey traps to ensnare murder victims strikes me as catering to rather a niche market. The question is whether you sought out that market, or whether it came to you. And whether you're an accessory, a co-conspirator or a killer.'

'Was it really necessary to drag me all the way in here?' Ramona complained, as Rebecca sat opposite her in an interview room made unnecessarily gloomy by a shortage of functioning lightbulbs. 'I have a stupid amount of work to get through today without an added detour.'

'You're not the only one who's busy,' Rebecca returned, curtly. 'We only have so much time to run back and forth across London hearing one iteration of events after another.'

Ramona made no reply, but shifted slightly in her chair, folding her arms beneath her breasts.

'When I spoke to you yesterday, you didn't mention having any visitors on Friday night.'

'I didn't.'

'So Tim Bateman didn't pay you a visit?'

'Who?'

'Tim Bateman,' Rebecca repeated, clearly. 'Your lover, if his statement is anything to go by. I'm not sure how sleeping with another woman's husband squares with the feminist worldview, but I –'

'I think you'll find the playing field is pretty level where adultery is concerned,' Ramona retorted, sharply.

'Are you referring specifically to Tim's marriage, or to society as a whole?'

There was a momentary pause before Ramona replied. 'Both.'

'So you admit to sleeping with him.'

'Not a crime, is it?'

'No. So why deny knowing him?'

She shrugged.

'You must have had a reason.'

'Embarrassed, I guess,' Ramona excused herself, at length. It wasn't a convincing answer, but there was no way of disproving it and Rebecca decided it wasn't worth pursuing.

'How did you meet?'

'I was supposed to be interviewing Natalie. She asked me to come to the house, but when I arrived she wasn't there.'

'And he was?' Rebecca assumed.

'Yes. He invited me in to wait. It turned out to be rather a long wait.' She lifted her eyebrows expressively as she spoke the word *long*.

'When was this?'

'May.'

'Is that when the affair began?'

'More or less.'

'Did you see Tim last Friday night?'

'For a couple of hours.'

'Can you run through what happened in that time?'

'He arrived not long after I got in,' Ramona revealed. 'We shared a bottle of wine, then went to bed.'

'Did you leave the apartment at any time?'

'No.'

'You didn't go to the pub?'

'No. We never go *out* together.'

'Not even for a drink?'

'No.'

'Why not?'

Ramona snorted in disbelief. 'That's rather obvious, don't you think?'

'Not really, no,' Rebecca disagreed. 'Given that Natalie is herself guilty of infidelity, I'm not clear why Tim should be so determined to keep your relationship under wraps.'

'Do you not think that's something you should be asking him?'

'I'm asking you.'

'And what makes you think I know?'

Rebecca smiled wryly. 'I can't imagine you jumping unquestioningly just because a man said jump.'

Ramona maintained eye contact for a couple of seconds before yielding. 'They have a prenup. If he's caught cheating, she's entitled to half his wealth. He wanted to be the one to petition for divorce.'

'So he would have been less than thrilled to learn that Steve knew about your affair.'

Ramona blinked. 'What?' She exclaimed. 'Steve knew nothing about it!'

'Not according to our information.'

Ramona regarded Rebecca closely for several seconds before shaking her head. 'You're bluffing,' she concluded. 'I don't know what you're trying to get me to say, but I do know Steve had no clue about me and Tim.'

'What makes you so sure?'

'Well, for starters, he thought I was a raging lesbian, so I very much doubt he would ever have even suspected me of having an affair with a *man*. And there's no way he could have known unless he bugged my desktop phone, which he had no reason to do. Tim's so paranoid about being found out, he doesn't even call my mobile.'

'You must mean a lot to him if he's prepared to take the risk of being with you despite that.'

Ramona shrugged, saying nothing.

'I wonder what other risks he might be prepared to take on your behalf?'

Ramona frowned. 'I don't follow.'

'After our conversation yesterday I had a read of some of the articles you've penned for publications other than the chronicle. You've written quite widely on topics such as domestic violence, sexual harassment, stalking and rape. What made you focus on those issues?'

'They're crimes that disproportionately affect women, are woefully under-reported to the authorities and have shockingly low conviction rates, in no small part because of society's misconceptions about them.'

Rebecca nodded thoughtfully, cognizant of the fact Lisa had said something similar the previous day. Although, she reflected, that wasn't necessarily meaningful, it was hardly a niche view. And, whatever the whys and wherefores, Ramona was right about one thing – the crimes she had outlined did frequently go unreported, and even more frequently unpunished.

'Do you think the police bear some responsibility for that?' Rebecca asked.

'I think everybody bears some responsibility for that.'

'Have you ever considered doing more than writing about it?'

'What, like chaining myself to the railings outside parliament?'

'No, like taking the law into your own hands.'

'Seriously?' Ramona exclaimed. 'You think I killed Steve because he harassed me? Does that seem like a proportionate response to you?'

'Is that all he did?'

Ramona's eyebrows contracted fractionally. 'Yes, that's *all*,' she retorted, sarcastically, as if Rebecca had chosen the word to trivialise Steve's behaviour rather than to exclude other possibilities. 'And if you want the log I was keeping for HR, I can give it to you! That's all *I* did. I might have strong views, but that doesn't make me an extremist. I'm not completely bloody mad!'

Lawrence felt shallow admitting it even to himself, but, scrolling through the photographs Lisa had reportedly supplied to Tim as evidence of his wife's infidelity, he could understand the contention of many a gossip columnist that Natalie Bateman was way out of her husband's league. Although slender, she had presumably filled out somewhat since her modelling days, possessing as she did femine curves rather than the malnourished, androgynous physique synonymous with the international catwalk. Facially, she had been blessed with fine bone structure and soft features, and the range of natural expressions Lisa had caught on camera indicated the woman was no botox devotee. She apparently favoured business wear with a twist, with asymmetric cuts, unconventional fabrics and unusual items of haberdashery providing stylish updates to such staples as the shift dress and blazer, and hairstyles that secured her rusty blonde mane away from her face: a French twist in one set of pictures, a chignon in another. She was, as Rebecca had said, stunning.

By contrast, the balding, bespectacled middle-aged man who accompanied Natalie in the pictures wasn't anything more to look at than her husband, so perhaps it wasn't fair to assume she had been attracted principally to Tim's wallet. Of course, it was equally possible her affair had also been governed by ulterior motive – assuming she genuinely was involved with the other man. Frustratingly, Tim had declined to provide the allegedly incriminating video footage, insisting he would do so only if served with a warrant. And while some of the snapshots he had been willing to share hinted at a relationship greater than friendship – capturing moments of unnecessary physical contact – they afforded no definitive proof.

Lawrence had downloaded the contents of the DVD Tim had provided, then sent the disc and its plastic wallet for fingerprinting before sitting down to run through the pictures and come to a decision about whether it would be necessary to apply for a warrant. His younger self might well have sought one on principle, but these days he favoured economy of effort, and he wasn't convinced the footage – assuming it existed – would add anything to the investigation.

Had Tim fabricated the reason for his association with Lisa, the question of Natalie's fidelity could be viewed as incidental. Not everyone hiring a private detective to trail a spouse would have their suspicions confirmed, so even photographs that proved nothing could be presented as evidence of sorts, and had Tim and Lisa gone to the considerable trouble of creating such a pretext, it seemed unlikely he would have blown it upfront with a lie about a video. And even if Lawrence could confirm the video existed, that still wouldn't rule out the possibility of its being an elaborate decoy. He sighed.

'Social Services turned up a file for Lisa,' Rebecca informed him, without preamble, as she entered his office. 'It seems one of her schoolteachers raised concerns about sexual abuse by her stepfather when she was fourteen.'

'Did anything come of that?'

'No – the teacher came under scrutiny himself for being too close to Lisa, and she wouldn't say a word against either party, so the end result was nothing more than some pages in a file.'

Lawrence could well understand how frustrating that must have been for those involved. Over the years, he'd seen a lack of evidence lead to too many police investigations culminating in little more than a pile of paperwork, and there were few things worse than feeling you'd failed a vulnerable minor. He couldn't begin to imagine how people dealt with being in that kind of position on a regular – perhaps even daily – basis.

'She also has a brother,' Rebecca continued. 'He still lives at the family home in Orpington. And it seems she uses her computer more than we thought. Alvin found thousands of photographs in cloud storage – although given what she does for a living that's hardly surprising – and each batch of pictures has an associated Word file. I've had a quick read of a couple of those, and they seem like legitimate notes on the sort of work she claims to do.'

'I'm sure at least some of them are,' Lawrence replied. 'Can you get everyone available onto looking through those? Aside from the obvious, I'm interested in any pictures – or videos – featuring Natalie Bateman.'

'Sure,' Rebecca nodded, turning to go. He stopped her with another question.

'Have you had anything through from the bank yet?'

'Nothing useful. No transactions of note have gone through Lisa's current account or the credit cards in her purse over the past year. She does most of her spending on credit, and she pays those bills in cash. And, according to the HMRC, she submits tax returns and pays NI, so I've no idea why she conducts her business in cash. Unless she's only declaring some of her earnings.'

'Either way, she must be maintaining accounts of some sort if she's reporting her earnings,' Lawrence replied. 'Was there anything else on the laptop?'

'Not that looked like accounts. There's very little saved on the laptop itself, most of it's in the cloud. Besides that, there are reams of Internet history. I've not had a chance to go through that in detail, but at first glance there was nothing to indicate she uses the web for anything more than the rest of us – social media, shopping, banking –' she shrugged.

'You'd think we'd all have more spare time these days, given we do so many things at the click of a mouse.'

'We do,' Rebecca smiled. 'We spend it surfing the net.'

Lawrence chuckled. 'True.'

Rebecca's mobile interrupted the exchange, and she answered it with an efficient, 'DS Palmer.' Several seconds passed before she said, 'Oh, hello, thanks for getting back to me so quickly. Did you –' she stopped, presumably in response to the other person speaking. There was a long pause before her eyebrows jumped dramatically. 'What date did you say that was?' Another pause. 'Uh-huh. Yes. Thank you, that's very helpful.' She hung up, her animated expression indicating she'd learned something of note. 'I requested further information on Lisa's stepfather,' she said, tantalisingly.

'And?' Lawrence chivvied, impatiently.

'He's dead.'

Lawrence could already guess the answer to his next question, but asked it anyway. 'How?'

'Suicide,' Rebecca revealed, lifting her eyebrows pointedly. 'It seems he hanged himself in the same month Lisa turned eighteen. How's that for a coincidence?'

Sixteen

It was almost immediately apparent that Lisa's brother, Lucas, couldn't have played any great part in Patrick's death. He answered the door on crutches, his leg in plaster as a result of being knocked off a bicycle three weeks earlier. A quick telephone call was all it took to confirm the details of the accident, and a handful of questions soon established that he also had a reliable alibi for the night of Steve's death.

Abandoning that line of enquiry, Lawrence turned the interview to the subject of the man's sister, but once again the answers proved disappointing. No, Lucas didn't see or hear much from Lisa; no, she didn't share anything about her work or personal life; and no, she'd not been home in months – at least, not as far as he knew. He doubted their mother would be able to help much either, she and Lisa had never had a particularly good relationship. But Lawrence and Rebecca were welcome to have a look around Lisa's old bedroom – if they didn't mind finding it themselves, that was, steps being quite an undertaking on crutches. It was the first room on the left at the top of the stairs. And could he offer them anything to drink?

The bedroom provided considerably more information about the teenage Lisa than Rebecca had learned from the rented room in Lewisham about Lisa the adult. There were pretty pastel files still containing school work, a display unit populated by small china animals, a carved wooden musical box, a collage of postcards from a range of destinations blutacked to the wall above the white melamine desk, and a hand-knitted patchwork blanket that covered the single bed. The chest of drawers was partially occupied, holding a handful of t-shirts and jumpers, and a smattering of items hung in the wardrobe. Likewise, the desk had been only partly stripped of its contents: one half-empty drawer was stacked with sheets of ruled A4 paper, a tin of colouring pencils and a sketch pad featuring a selection of rather gothic-looking faries at various stages of composition; another was scattered with scented lip balms, a tangle of colourful plastic strings, some woven into bracelets, and several pairs of different-sized knitting needles.

As illuminating as many of the possessions left abandoned in the room were, none appeared to have any real bearing on the investigation. As a last resort, Rebecca began to flick through the pages of each of the books lining the bookcase: To Kill a Mockingbird, The Lovely Bones, Jane Eyre, Watership Down, the CTS New Catholic Bible. Pausing with the heavy volume in her hands, it struck her that Lisa's room in Lewisham had been devoid of a copy, which seemed more than a little odd for a woman whose only item of jewellery was a Saint Christopher and whose business card bore a Bible quotation. Perhaps, in reality, her interest in religion had less to do with belief than justification for her involvement in multiple murder.

Lucas glanced up from the laptop balanced on his good leg as Rebecca looked into the living room.

'Are you done?'

'I've a few more questions, if you don't mind.'

He shook his head, lifting the laptop and setting it down beside himself on the sofa.

'Your sister's a Catholic, is that right?'

'I s'pose. We were both Christened.'

'Was that the limit of your exposure to the church?'

He wrinkled his nose. 'We went to Sunday school as kids, but that was about it.'

'Do you know why Lisa wears a Saint Christopher, if she's not a practising Christian?'

'Dad gave it to her. She's worn it ever since he died.'

'Ah,' Rebecca nodded, at least a part of the puzzle now making sense. 'I'm sorry to ask, but would you mind telling me how he died?'

'He was shot while on duty,' Lucas replied, before adding, helpfully, 'He was a police officer.'

'Is that why Lisa wanted to join the police force?' Rebecca asked, thinking back to the comment the woman had made during their first interview.

'Yes.'

'Do you have any idea why she didn't follow that through?'

'She failed the medical.'

'On what grounds?'

He shrugged. 'She never said.'

'Did you find that strange?'

'Not really. She's never confided in me. I used to worry she didn't like me, but these days I don't let it bother me. I'm not sure she's ever particularly liked anyone.'

Spotting Jon in the lab as he passed, Leighton put his head around the door. His friend was sitting at the bench, peering through the eyepiece of a microscope and adjusting the focus with the fingers of his right hand.

'Can I interest you in a beer?'

'I'd be more than interested in a beer, believe me,' Jon replied, lifting his gaze. 'But unfortunately I'm nowhere near done.'

'Well that's no good,' Leighton responded, amiably, releasing the lab door and approaching the bench. He had been looking for an excuse to delay going home; Tom had yet to move on, and Leighton was beginning to suspect he had nowhere else *to* go. On Monday night he had been contrite and apologetic after Sunday's outburst, but by Tuesday evening his good humour had deserted him, and Leighton had spent the best part of six hours walking on eggshells. He had already passed too many years of his life tiptoeing around his father's unpredictable temper, and had no intention of returning to doing as much as an adult, but thus far had failed to find the words with which to broach the subject of his brother's continued occupation. And, as with so many other things in life, while he could put it off, he would.

'D'you need a hand?'

'Thanks, but I can hardly give you half a PM,' Jon smiled, ruefully. 'I was going to ask you to take a quick look at something for me, though.' He cast his eyes over a selection of glass slides lying on the bench to his left before reaching for one and exchanging it with that on the microscope's viewing platform.

'What is it?

'A seed of some sort,' Jon replied, slipping down from the stool to allow Leighton to take his place in front of the microscope. 'Looks a bit like a squashed hedgehog.'

Laying his mobile on the bench, Leighton perched on the stool and peered at the field of view, tweaking the wheel at the side of the device. An extreme close-up of part of something brown came into sharp focus, prompting him to twist the nosepiece through 120 degrees in favour of a less powerful lens.

Anything plant-related generally found its way to him sooner or later. Forensic botany hadn't been an officially sanctioned thesis option when he'd studied for his master's in analytical and forensic chemistry; the Nobel committee might not know the difference between chemistry and biology, his professor had lamented, but he wasn't about to be as imaginative with his interpretation, thank you very much. He was running a faculty of chemistry, not Kew bloody Gardens. Never easily deterred, Leighton had cited case after case in which forensic evidence involving plant traces had proved central to a conviction, and the professor had eventually yielded, muttering something about his having the persistence of a terrier with a hold on a postman's trousers. Leighton still wasn't entirely sure whether the man had been pleased or pissed off when the plant scientists co-opted to assist in the marking process had opted to award him a first.

'I think it's some kind of campion,' he said, looking back around at Jon. 'Does that help?'

'What are they when they're at home, then?' Jon asked, before adding, 'The only way I'll ever grow green fingers is if they turn gangrenous. Plants get suicidal around me.'

Leighton smiled. If he was honest, his interest in vegetation didn't extend much further than the lab; as it was he barely had time to maintain the small patch of lawn beyond the decking. As far as he was concerned, his garden was more of a seasonal extension of his living room than an entity in its own right – a place to drink beer, barbecue sausages and let off fireworks. And, depending on the weather and her mood, a sun trap or mouse trap for Pandora.

'Wild flowers,' he said, as he vacated the stool, allowing Jon to return to his previous position behind the microscope. 'You find them in woodlands and hedgerows.'

'Common, then,' Jon said, gloomily, as he reclaimed his seat.

'As mud.'

'Sodding typical,' Jon replied, shifting the slide out from under the clips that held it beneath the lens and reaching for another. 'I was hoping they'd give me some sort of hint about location.'

'Run it past an expert, I could be wrong. And even if I'm not, you might get lucky and discover it's one of the less common species.'

Jon nodded, turning his attention to the latest object of magnification. Leighton glanced towards his phone as it buzzed on the workbench and, seeing a familiar email address flash up on the screen, swiped it open. Scrolling down, he scanned the pertinent bits of the message. Despite having requested a few very specific tests in the wake of the postmortem on Patrick Copeland, he'd not really been expecting any of them to come back positive, and felt apprehensive rather than triumphant when he saw that one of them had. The result was likely to take some explaining. He could only hope Lawrence wouldn't shoot the messenger.

'Any progress?' Leighton asked, as Lawrence joined him in an empty interview room along the corridor from the one in which he had left Lisa. The pathologist was perching on the table, his feet resting on a nearby chair, rucksack tucked between them. It was a relaxed pose, but Lawrence sensed a slight wariness in his colleague's tone, and guessed he hadn't simply stopped by for an update on his way home.

'None. She's stonewalling,' he sighed, pulling one of the unoccupied chairs out from the table and sitting down. 'She's clearly at least an accessory, but as it stands we have nothing that isn't circumstantial, and I suspect she knows that if she keeps schtum she'll probably walk. I think we're going to have to go over everything we've got again in the hope of identifying her accomplice another way – she's certainly not going to give him up.'

'I'm not sure she has one,' Leighton admitted, uneasily. 'I think she may be our man, as it were.'

Lawrence frowned. 'What?'

'You know you queried the sex of that DNA profile?'

'And you told me it was definitely male,' Lawrence reminded him, his frown deepening as he anticipated an error belatedly coming to light.

'It is,' Leighton replied, quickly. 'But DNA profiling isn't foolproof. It only compares a small number of highly variable sequences that add up to be more or less as individual as a fingerprint. It doesn't sequence every gene, or tell you much about the person the sample came from. For that you need to sequence a whole lot more, which is time-consuming and costly. With the equipment we have, at any rate.'

'Better science exists, but we can't use it, you mean,' Lawrence said, wearily. He'd heard similar justifications for the shortcomings of forensic science before, as well as the regular refrain of pathologists and scenes of crime officers alike that TV dramas painted a totally unrealistic picture of what the available technology was capable of.

'Yeah. But when I did Patrick's PM – after you'd queried the results in Steve's case – I sent a few samples for specific single-gene sequencing. Those results have just come through, and it's likely you're looking for a person who is genetically male but appears to be female.'

Lawrence massaged his brow as he tried to make sense of what his colleague was saying. After so many hours in the artificial lighting of interview rooms, his head was beginning to ache. 'But not trans?'

'No. Intersex.'

'Run that past me again.'

'Genetically, sex is determined very simply by two chromosomes,' Leighton began, leaning backwards and wrapping his left hand around the far side of the table to support himself. 'But the physical traits we associate with each sex result from the expression of a whole range of genes.'

Lawrence nodded. 'Ok.'

'Male sexual characteristics develop in response to hormones called androgens. For those to have an effect, a person's cells need to carry a particular type of receptor. If they don't – if a mutation in the gene for the receptor prevents it from being made – male characteristics never develop, and you end up with someone who looks female.'

'How female?'

'Completely. Breasts, hips, the works. Externally even the genitalia look female.'

'Right.'

'I'm sorry incomplete science sent you around the houses. Hopefully we'll get a definitive answer when the result of Lisa's DNA profile comes back tomorrow.'

'That's likely to be about as much use as the proverbial stable door,' Lawrence responded, irritably. 'If we don't come up with something in the next eight hours, I've no choice but to release her. You might have mentioned the DNA test's potential to mislead before now.'

'If I'd started by listing all the caveats attached to DNA profiling, we'd still be working through them now,' Leighton countered, defensively. 'And the prevalence of something like complete androgen insensitivity is incredibly low – you're talking about a few cases per hundred thousand. Hardly the kind of odds you'd give much weight to.'

'Maybe not, but you clearly gave them enough to run the test in the first place. It wouldn't have taken much effort to give me a heads up, would it?'

'Effort had nothing to do with it. Listing every outside possibility at every turn would be more hindrance than help. It'd be information overload.'

'I'm not asking for every outside possibility, just the important ones!'

'You could make a case for a whole lot of results being important *if* they come up positive.'

'Well, I suppose I'll have to take your word for that.'

'I don't know what you want me to say. You know the science has limitations, and –'

'No no no,' Lawrence stopped him. 'Don't you try to put the responsibility for this on me! I'm aware there are limitations, but not what most of them are, and making those clear is *your* responsibility!'

'That's not what I meant. It isn't a question of apportioning responsibility. All I'm saying –'

'I think that's a matter of opinion!'

'There's no need to shout at me,' Leighton responded, coolly. 'We run a lot of tests on the off-chance. We don't flag every one in advance to avoid *likely* drowning in a sea of *possibles.* I realise the circumstances are frustrating, but I didn't withhold information, I just followed procedure. If you think the procedure needs revising, you're welcome to take it up with Max.'

Lawrence regarded him in silence, undecided as to whether he himself was being unreasonable or whether his colleague was making excuses. He had no way of knowing what proportion of test results revealed nothing and so never made it as far as his desk, and no intention of bleating to Max about the situation unless there was a genuine case to answer.

The pathologists and scenes of crime officers were no strangers to speculation in the face of the wait – often prolonged – for many of the DNA, toxicology and other results to come in, although Lawrence knew Max encouraged prudence. Conjecture had a place in the scientific process, he acknowledged, but was only a minor player compared with experimentation and investigation. However, it would be easy enough for medics and forensic technicians to take advantage of others' limited understanding of their subjects to explain away errors in method or judgement, and Lawrence didn't doubt there were those who readily did as much. To be fair, Leighton probably wasn't one of them; he'd held his hands up to mistakes on several occasions in the past, and could hardly be described as a slave to procedure, so had presumably adhered to it for good reason. And, given that on a couple of occasions he had offered to run his own tests in order to expedite the scientific process, he was unlikely to have delayed anything unnecessarily.

'All right,' Lawrence conceded, eventually, with a heavy sigh. 'All right. Let's move on. We're looking for a woman, not a man, is effectively what you're saying, yes?'

'More or less.'

'Which does make sense. But I don't think we've a hope in hell of getting her to confess to anything. At least, not without more than we have at the moment.' A movement to his left caught his eye and he turned to see Rebecca standing in the doorway, her expression triumphant.

'Lisa *does* have a storage unit,' she imparted, breathlessly, the moment his eyes met with hers. 'It's paid for via a credit card she seems to keep solely for the purpose, there've been no other transactions through the account in the past six months and it isn't among the cards in her purse.'

'So where did you find it?'

'I didn't. I worked out that she had a Santander account from the reams of Internet history and followed up with them. She'd checked it online a couple of times, and although she'd cleared the browser history I guess she didn't realise the computer might have cached the information.'

'Where is the unit?'

'Peckham. Shall I head over there now?'

Lawrence nodded. 'Yes. And I'll see whether the pressure of that discovery squeezes any more information out of Lisa. If it doesn't, perhaps the contents of the unit will.'

Leighton had offered Rebecca a lift to the storage depot, pointing out that it required only a brief detour on his route home, but instead of dropping her at the gates he pulled into the car park and eased his Aston Martin into a space. Switching off the ignition, he reached behind the passenger seat for a bag of forensic equipment before moving to climb out of the vehicle.

'I doubt she's been storing bodies in there,' Rebecca remarked as she opened the passenger door.

'Probably not. Although I reckon someone somewhere will be.'

'You know what I mean,' she replied, hauling herself out of the comfortable but low-slung leather seat and resting her forearms on the roof of the car. 'If there's anything to see I can get a couple of SOCOs out to look after it. You don't have to give up your evening.'

'I don't know, always trying to do me out of the fun jobs,' Leighton tutted, with a jaunty smile.

Rebecca instinctively returned the smile, rolling her eyes and shaking her head as she moved to close the car door. 'Well don't say I didn't offer.'

The storage facility was modern, well-lit and spotlessly clean, its yellow-doored units arranged back-to-back in parallel banks like oversized changing-room lockers, with ceiling-mounted signs clearly demarcating aisle and unit numbers. These made locating Lisa's unit simple enough; getting inside required a little more effort. Rebecca had anticipated the need for heavy-duty bolt cutters, and, having never used them before, had also brought along instructions on how to adjust them for best effect. Leaning the cutters against the unit door, she unfolded the eHow printout and began to read. She was a few sentences in when Leighton said, tentatively, 'If I offer to do the breaking and entering will I get told off for being sexist?'

'Only if you've no more idea than I have what to do with these things,' she indicated the bolt cutters.

Leighton didn't reply, he simply held out a hand for the spanner and safety glasses grasped in her left hand. Rebecca gave them up and watched as Leighton crouched down and deftly adjusted the spanner before applying it to the hexagonal screw at the head of the bolt cutters, stealing an occasional glance at the combination padlock on the unit door.

'Ok, you need to stand back unless you've another pair of goggles,' he advised, slipping the glasses on and straightening up.

Rebecca retreated a couple of metres down the aisle, and watched him grasp the long handles of the cutters and position the jaws around the shackle of the lock.

'I've never done this with a police escort before,' he remarked, before applying pressure to the tool's arms and slicing the thick metal band in two.

'That's probably just as well,' Rebecca replied, rejoining him at the door as he unhooked the padlock.

'Probably,' he concurred, with a grin, tossing the padlock into his bag and pulling out a pair of blue nitrile gloves. Rebecca hurriedly located the vinyl gloves in her own bag and had just wriggled her fingers into position when her colleague reached to open the door.

'Ready?'

Rebecca's mental image of a storage unit's interior had been akin to the view from the garage door at her parents' Norwich home: a semi-organised but largely impenetrable arrangement of boxes, crates, furniture and other miscellany too large or awkward to be packed away. Lisa's small storage vault had more in common with a walk-in wardrobe. A basic shelving unit stood against the back wall, lined with identical cardboard archive boxes, while a hanging rail ran along the left-hand wall with several outfits dangling from it, all of them black and scarcely visible in the gloom of the unlit room. Rebecca lifted the first out into the light of the corridor to reveal a studded leather bodice attached to a thick choker by a handful of buckled straps.

'Oh, now I can see you in that,' Leighton teased, flicking on a torch and stepping into the chamber.

Rebecca smiled to herself, wondering what her colleagues might make of some of the more risqué outfits she'd worn on nights out in the not so distant past. Or rather, what they'd make of the idea of *her* wearing them. The pencil skirts, tailored trousers and smart blouses that comprised her work wardrobe were far removed from her choice of attire for rock bars and clubs.

Next along Lisa's rail was a camisole designed to look like a corset without similarly restricting the wearer, with black cords criss-crossing between eyelets at the sides and a series of buckles that served nothing but decorative function lined up down the front. This was followed by a pair of leather hotpants; beyond those was a PVC bodysuit.

'Well these are certainly a little different from the contents of her wardrobe at home,' Rebecca observed.

'I think these might be the associated accessories,' Leighton replied, holding out a box, his torch beam trained on the contents. Several unopened pairs of fishnet stockings and packets of hair extensions were lined up side-by-side at one end, the rest of the box given over to paraphernalia including theatrical eye masks, black leather gloves and more than one pair of heavily padded leather handcuffs.

'Not quite what I was expecting,' Rebecca admitted.

'Looks like Forrester had the right idea all along.'

'In what sense?'

'In that it's not necessarily a huge leap from sex games to strangulation.'

'Would you give some girl you'd never met that kind of control?'

'Things aren't necessarily that black and white in the heat of the moment. A lot of people have surprisingly little regard for their own safety where sex is concerned, especially after a few drinks. Despite the risks, how many of your friends have gone home from a bar or a club with someone they didn't know from Adam? And how many people do you know who don't always practise safe sex when they ought to know better?'

It was a fair point. Rebecca even remembered one friend of a friend who'd gone home with a man she'd met on the night bus. She herself had never had a one-night stand. She couldn't imagine being so intimate with someone she barely knew.

'Besides,' Leighton continued, 'There are plenty of warnings about date rape, but nobody ever says *hey guys, watch out some chick doesn't try to engage you in a little light bondage and then choke you to death.*'

'Do they not?'

'It's a grave failing of sex education,' he joked, setting the box down on the floor and reaching for an evidence bag. Abandoning the collection of outfits, Rebecca crouched down to reach for one of the boxes on the bottom shelf, and was surprised to spot a spiral-bound shorthand notebook resting on the lid. Given the orderly nature of both the unit and Lisa's bedroom, she guessed it had been purposefully excluded from the boxes. Pulling it out by the wire coil across its top, she turned back the thin cardboard cover and fixed the beam of her small LED torch on the first page.

One word – the name Amanda – was double-underlined as a heading, and below it appeared a date and a series of bullet points. Several of these were penned in a combination of inks, as if they had been added to at some stage after their inception, and in a couple of places words had been repeatedly ringed for emphasis. It didn't take Rebecca long to establish that the bulleted list related to the details of a sexual assault reportedly committed by one Darryl Hayden – presumably on a woman called Amanda – as well as a selection of his personal details. These included his home address and, she discovered on turning the page, the name and location of his place of work. A third page contained several other snippets of information about him, after which a couple of blank ones were followed by another list headed with a different woman's name.

Rebecca flicked quickly through the rest of the notebook and, finding it almost half full, pushed herself back up from the floor to head for the better light of the corridor. The book looked to contain Lisa's notes on calls to her helpline, and there seemed a good chance of Patrick, and perhaps Steve, featuring somewhere in the compendium. The possibility that she'd unearthed the smoking gun they needed was exhilarating.

Disappointingly, there was no mention of either man in the notebook. However, the combined thickness of the pages didn't match the diameter of their helical binding, suggesting some leaves had been removed, and making it possible the book contained more information than was immediately apparent. Leighton offered to see what he could lift from it, and, having looked into the Yard to update Lawrence on what they had gathered from Lisa's storage vault thus far, Rebecca made her way to the pathology unit. On arrival, its dimly lit corridors were the only part of the department not shrouded in darkness, and in the end she had to call Leighton to ask where he was. He directed her up the back staircase to the fourth floor, where he met her at the security door. From there, he led her down a corridor, past several darkened rooms, before swiping open the secure door to a small, minimalist laboratory stocked with a few sizeable pieces of equipment and little else. Shoving his access pass into his pocket, he headed straight for a largely featureless oblong metal box, snapped on a pair of gloves and reached for a bundle of A5 pages that lay on the workbench.

'I didn't know you had labs up here,' Rebecca said, her voice lowered as if in fear of disturbing someone. As she spoke, she wondered why being in a deserted building at night time automatically elicited that response.

'Technically, *we* don't,' Leighton came back, setting one of the pages down on the glass platform atop the device in front of him before starting to leaf through the others.

'Do you have permission to be in here?'

'Not exactly,' he admitted, adding another page to the glass and returning the rest of the bundle to the bench.

Rebecca felt uneasy. 'You didn't break in, did you?'

Leighton glanced up, opening his mouth wide and raising his eyebrows in mock indignation. 'Would I?'

'I'm serious. If you want to break the law that's your prerogative, but I can't get involved.'

'I didn't break in,' he replied, shortly, reaching to cover the two sheets of paper with what looked like clingfilm and smoothing away a few wrinkles with his fingertips.

'So?' Rebecca persevered.

'One of the lab technicians may have slipped me a pass.'

'In exchange for what?'

'Nothing.'

'Why would someone risk their neck for nothing?' Rebecca asked, suspiciously.

Leighton sighed, looking back up from the machine on the bench. 'It was a favour, all right? Not everybody works only on a quid pro quo basis.'

Rebecca held his gaze, still not entirely convinced. Leighton had always been prepared to bend the rules – admittedly often to the Met's advantage – and Rebecca wouldn't have put it past him to bend the law as well. He had a curious knack of getting away with things most people didn't, from routinely turning up late to work to charming his way out of parking tickets, and she suspected it was only a matter of time before he pushed his luck too far. But she could also imagine people being willing to go out of their way on his behalf. He was one of those chatty, friendly people who seem to know and have time for just about everyone, from the postman to the chief executive. And he probably wouldn't hesitate to put himself out for others in return.

'We're all funded by the Home Office,' he added, as if in mitigation. 'It's not as if I'm stealing anything. If I put in an official request for this job, someone else will end up using this machine to do it tomorrow. All I'm trying to do is speed things up.'

Rebecca smiled. 'Any chance you could speed up that DNA test?'

'I may be good, but I'm not *that* good,' he returned, affably. 'I can't warp space-time. PCR takes as long as it takes.'

He flicked one of the two switches on the front of the device on the bench, and it immediately began buzzing in a manner that reminded Rebecca of a Nespresso coffeemaker. She had never owned one, viewing the machines as just another gadget to clutter up limited kitchen workspace, but suspected she would quickly grow all too fond of the one Perry had moved in at the weekend. Getting used to having a flatmate again might take longer. At present, things were still at the awkward, polite stage, and were destined to remain that way for as long as Rebecca was home for little more than to sleep. Still to come were discoveries of how mismatched their expectations were on matters of cleanliness and order, how compatible they were when it came to bringing their social lives home, and whether they had anything in common besides an address.

Leighton reached for a grey metal bar some twelve inches long and, holding it millimetres above the pages in front of him, moved it slowly towards himself. As it drew level with the front of the glass platform, he turned it back in the opposite direction and, on reaching the back, repeated the exercise. Rebecca stood watching for a few moments before sitting on a nearby stool. After a matter of seconds, Leighton put the bar down, grasped hold of the right side of the glass and lifted it through forty-five degrees. Holding it in position with one hand, he lifted a pot of grey powder from the workbench with the other and shook it over the plastic film, dispensing small quantities as his hand travelled back and forth. Additional words began to appear, overwriting those on the pages, and after a few seconds he returned the pot to the bench and switched the machine off.

Taking what looked like a sheet of waxed paper from a tray on a nearby shelf, he peeled a sheet of sticky-backed plastic away from the wax and overlaid it on the film, ironing out the air bubbles between the two with a gadget akin to the small rollers designed for painting behind radiators. He then slowly lifted the resulting transparency, which crackled as if with static as it peeled away from the glass and paper beneath.

'Et voila,' he announced, presenting it to Rebecca with a flourish and a smile.

Rebecca had never previously watched the process used to reveal indented writing, and it was far quicker – and simpler – than she had imagined. She didn't say as much, however, returning the smile and voicing her thanks as she took the transparency. Leighton replaced the pages on the glass with two others, and set about repeating the steps he'd just performed. Rebecca headed for a clear stretch of bench, drew up a stool and sat down to read.

'Anything?' Leighton asked, returning to the lab with two mugs of coffee. He had left Rebecca to read through the last of the transparencies he'd made from the inscribed section of Lisa's pad, and headed for the kitchenette further down the corridor in search of caffeine. The bulk of the pages had revealed nothing of note, and he hadn't been holding out a lot of hope that the last few would be any different.

Rebecca shook her head, thanking him as he handed her one of the mugs. 'There's a lot of information that might be relevant in a larger sense, but nothing that obviously relates to known victims.'

'Bollocks,' Leighton muttered, glancing at his watch. It was almost ten-thirty. 'What've we got left, two hours?'

'Pretty much.'

He sighed.

'I might try reading the original text again, make sure we've not missed anything,' Rebecca suggested.

Leighton reached for the stack of evidence bags containing the pages of succinct ballpoint notes and passed them to her, then turned around and leaned against the bench, inhaling the steam that rose off his coffee. Logically, he knew he wasn't to blame for the deceptive nature of the DNA test results, but that didn't stop him *feeling* responsible. Nor, he suspected, did it stop his colleagues – or at least Lawrence – thinking likewise. He tapped his fingers against the mug in his hands, re-reading the words printed across the white china for the umpteenth time. *Feel safe at night: sleep with a police officer.* That would be one way to get shot of Tom, he reflected, cynically. His brother's antipathy towards the police long predated any of his arrests, a view inherited, no doubt, from their father. Perhaps that was why the idea of working with the police had so appealed to Leighton.

He'd often been asked at what stage during his medical training he'd decided to pursue a career in forensic pathology, and people almost invariably seemed surprised to hear it had always been his intent. The seeds of the idea had been sown on a rainy weekday afternoon when his GCSE chemistry teacher had taken advantage of the macabre appeal of three recent grisly murders to engage a generally disinterested group of teenagers. One hour of basic forensic chemistry later, Leighton had asked what he'd need to do to get a job in the field. His teacher's initial dry response had been 'some work would be a good start'. The following week, presumably realising few pupils were likely to admit to any interest in academia in front of their peers, the man had kept him behind after class on the basis of some spurious infraction in order to lend him a book on the subject. 'Any questions,' he had said, rather gruffly, as he handed it over, 'Put them in the back of your book.'

Using the back pages of exercise books, whether for glossaries, notes or language tables, had been popular practice at the school, and with that in mind Leighton set his mug down and reached for a box of disposable gloves. Pulling a pair on, he flipped through the blank remains of Lisa's notebook and examined the last page. A faint score mark ran the length of it. Reaching for a scalpel, he carefully sliced the paper crenellations running along the top of the sheet to free it from its spiral binding, then carried it to the electrostatic detector and restarted the machine. He charged the film, scattered toner over it and fixed the image before laying the transparency on the adjacent workbench.

The trace didn't immediately make much sense: a single line ran down the centre of the page, irregularly marked on either side with tiny arrows pointing in seemingly random directions. Single words that looked like names – Disraeli, Werter, Montserrat – appeared at intervals, and, next to one of them, the number 54. He deferred to his mobile phone's search engine. *If in doubt*, as Jon was fond of saying, *Google.*

Seventeen

Lawrence laid several pages of Lisa's notebook – each in its own evidence bag – side by side on the interview room table before asking why she had taken notes on her conversations with women calling her helpline.

'I wanted to make sure I didn't forget anything important between calls,' she replied, simply. 'There's nothing worse than feeling you're not being listened to.'

'So why do you have no notes on Jodie's calls?'

Lisa hesitated. 'I didn't have the book to hand.'

'I'm surprised you ever had it to hand, given where we found it. Do you normally rush down to your storage unit every time you receive a call?'

'Of course not. I just leave things at the unit for safekeeping while I'm working. You brought me in here in the middle of the day, remember?'

'Because a notebook wouldn't be safe with your flatmate around?' Lawrence responded. 'Or because after our first visit you guessed we might come back?'

'That's not what I meant.'

'What did you mean?'

'Those women told me what they did in confidence. I didn't want it lying around for anyone coming into the house to read.'

'Given that you've listed only their first names I think they could be assured their anonymity in a city the size of London, don't you? Besides, most of the information you've gathered seems to relate not to the women, but to the men they accuse of assault.'

'Hardly surprisingly, when those men were their reason for calling.'

'And why did you need to remember more than the men's names? How was where they lived relevant? Or where they worked? Were those crucial details to making people feel listened to?'

'I didn't analyse it in that much depth,' Lisa shrugged off the question. 'I just made notes.'

'So where are your notes on the conversations you had with Jodie?'

'I'm not sure. I can't remember.'

'You can't *remember*?' Lawrence echoed, incredulously. 'Well that's not going to be much use for helping Jodie feel listened to when she next calls, is it? And it doesn't do a lot to guarantee the confidentiality you've repeatedly avowed dedication to.'

'I'm tired,' Lisa defended herself. 'I've been here since yesterday afternoon.'

'Well let me help you narrow things down. Jodie's name doesn't appear in any notes in your flat, your car, your family home or your storage unit. Where else do you keep things?'

Lisa made no reply.

'Nowhere,' he concluded. 'As I thought. No doubt you disposed of them not long after you did the same with Patrick. Let's move on from Jodie and Patrick to Steve Golding.'

'How many times?' Lisa demanded, her voice sounding strained. 'I've never heard of him!'

'You're certain of that?'

'Yes.'

'So why did you hand draw a map of the streets around his home, complete with his address?' Lawrence asked, sweeping the pages of her notebook to one end of the table and laying the transparency depicting Putney High Street and the roads leading off it in front of her, planting his finger on the number 54 that marked Steve's flat.

Lisa paled. 'I didn't,' she protested, weakly.

'No?' Lawrence queried, disbelievingly. 'Because that looks just like your handwriting, and I'm guessing if we get an expert to analyse it they'll agree.'

Lisa didn't reply.

'I'll ask again. Why did you draw this map?'

Still no answer.

'It's not as if you'd need a map to Steve's place if your plan was to chat him up in a local pub and then accompany him home, is it?' Lawrence continued. 'He knew where he lived.' He waited a few seconds to see whether she would speak, and, when she didn't, went on, 'But, of course, you didn't want to leave any unnecessary evidence behind. Which is presumably why you noted down the position and angle of every CCTV camera on Putney High Street and beyond.' Using his forefinger, he traced an imaginary dot-to-dot between the series of arrows scattered across the map, which Leighton and Rebecca had identified with the aid of Google Street View. 'You took great care to keep your face turned away from every camera you passed, and you used hair extensions to disguise the back of your head,' he placed a bag containing a bundle of long blonde hair beside the map. 'All very well thought out, I'll give you that. Ironic, really, that you only came to our attention thanks to a completely different disguise you used to do your research.'

Lisa didn't acknowledge any of these conjectures, keeping her hands in her lap and eyes focused on the table. Lawrence wondered what she was thinking.

'And, at a guess, you used these to help immobilise your victims,' he said, adding one of the pairs of padded handcuffs to the table. 'Strangulation generally renders people unconscious within a matter of seconds, although it probably feels like a thousand times that. I can only imagine what went through their minds as you choked the life out of them.'

Lisa finally raised her eyes. 'How long do you suppose every second lasts when you're being raped?' She returned, coldly. 'What do you *imagine* that might be like? Assuming you have any real capacity to understand?'

'Nobody's suggesting rape isn't just as terrifying. But I'm not interviewing a rapist, am I? Because you chose to administer your own justice.'

'You say that as if I might believe you stand any real chance of getting the likes of Steve convicted. We've already been over the failings of the British justice system.'

'I don't deny the system isn't perfect, but at least both sides stand a chance. Did you give your victims an opportunity to state their cases?'

Lisa uttered something approaching a sardonic laugh.

'I presume that's a no.'

She said nothing, simply lifting her shoulders and eyebrows in a provocative shrug.

'I can understand how men might be persuaded to engage in a game involving handcuffs, but how did you go about slipping a noose around their necks without giving the game away?'

'I didn't.'

'We both know that's not true.'

'I had no part in it,' Lisa maintained, before her lips twisted into a smirk and she added, derisively, 'They did it themselves.'

Lawrence frowned. 'I'm not sure I follow.'

'Men are so easy to manipulate in the bedroom. Tell them something turns you on, and you can almost guarantee they'll do it.'

Mentally scanning through the details of each crime scene, Lawrence made the connection. 'You asked them to wear a tie in bed.'

Lisa didn't confirm or deny it, she simply gave the same

infuriating shrug.

'Was your stepfather wearing a tie the last time he forced himself on you?'

This had more effect, and Lisa swallowed hard. 'I only pulled it to try to get him off me,' she revealed, after a moment. 'But I didn't know what he might do if I let go.' She paused. 'So I didn't.'

Although the memory obviously stirred some emotional reaction, her tone was oddly dispassionate. There was no sense of contrition in any of her admissions, just facts and contempt. Lawrence suspected she had no real capacity to empathise with others, and had simply given the women calling her helpline the impression she cared because to do so served her own ends. Despite having brought up the subject, he very much doubted her actions had been rooted in any real desire to administer justice; more likely Lisa felt driven, for whatever deep-seated psychological reason, to re-enact that final experience with her stepfather. Whether there was any therapeutic or pharmaceutical way with which to manage that desire – or, indeed, her lack of empathy – and how one would ever know whether it had been achieved, he had no idea. He certainly didn't envy the person who would one day have to make that call.

A note from Sadie

Thank you for choosing to read this book. If you have enjoyed *Shadow Lines*, I would be very grateful if you would consider rating it, or even writing a review – just a few words can make a difference in helping to persuade others to give my books a try!

If you would like to hear about new releases and offers, you can sign up to my mailing list on my website:

https://www.sadiegordonrichmond.co.uk

Printed in Great Britain
by Amazon